"Ian Hamilton's *The Water Rat of Wanchai* is a smart, action-packed thriller of the first order, and Ava Lee, a gay Asian-Canadian forensics accountant with a razor-sharp mind and highly developed martial arts skills, is a protagonist to be reckoned with. We were impressed by Hamilton's tight plotting; his well-rendered settings, from the glitz of Bangkok to the grit of Guyana; and his ability to portray a wide range of sharply individualized characters in clean but sophisticated prose." — Judges' Citation, Arthur Ellis Award for Best First Novel

"Ava Lee is tough, fearless, quirky, and resourceful, and she has more — well, you know — than a dozen male detectives I can think of… Hamilton has created a true original in Ava Lee." — Linwood Barclay, author of *No Time for Goodbye*

"If the other novels [in the series] are half as good as this debut by Ian Hamilton, then readers are going to celebrate. Hamilton has created a marvellous character in Ava Lee…This is a terrific story that's certain to be on the Arthur Ellis Best First Novel list." — *Globe and Mail*

"[Ava Lee's] lethal knowledge…torques up her sex appeal to the approximate level of a female lead in a Quentin Tarantino film." — *National Post*

"The heroine in *The Water Rat of Wanchai* by Ian Hamilton sounds too good to be true, but the heroics work better that way…formidable…The story breezes along with something close to total clarity…Ava is unbeatable at just about everything. Just wait for her to roll out her bak mei against the bad guys. She's perfect. She's fast." — *Toronto Star*

"Imagine a book about a forensic accountant that has tension, suspense, and action...When the central character looks like Lucy Liu, kicks like Jackie Chan, and has a travel budget like Donald Trump, the story is anything but boring. *The Water Rat of Wanchai* is such a beast...I look forward to the next one, *The Disciple of Las Vegas*." — *Montreal Gazette*

"[A] tomb-raiding Dragon Lady Lisbeth, *sans* tattoo and face metal." — *Winnipeg Free Press*

"An enjoyable romp with a feisty, ingenious heroine whose lethal martial arts skills are as formidable as her keen mind." — *Publishers Weekly*

"Readers will discern in Ava undertones of Lisbeth Salander, the ferocious protagonist of the late Stieg Larsson's crime novels...She, too, is essentially a loner, and small, and physically brutal...There are suggestions in *The Water Rat of Wanchai* of deeper complexities waiting to be more fully revealed. Plus there's pleasure, both for Ava and readers, in the puzzle itself: in figuring out where money has gone, how to get it back, and which humans, helpful or malevolent, are to be dealt with where, and in what ways, in the process...Irresistible." — Joan Barfoot, *London Free Press*

"*The Water Rat of Wanchai* delivers on all fronts...feels like the beginning of a crime-fighting saga...A great story told with colour, energy, and unexpected punch." — *Hamilton Spectator*

"The best series fiction leaves readers immersed in a world that is both familiar and fresh. Seeds planted early bear fruit later on, creating a rich forest that blooms across a number of books...[Hamilton] creates a terrific atmosphere of suspense..." — *Quill & Quire*

"The book is an absolute page-turner...Hamilton's knack for writing snappy dialogue is evident...I recommend getting in on the ground floor with this character, because for Ava Lee, the sky's the limit." — *Inside Halton*

"Seldom does one get a thriller about white-collar crime, with an intelligent, independent lesbian and Asian protagonist. It's also rare to find a book with such interesting and exotic settings...Readers will find great amusement in Ava's unconventional ways and will certainly enjoy accompanying her on her travels." — *Literaturkurier*

PRAISE FOR *THE DISCIPLE OF LAS VEGAS*
FINALIST, BARRY AWARD FOR BEST ORIGINAL TRADE PAPERBACK

"I started to read *The Disciple of Las Vegas* at around ten at night. And I did something I have only done with two other books (Cormac McCarthy's *The Road* and Douglas Coupland's *Player One*): I read the novel in one sitting. Ava Lee is too cool. She wonderfully straddles two worlds and two identities. She does some dastardly things and still remains our hero thanks to the charm Ian Hamilton has given her on the printed page. It would take a female George Clooney to portray her in a film. The action and plot move quickly and with power. Wow. A punch to the ear, indeed." — J. J. Lee, author of *The Measure of a Man*

"I loved *The Water Rat of Wanchai*, the first novel featuring Ava Lee. Now, Ava and Uncle make a return that's even better...Simply irresistible." — Margaret Cannon, *Globe and Mail*

"This is slick, fast-moving escapism reminiscent of Ian Fleming, with more to come in what shapes up as a high-energy, high-concept series." — *Booklist*

"Fast paced...Enough personal depth to lift this thriller above solely action-oriented fare." — *Publishers Weekly*

"Lee is a hugely original creation, and Hamilton packs his adventure with interesting facts and plenty of action." — *Irish Independent*

"Hamilton makes each page crackle with the kind of energy that could easily jump to the movie screen...This riveting read will keep you up late at night." — *Penthouse*

"Hamilton gives his reader plenty to think about...Entertaining."
— *Kitchener-Waterloo Record*

PRAISE FOR *THE WILD BEASTS OF WUHAN*
LAMBDA LITERARY AWARD FINALIST: LESBIAN MYSTERY

"Smart and savvy Ava Lee returns in this slick mystery set in the rarefied world of high art...[A] great caper tale. Hamilton has great fun chasing villains and tossing clues about. *The Wild Beasts of Wuhan* is the best Ava Lee novel yet, and promises more and better to come."
— Margaret Cannon, *Globe and Mail*

"One of my favourite new mystery series, perfect escapism."
— *National Post*

"As a mystery lover, I'm devouring each book as it comes out...What I love in the novels: The constant travel, the high-stakes negotiation, and Ava's willingness to go into battle against formidable opponents, using only her martial arts skills to defend herself...If you want a great read and an education in high-level business dealings, Ian Hamilton is an author to watch." — *Toronto Star*

"Fast-paced and very entertaining." — *Montreal Gazette*

"Ava Lee is definitely a winner." — *Saskatoon Star Phoenix*

"*The Wild Beasts of Wuhan* is an entertaining dip into potentially fatal worlds of artistic skulduggery." — *Sudbury Star*

"Hamilton uses Ava's investigations as comprehensive and intriguing mechanisms for plot and character development." — *Quill & Quire*

"You haven't seen cold and calculating until you've double-crossed this number cruncher. Another strong entry from Arthur Ellis Award–winner Hamilton." — *Booklist*

"An intelligent kick-ass heroine anchors Canadian author Hamilton's excellent third novel featuring forensic accountant Ava Lee... Clearly conversant with the art world, Hamilton makes the intricacies of forgery as interesting as a Ponzi scheme." — *Publishers Weekly*, *Starred Review*

"A lively series about Ava Lee, a sexy forensic financial investigator." — *Tampa Bay Times*

"This book is miles from the ordinary. The main character, Ava Lee is 'the whole package.'" — *Minneapolis Star Tribune*

"A strong heroine is challenged to discover the details of an intercontinental art scheme. Although Hamilton's star Ava Lee is technically a forensic accountant, she's more badass private investigator than desk jockey." — *Kirkus Reviews*

PRAISE FOR *THE RED POLE OF MACAU*

"Ava Lee returns as one of crime fiction's most intriguing characters. *The Red Pole of Macau* is the best page-turner of the season from the hottest writer in the business!" — John Lawrence Reynolds, author of *Beach Strip*

"Ava Lee, that wily, wonderful hunter of nasty business brutes, is back in her best adventure ever... If you haven't yet discovered Ava Lee, start here." — *Globe and Mail*

"The best in the series so far." — *London Free Press*

"Ava [Lee] is a character we all could use at one time or another. Failing that, we follow her in her best adventure yet." — *Hamilton Spectator*

"A romp of a story with a terrific heroine." — *Saskatoon Star Phoenix*

"Fast-paced…The action unfolds like a well-oiled action-flick."
— *Kitchener-Waterloo Record*

"A change of pace for our girl [Ava Lee]…Suspenseful." — *Toronto Star*

"Hamilton packs tremendous potential in his heroine…A refreshingly relevant series. This reader will happily pay House of Anansi for the fifth installment." — *Canadian Literature*

PRAISE FOR *THE SCOTTISH BANKER OF SURABAYA*

"Hamilton deepens Ava's character, and imbues her with greater mettle and emotional fire, to the extent that book five is his best, most memorable, to date." — *National Post*

"In today's crowded mystery market, it's no easy feat coming up with a protagonist who stands out from the pack. But Ian Hamilton has made a great job of it with his Ava Lee books. Young, stylish, Chinese Canadian, lesbian, and a brilliant forensic accountant, Ava is as complex a character as you could want… [A] highly addictive series… Hamilton knows how to keep the pages turning. He eases us into the seemingly tame world of white-collar crime, then raises the stakes, bringing the action to its peak with an intensity and violence that's stomach-churning. His Ava Lee is a winner and a welcome addition to the world of strong female avengers." — *NOW Magazine*

"Most of the series' success rests in Hamilton's tight plotting, attention to detail, and complex powerhouse of a heroine: strong but vulnerable, capable but not impervious… With their tight plotting and crackerjack heroine, Hamilton's novels are the sort of crowd-pleasing, narrative-focused fiction we find all too rarely in this country." — *Quill & Quire*

"Ava is such a cool character, intelligent, Chinese Canadian, unconventional, and original… Irresistible." — *Owen Sound Sun Times*

PRAISE FOR *THE TWO SISTERS OF BORNEO*
NATIONAL BESTSELLER

"There are plenty of surprises waiting for Ava, and for the reader, all uncovered with great satisfaction." — *National Post*

"Ian Hamilton's great new Ava Lee mystery has the same wow factor as its five predecessors. The plot is complex and fast-paced, the writing tight, and its protagonist is one of the most interesting female avengers to come along in a while." — *NOW Magazine* (NNNN)

"The appeal of the Ava Lee series owes much to her brand name lifestyle; it stirs pleasantly giddy emotions to encounter such a devotedly elegant heroine. But, better still, the detailing of financial shenanigans is done in such clear language that even readers who have trouble balancing their bank books can appreciate the way conmen set out to fleece unsuspecting victims." — *Toronto Star*

"Hamilton has a unique gift for concocting sizzling thrillers." — *Edmonton Journal*

"Hamilton has this formula down to an art, but he manages to avoid cliché and his ability to evoke a place keeps the series fresh." — *Globe and Mail*

"From her introduction in *The Water Rat of Wanchai*, Ava Lee has stood as a stylish, street-smart leading lady whose resourcefulness and creativity have helped her to uncover criminal activity in everything from illegal online gambling rings to international art heists. In Hamilton's newest installment to the series, readers accompany Ava on great adventures and to interesting locales, roaming from Hong Kong to the Netherlands to Borneo. The pulse-pounding, fast-paced narrative is chocked full of divergent plot twists and intriguing personalities that make it a popular escapist summer read. The captivating female sleuth does not disappoint as she circles the globe on a quest to uncover an unusually intriguing investment fiasco involving fraud, deception and violence." — *ExpressMilwaukee.com*

"Ava may be the most chic figure in crime fiction." — *Hamilton Spectator*

"The series as a whole is as good as the modern thriller genre gets." — *The Cord*

PRAISE FOR *THE KING OF SHANGHAI*

"The only thing scarier than being ripped off for a few million bucks is being the guy who took it and having Ava Lee on your tail. If Hamilton's kick-ass forensic accountant has your number, it's up." — Linwood Barclay

"One of Ian Hamilton's best." — *Globe and Mail*

"Brilliant, sexy, and formidably martial arts-trained forensic accountant Ava Lee is back in her seventh adventure (after *The Two Sisters of Borneo*)...Ever since his dazzling surprise debut with *The Water Rat of Wanchai*, Hamilton has propelled Ava along through the series with expanded storytelling and nuanced character development: there's always something new to discover about Ava. Fast-paced suspense, exotic locales, and a rich cast of characters (some, like Ava's driver, Sonny, are both dangerous and lovable) make for yet another hugely entertaining hit." — *Publishers Weekly*, *Starred review*

"A luxurious sense of place...Hamilton's knack for creating fascinating detail will keep readers hooked...Good fun for those who like to combine crime fiction with armchair travelling." — *Booklist*

"Ava would be a sure thing to whip everybody, Putin included, at the negotiating table." — *Toronto Star*

"After six novels starring Chinese Canadian Ava Lee and her perilously thrilling exploits, best-selling Canadian author Ian Hamilton has jolted his creation out of what wasn't even yet a rut and hurled her abruptly into a new circumstance, with fresh ambitions." — *London Free Press*

"It's a measure of Hamilton's quality as a thriller writer that he compels your attention even before he starts ratcheting up the suspense."
— *Regina Leader Post*

"An unputdownable book that I would highly recommend for all."
— *Words of Mystery*

"Ava is as powerful and brilliant as ever." — *Literary Treats*

PRAISE FOR *THE PRINCELING OF NANJING*
NATIONAL BESTSELLER
A KOBO BEST BOOK OF THE YEAR

"The reader is offered plenty of Ava in full flower as the Chinese Canadian glamour puss who happens to be gay, whip smart, and unafraid of whatever dangers come her way." — *Toronto Star*

"Hamilton's Chinese Canadian heroine is one of a kind … [An] exotic thriller that also offers a fascinating inside look at fiscal misconduct in China … As a unique series character, Ava Lee's become indispensable." — *Calgary Herald*

"Ava Lee has a new business, a new look, and, most important, a new triad boss to appreciate her particular financial talents … We know that Ava will come up with a plan and Hamilton will come up with a twist." — *Globe and Mail*

"Like the best series writers — Ian Rankin and Peter Robinson come to mind — Hamilton manages to … keep the Ava Lee books fresh … A compulsive read, a page-turner of the old school … *The Princeling of Nanjing* is a welcome return of an old favourite, and bodes well for future books." — *Quill & Quire*

"Hamilton uses his people and plot to examine Chinese class and power structures that open opportunities for massive depravities and corruptions." — *London Free Press*

"As usual with a Hamilton-Lee novel, matters take a decided twist as the plot unrolls." — *Owen Sound Times*

"One of those grip-tight novels that makes one read 'just one more chapter' and you discover it's 3 a.m. The novel is built on complicated webs artfully woven into clear, magnetic storytelling. Author Ian Hamilton delivers the intrigue within complex and relentless webs in high style and once again proves that everyone, once in their lives, needs an Ava Lee at their backs." — *Canadian Mystery Reviews*

"The best of the Ava Lee series to date...*Princeling* features several chapters of pure, unadulterated financial sleuthing, which both gave me some nerdy feels and tickled my puzzle-loving mind." — *Literary Treats*

"*The Princeling of Nanjing* was another addition to the Ava Lee series that did not disappoint." — *Words of Mystery*

PRAISE FOR *THE COUTURIER OF MILAN*
NATIONAL BESTSELLER

"The latest in the excellent series starring Ava Lee, businesswoman extraordinaire, *The Couturier of Milan* is another winner for Ian Hamilton...The novel is a hoot. At a point where most crime series start to run out of steam, Ava Lee just keeps rolling on." — *Globe and Mail*

"In Ava Lee, Ian Hamilton has created a crime fighter who breaks the mould with every new book (and, frankly, with every new chapter)." — CBC Books

"The pleasure in following Ava's clever plans for countering the bad guys remains as ever a persuasive attraction." — *Toronto Star*

"Fashionably fierce forensics...But Hamilton has built around Ava Lee an award-winning series that absorbs intriguing aspects of both Asian and Canadian cultures." — *London Free Press*

PRAISE FOR *THE IMAM OF TAWI-TAWI*

"The best of the series so far." — *Globe and Mail*

"One of his best … Tightly plotted and quick-moving, this is a spare yet terrifically suspenseful novel." — *Publishers Weekly*

"Combines lots of action with Ava's acute intelligence and ability to solve even the most complex problems." — *Literary Hub*

"Fast-paced, smoothly written, and fun." — *London Free Press*

"An engrossing novel." — *Reviewing the Evidence*

"Hamilton's rapid-fire storytelling moves the tale along at breakneck speed, as Ava globe-trots to put clues together. Hamilton has always had a knack for combing Fleming-style descriptors with modern storytelling devices and character beats, and this book is no different." — *The Mind Reels*

"An engaging and compelling mystery." — *Literary Treats*

PRAISE FOR *THE GODDESS OF YANTAI*
NATIONAL BESTSELLER

"Ava at her most intimate and vulnerable." — *Toronto Star*

"This time, [Ava's] crusade is personal, and so is her outrage." — *London Free Press*

"In *The Goddess of Yantai* … Ava's personal and professional lives collide in a manner that shakes the usually unflappable character." — *Quill & Quire*

"Told in his typical punchy and forthright style, Hamilton's latest thriller is a rapid-fire read that leaves the reader breathless and eagerly anticipating the next installment...This is a series of books that just seems to get better and better."— *The Mind Reels*

"I wanted to just rip through this book...If you love great writing, an intense pace, and a bit of a thrill, then [the Ava Lee novels] are perfect for you."— *Reading on the Run*

"Action packed and thrilling."— *Words of Mystery*

PRAISE FOR *THE MOUNTAIN MASTER OF SHA TIN*

"Whether it's the triad plot lines or the elegant detective skills of Lee, Ian Hamilton has managed to maintain a freshness to his stories. *The Mountain Master of Sha Tin* is as slick and smart as *The Water Rat of Wanchai*, the first Ava Lee novel...This is one of Canada's best series by one of our best writers."— *Globe and Mail*

"Propulsive."— *London Free Press*

"Hamilton's punchy, fast-paced style has woven a tapestry in over a dozen novels that have introduced us to a variety of characters... This novel, like the previous tales, rockets along."— *The Mind Reels*

"Hamilton provides a fascinating peek into a disturbingly glamorous world."— *Publishers Weekly*

"Another action-packed entry in a solid series."— *Booklist*

PRAISE FOR *THE DIAMOND QUEEN OF SINGAPORE*

"With crisp, taut storytelling, Hamilton whips us around the globe with his captivating prose that delivers like a phoenix strike...Hamilton's

Fleming-esque style of description elicits images and sensations that bring Ava's realm to colourful, glittering life... The perfect summer read, completely engaging, entertaining, and unputdownable." — *The Mind Reels*

"Hamilton takes great care to make sure that the Ava Lee universe and the characters feel authentic, and it especially shows in this book... I'm looking forward to the next book and to seeing Ava take on an even bigger opponent." — *Words of Mystery*

"Another fantastic addition to Hamilton's box of jewels." — *The Bowed Bookshelf*

THE GENERAL OF TIANANMEN SQUARE

The Ava Lee Series

The Dragon Head of Hong Kong: The Ava Lee Prequel
(ebook)

The Water Rat of Wanchai

The Disciple of Las Vegas

The Wild Beasts of Wuhan

The Red Pole of Macau

The Scottish Banker of Surabaya

The Two Sisters of Borneo

The King of Shanghai

The Princeling of Nanjing

The Couturier of Milan

The Imam of Tawi-Tawi

The Goddess of Yantai

The Mountain Master of Sha Tin

The Diamond Queen of Singapore

The Sultan of Sarawak

The Lost Decades of Uncle Chow Tung

Fate

Foresight

Fortune

Finale

Bonnie Jack

THE GENERAL OF TIANANMEN SQUARE

AN AVA LEE NOVEL
THE TRIAD YEARS

IAN HAMILTON

SPIDERLINE

Published in Canada in 2023 and the USA in 2023 by House of Anansi Press Inc.
www.houseofanansi.com

House of Anansi Press is committed to protecting our natural environment.
This book is made of material from well-managed FSC®-certified forests,
recycled materials, and other controlled sources.

House of Anansi Press is a Global Certified Accessible™ (GCA by Benetech)
publisher. The ebook version of this book meets stringent accessibility standards
and is available to readers with print disabilities.

27 26 25 24 23   1 2 3 4 5

Library and Archives Canada Cataloguing in Publication

Title: The general of Tiananmen Square : the Triad years / Ian Hamilton.
Names: Hamilton, Ian, 1946- author.
Series: Hamilton, Ian, 1946- Ava Lee series.
Identifiers: Canadiana (print) 20220401810 | Canadiana (ebook) 20220401845 |
ISBN 9781487010218 (softcover) | ISBN 9781487010225 (EPUB)
Classification: LCC PS8615.A4423 G46 2023 | DDC C813/.6—dc23

Book design: Lucia Kim
Text design: Alysia Shewchuk
Cover image: Dashu83 @ iStock Photo

*House of Anansi Press respectfully acknowledges that the land on which we
operate is the Traditional Territory of many Nations, including the Anishinabeg,
the Wendat, and the Haudenosaunee. It is also the Treaty Lands of the
Mississaugas of the Credit.*

With the participation of the Government of Canada
Avec la participation du gouvernement du Canada

*We acknowledge for their financial support of our publishing program the Canada
Council for the Arts, the Ontario Arts Council, and the Government of Canada.*

Printed and bound in Canada

To my first readers — John, Catherine, Robin, Carol, Lam and CC — a huge thanks for the contributions you have made over the course of many books.

Saint-Jean-Cap-Ferrat
May

IT WAS AVA LEE'S FIRST VISIT TO THE FRENCH RIVIERA,
and as she sat on the terrace of her hotel suite looking out
onto the Mediterranean Sea, she knew it wasn't going to be
her last. What she couldn't understand was why she hadn't
discovered it until now.

It was an early morning in the third week of May. The
weather was perfect, with clear skies and temperatures that
were warm but not humid, and every morning when Ava
sat on the terrace to have coffee she was greeted by a gentle
breeze infused with an aroma that was a combination of
flowers and the sea.

The hotel — the Grand-Hôtel du Cap-Farrat — was as
magnificent as the weather. It had been chosen by Ava's business partner May Ling Wong. Ava had initially had doubts
about staying there because it was more than forty kilometres from Cannes, and Cannes — specifically the Cannes
Film Festival — was the reason they were in the south of

France. But May had been told about the hotel by a friend whose taste she trusted and who thought its tranquil atmosphere would be more to their liking than the craziness that was Cannes during festival time.

Eighteen months previously, Ava could never have imagined being at the film festival for any reason, let alone having a film in it. But a series of events involving Ava's lover, the actor Pang Fai, had led Ava to a chance meeting with Fai's former husband, Lau Lau. There was a time Lau Lau had been regarded as China's leading film director, but when Ava met him, he was a drug-addicted, unemployable wreck of a human being. But as she spoke to him at that first meeting, memories of the great films he'd made flooded over her and she found herself wondering *what if?*

What if — at her expense — she could convince him to go into rehabilitation? What if she offered to pay him to write a script? What if he created one that was good enough to be filmed? What if she provided the money to make that happen? What if Lau Lau could be trusted to direct it? What if he could stay clean throughout the filming — and beyond, into editing and promotion? The result of all those "ifs" was a film named *Tiananmen,* and an invitation to submit the film for consideration at Cannes.

"What are you thinking about? You look like you're completely lost in thought," a voice asked from the terrace doorway.

She turned towards Fai. They had been lovers and constant companions for more than two years. It was the most intense and happiest relationship of Ava's life. Tall, willowy, and elegant, Fai was stunningly beautiful, but when it came to the roles she chose, she never cared about how she looked. Lau Lau had discovered her at the Central Academy of Drama in Beijing, and she had starred in all of his most successful films. Those films were hard-hitting and emotionally challenging, as they dealt with ordinary people trying to cope with the brutal realities of events like the Great Leap Forward and the Cultural Revolution. There was nothing glamorous about many of the characters she had played, but she had always been willing to mute her personality and appearance to fit the role.

"I was remembering meeting Lau Lau for the first time at that artists' commune in Beijing," said Ava, smiling as Fai stepped behind her and wrapped her arms around Ava's shoulders.

"What a mess he was. The world had decided he wasn't fit to be part of it, and he had accepted the world was right until you came along," said Fai. "Chen and I were speaking about that last night. We still don't know what you saw in Lau Lau that made you think he was salvageable."

Chen Jie had been Fai and Lau Lau's agent, but had been recruited by Ava to produce *Tiananmen*. He was sharing another suite at the hotel with Silvana Foo, who along with Fai was starring in the film. "I wasn't sure he was. I just thought he was worth the effort," Ava said. "Even if he was half the director he had been, I thought he'd still turn out better work than the schlock that dominates Chinese cinema these days."

"It turns out he's a lot more than half of what he was. In fact, Chen, Silvana, and I think this could be the best film he's ever made," Fai said, moving alongside. She looked at her watch. "But in half an hour we'll have the first indication of what the international film community thinks of it.

I don't imagine either Lau Lau or Chen slept much last night, thinking about this morning."

"Amanda also didn't sleep well. She called me fifteen minutes ago from Hong Kong to ask me if we'd heard anything yet," said Ava, referring to Amanda Yee, the third partner in Three Sisters. She was also Ava's sister-in-law through her marriage to Michael, Ava's half-brother. "She thought it was crazy that they would schedule *Tiananmen*'s first viewing at seven thirty in the morning. I repeated what you told me about the tradition of morning screenings for critics and other industry people, but Amanda still can't help thinking they're slighting us somehow."

"I thought it was strange the first time I came here, but it's the way things have always been done — the morning screening for critics, and the evening premiere for the public. The premiere is the main event, and the critics are expected to hold back their reviews and opinions until it's over, but word always leaks out. And in this case, we have Harris Jones on the inside. He told Chen he'd call him as soon as the screening is finished."

"Are we paying him to do that, or is he simply being unethical on our behalf?" Ava asked with a smile.

"Harris is a film critic, and even if it is for London's most prestigious newspaper, the job doesn't require him to pass a morality test," Fai said. "Besides, I also think he genuinely fell in love with our movie when he saw the rough cut in Taipei. It was very shrewd of Chen to let him be the first outsider to see it. He became our champion and promoted the hell out of it to the programmers at Cannes. And when Harris champions, people listen. Chen says he's the most influential film critic in the English language since Pauline Kael."

"All those months of work, all those months of anticipation, and it all comes down to what a bunch of strangers think of your work at seven in the morning," Ava said. "What amazes me is how calm you are."

"Lau Lau has made a great film. I'll believe that regardless of what the critics think."

"Looking back, I remember you were as calm in London when we launched the PÖ line at Fashion Week," Ava said. "The rest of us were running around like chickens with our heads cut off, and you were an island of serenity. When I mentioned it to you, you said, 'I love Clark's clothes and I know how to model them to their greatest advantage. I am an actor, you know. This isn't a stretch.' And model them you did. You were spectacular. There had been no need for any of us to worry."

"What made me nervous that day was the lunch after the London show. I decided to flirt with you — except you didn't pick up on it," said Fai.

"I was too star-struck to believe it was possible you could be interested in me."

"Well, it was a good thing that I persisted," Fai said, and then kissed Ava gently on the lips.

"Do you want to go back to bed?" Ava asked.

Fai smiled, but before she could say anything, her phone rang. She almost leapt at it. "*Wei*," she answered, listened for a few seconds, and then said, "Chen, you have to slow down. I can barely understand what you're trying to tell me."

Ava couldn't hear Chen, but she kept her eyes locked on Fai and tried to discern her reaction. Her face was impassive until her eyebrows rose and her mouth formed a large O. "That should make tonight's preview more interesting," Fai said. "We'll see you at five-thirty in the lobby."

"Well?" Ava asked as Fai put down the phone.

"Jones told Chen that people stood and clapped when the film ended. Chen is so overwhelmed he could hardly talk," she said.

"What a relief. I'm so happy for Lau Lau," Ava said. "So that's one group down and one to go. I pray that the public screening goes as well."

"That's never a guarantee, but this is a wonderful start."

"Are Chen and Silvana going to join May and us for lunch today? I'd like to hear everything Jones had to say," said Ava.

"I don't think we'll see Chen. We still need to find a distributor, and he'll want to initiate more talks while the iron is hot," Fai said.

"He did explain his strategy to me. I wasn't sure it was smart to gamble so much on Cannes and hoped we'd be able to land a deal with one of the big international distribution companies here, but if this morning went as well as Jones said then Chen may be right again.

"And if he is, you'll get back the money you invested, and maybe even more, and if we don't get a mega-deal then he can still piece together a bunch of smaller, regional ones."

"What would the impact be if we managed to win the Palme d'Or?" Ava asked.

"It is almost too much to imagine, but I can't deny that Chen and I have fantasized about it. But that's what it is, a fantasy. I'm just happy we're here and that our film is being seen."

TIANANMEN WAS SCHEDULED TO BE SHOWN AT SEVEN
thirty that night, and a public relations firm Chen had hired
would manage Fai, Ava, and May's arrival at the Palais des
Festivals, guide them up the red carpet, handle the media
and photographers who would be there, and get them into
their seats in time for the start of the film.

Ava and May had been reluctant to do the red carpet, but
Fai and Chen insisted they join them. May actually didn't
put up much protest, and spent a day in Shanghai with Clark
Po looking at dresses he had created for her before flying
into Nice.

Fai didn't visit with Clark, but they had communicated
online. She had always worn Chinese dresses at premieres,
and asked him to carry on the tradition. He had made two
cheongsams for her, and she insisted Ava decide which one
she should wear.

The first was made of red silk with fine ribbons of green
and silver, but was rather traditional with a short collar and
sleeves, and a moderate slit up one leg.

The second was an electric-blue colour shot through with

bright gold strands, a collar that reached almost to Fai's cheekbones, bell-shaped split sleeves that dangled over her wrists, and a slit that went all the way to her upper thigh.

"What do you think?" Fai asked. "The red one is beautiful, but rather safe, while the blue dress is unlike anything I've ever worn. Is it too much?"

"It will certainly attract attention, but what's the point in coming to Cannes and walking the red carpet if you don't do that?" Ava said. "Truthfully, the dress by itself is fantastic, and on you it is even more fantastic. This is a special night. The blue cheongsam is a special dress. It's the one to wear."

"Then that is what I'll have on," Fai said. "I have to say, though, I wish you would wear something a little more colourful than your black dress."

"Clark made it for me to wear at the reception the night before we introduced the PÖ brand in Shanghai. It makes me feel really feminine. It has also been lucky, and you know how I value luck."

"Well, it is sexy. Every time I see you in it, it makes me amorous."

"I'm sure that would make Clark very happy."

"It should, and so will the fact he'll have four dresses on the red carpet tonight, when you count May and Silvana."

Ava hadn't yet seen what May and Silvana were going to wear, and the way their day was structured, there wouldn't be the chance until it was time to get into the limos. After the call from Chen, Ava and Fai had gone back to bed and then spent the rest of the morning by the pool. The women were excited when they met for lunch with May and Silvana, where they talked about the critics' screening, and then they went to their suites to wait for the hairstylists and makeup artists hired by the public relations company.

Ava rarely wore makeup other than a touch of mascara and lipstick, and her hair hadn't changed in years. She either wore it parted down the middle and let it hang to her shoulders, or pulled it back and fastened it with a chignon pin. Her trips to the hairdresser were for trims and not much more. The last time she had experienced anything different was when she was a maid of honour at Amanda's wedding and had to undergo her hair being piled on top of her head and sprayed into a solid block. She had hated it, and was determined not to let anyone do that again, so when the hairstylist arrived at her and Fai's suite, Ava waved off the attempt to sculpt her hair. She did submit to some extra makeup when the artist pointed out that, without some colour added to her cheeks and lips, her skin was going to look washed out under the camera flashes.

While the beauty crew worked on Fai, Ava slipped on her dress and went to sit on the terrace. Before partnering with May Ling and Amanda, she had been in the debt collection business with an elderly Hong Konger named Uncle. He was a wise man, and he had loved her like a granddaughter and provided her with advice that she continued to value and use. One of the things he'd said to her often was: "We should never get ahead of ourselves or assume too much. We should accept things for what they are and not what we want them to be." And that's what she thought as she waited for Fai's hairstylist to finish. It was terrific that the film had been well-received by the critics, but was that because they actually liked it, or was it possible that some had reacted positively because they wanted to see Lau Lau make a comeback and were willing to embrace whatever he made? The audience reaction that night would be a better gauge, she decided. Then her phone rang and she saw Chen's name on the screen.

"I thought we were meeting at five thirty, that's only minutes from now," she answered. "What happened that you can't wait until then? Have you already sealed a distribution deal?"

"No, but there is definite interest and we'll get offers," he said. "But I'm calling to give you and Fai a heads-up about tonight. When I was in Cannes today having lunch with a distributor, I found myself sitting two tables away from Mo and a group of his executives. They are here in force."

Ava hesitated. "Mo who is chairman of the China Movie Syndicate?"

"Yes, one and the same."

"What is he doing here?" she asked.

"Well, given that he manages the organization that has to approve every film made in China, and every film that foreign companies want to screen in China, it is logical that he would attend one of the most prestigious film festivals in the world," Chen said.

"Him being there, and so close, must have been awkward. Did you acknowledge each other?"

"More than acknowledge," Chen said. "He came to my table to say that he and his people had arrived in Cannes only that morning, had missed the critics' screening, and so unfortunately were going to be at our premiere. He said it wasn't something any of them were looking forward to. He was completely condescending and I responded by doing something I shouldn't have. I asked him if he had heard how well it had gone for us that morning."

"That was poking the dragon."

"I know, and I wish I hadn't because he became immediately angry, turned to the distributor, and told him that if he ever wanted to have another of his films shown in China then he should have nothing to do with me."

"So Mo knew him?"

"Mo knows a lot of distributors, but not all of them will bend to his threats."

"But some will?"

"Of course. Money talks, and China is a big, and growing, market."

"I wonder after seeing *Tiananmen* who he'll hate the most — the film or us?"

"I am quite certain he'll hate it and us with equal passion, but now that our film is made I don't know what he can do to cause us or it any harm," Chen said. "The only reason I told you I saw him was because I didn't want you or Fai to be unpleasantly surprised."

"Thanks for that, Chen. We'll see you at five thirty," Ava said, ending the call.

She stared out at the sea. An almost perfect day had just hit a speed bump, albeit maybe a small one. Mo was potentially the most powerful man in the world of Chinese film, and had the ability to not only approve what could be made and seen in China, but also make or break the career of anyone working in the industry. Fai had become a target of his displeasure when she'd refused to trade sex for roles. He'd threatened to end her career in China, and when that didn't get the result he wanted, Fai was blackmailed with sex tapes that would have exposed her true sexuality. Ava had intervened, and managed to pressure Mo into backing down when she discovered and promised to make public the fact that his son and only child was gay. It was something Ava regretted having to do, and she had felt immense relief when it became unnecessary.

"Every time I come out here, you seem to be staring out at the sea and lost in deep thought," Fai said from behind.

Ava turned to look at her. "Oh my god, you look just fantastic," she said.

"It's amazing what a brilliant designer dress and an hour or so with a fabulous hairstylist and makeup master can do for a woman," said Fai.

"You're going to light up that red carpet."

"I only hope that I'll be able to sit when we get inside the Palais. This dress is really tight around the hips. I think I've put on some weight."

"I'll help ease you into your seat," Ava said.

"That should make for an interesting few seconds. We can practise when I get into the limo," Fai said. "Speaking of which, we should probably think about heading downstairs."

"We'll go in a few minutes. Chen phoned me while you were finishing up inside. He had some news I wasn't thrilled to hear — Mo and his crew are in Cannes. Chen doesn't assign any particular importance to the fact. He just thought we should know so we're not surprised if he pops into view," Ava said, downplaying Chen's interaction with Mo.

"He has come to see *Tiananmen*."

"You said that with conviction."

Fai shrugged. "He will have read Harris Jones's article. It not only ran in the *Tribune*; it was picked up by at least ten other major newspapers. Mo will want to see for himself how the film deals with the events of June fourth."

"Jones focused as much on the human elements as the political."

"I doubt Mo and his cronies will care about that in the least."

"We always knew it could be controversial, especially in the short term. We have prepared as well as we can for that possibility," said Ava.

Fai nodded. "I know, but that doesn't stop me worrying. Last night in bed I kept asking myself what is best for all of us — that the movie be a huge hit or a flop? The artist part of me wants a hit; the realist believes it might be easier on all our lives if it isn't."

"Everyone I spoke to before I committed to this project warned me that there was nothing the Chinese government was more sensitive about than Tiananmen Square, so I didn't go into this with my eyes closed," Ava said. "You, Lau Lau, and Chen were among those who gave the warning. Yet here we all are in Cannes getting ready to screen a film that we knew ahead of time the Chinese government would detest and do everything possible to discredit and destroy. What does that say about us?"

"Lau Lau needed resurrection, and whatever happens to him can't be worse than the hell he was in. Chen has spent his entire career on the outside looking in. Now he has a chance to leave his mark, and I have to say he's relishing it. As for me, I was carrying a lot of guilt about Lau Lau, and quite honestly worried that I'd never find another role of which I could be proud. We are all getting something we want. But tell me, Ava, what are you getting?"

Ava smiled. "At the start it was all about Lau Lau. I couldn't stop thinking about the marvellous films he'd made, and I couldn't stop equating those with the mess of a human being I met. All I wanted to do was give him the chance to do great work again. I didn't expect a script about Tiananmen Square, but when we got it, and saw how powerful it was, how could I say no to it…? There are some truths too big to bury."

(3)

THE REST OF THEIR PARTY WAS IN THE HOTEL LOBBY
when Ava and Fai exited the elevator.

"What a handsome group," Ava said as she approached them.

Chen wore a standard tuxedo with a black bow tie; Lau Lau had on a black suit and a white silk shirt that was unbuttoned halfway down his chest; but Silvana Foo and May Ling were dressed more opulently. Silvana was short and plump, and Clark had designed an aqua-coloured two-piece silk outfit for her that made her appear a bit thinner and taller. The top was a billowy blouse with sleeves that went past her wrists. The skirt was heavier, pleated, and fanned out from her waist to her ankles. May wore a snug, knee-length, glittering red silk sheath dress that was cut in a straight line across her chest to accentuate her ample bosom.

"I can't remember ever being surrounded by so many stunning women," Chen said.

"I agree," Lau Lau said, almost shyly.

"Congratulations on this morning," Ava said to him. "I was thrilled to hear the film was so well-received."

Lau Lau smiled and slightly lowered his head.

"The PR people have been telling us that it has generated quite a buzz," Chen said. "And speaking of public relations, two of the assistants are outside waiting for us by the limousines, and I think we should join them. I thought I'd travel to Cannes in one limo with Silvana and Lau Lau."

"That's perfect," Ava said.

Two black Mercedes-Benz limos were parked in front of the hotel; the first in line had a young woman standing by the rear door, the other had a young man. Chen led Silvana and Lau Lau to the first.

"Good evening, my name is Henri," the young man said to Ava, Fai, and May as he opened the back door of the second vehicle for them. "Ms. Pang, it is a thrill to meet you. I am a big fan."

"Thank you," Fai said, eyeing the back seat. "Ava, you or May should sit in the middle. I don't want to slide all that way."

"*Momentai*," Ava laughed, then said to May, "Fai finds her dress is a bit tight."

"She's not the only one," May said. "I thought this fit perfectly when I tried it on in Shanghai. I must have put on a kilo or two since then. French food is more fattening than Chinese."

Henri waited for Ava to get into the middle seat, gently helped Fai climb in, and then ran around the car to open the other rear door for May. When they were settled, he sat in the front next to the driver, but immediately turned to face them. "Your film was a great success this morning. We saw some of the scorecards and the ratings were terrific."

"We heard, and it is very gratifying," Ava said. "Let's hope tonight will be as successful."

"If it isn't, we'll be shocked. One thing is already certain, you're going to be warmly welcomed. People have been crowding into the area surrounding the Grand Théâtre Lumière for hours. There will be thousands of them lining both sides of the red carpet and beyond."

"Ms. Wong and I are amateurs at this kind of thing, so I don't know if we're pleased or terrified to hear that," Ava said. "What is the plan when we get to Cannes?"

"The film is scheduled to screen at seven thirty, so our objective is to get you into the lobby by seven twenty. You will wait there until the theatre is quiet, and then we'll take you to your seats — which are obviously front row centre," Henri said. "We will arrive at the Palais right around seven, so you have twenty minutes or so to make your way up the red carpet."

"Will it really take twenty minutes? How long is the carpet?" Ava asked.

"When you leave the car, you'll walk about twenty metres or so to the first step. I'll be with you, and I expect some festival staff will be there to help. There are twenty-four steps to the theatre entrance. Fans will be screaming at you, photographers will want you to pose for pictures. It can be intimidating, but you should try to think of it as simply being fun," he said. "When you have climbed the first twelve steps, you will reach a platform where you'll be greeted by the festival president and the festival director. This is where the photographers are the most prevalent."

"What do you mean by 'prevalent'?" asked Ava.

"Last year there were close to three hundred photographers lining the carpet."

"Good god, I had no idea," Ava said. "How many people will be inside the theatre?"

"We were told it is a sellout, so approximately two thousand three hundred guests — and 'guests' are how the festival refers to them."

"Did you know it was going to be like this?" May said to Fai.

"This is my second time here. The first time both Lau Lau and I were doing drugs so my recollection is a bit hazy. But it seems to me it was much like Henri has explained."

"And we are expected to walk that carpet with Fai?" May asked Henri.

"Your names are on the list," he said.

"And I want the support, so don't think about backing out," Fai said.

"If we survived Fashion Week in London, I guess we can survive this," Ava said.

"It will be exciting," Henri said. "This is a once-in-a-lifetime experience for most people. Think of the memories you'll have — particularly when your film is well-received and adds to the enjoyment of the evening."

"Three hundred photographers, two thousand three hundred guests," May muttered.

"And beautifully dressed guests at that," said Henri. "The festival has a very strict dress code. Men who show up in less than formal wear are often turned away. We had one client last year who was refused entry because he was wearing brown shoes with his black tuxedo. Mind you, he wasn't an artist. They will sometimes turn a blind eye to someone inappropriately dressed if he or she is an important enough actor or director."

"Lau Lau isn't wearing a bow tie, or any tie for that matter. Will that be a problem?" said Ava.

"My colleague has a selection in the car. I'm sure that

between her and Mr. Chen they can persuade him to put one on."

"What if they can't?" May asked.

"Then I will," Ava said. "We haven't come this far to let something as minor as a tie ruin our evening."

"It won't be a problem," Fai said. "Lau Lau will never say no to Ava, he's totally afraid of her."

Ava looked out the car window. They were passing through a series of small towns, all connected to each other and built to offer as many views of the sea as possible. Traffic was heavy, but moving. "What do we do if we get to Cannes early?" she asked Henri.

"The festival has a reserved parking area near the theatre. We'll wait there until it's time to go to the theatre."

"They think of everything, don't they?" Ava said.

"They try, and they don't make many mistakes," said Henri.

The car became quiet as they continued towards Cannes. It was a huge night, Ava thought, and everyone had their own way of preparing for it. But rather than doing that, her mind returned to Chen's phone call about Mo. Although she had known it was inevitable that *Tiananmen* would catch his and the Chinese government's attention, she had hoped their reaction would be muted — perhaps thinking that ignoring it would draw less attention to it. Mo's attitude with Chen and the threats he'd made to the distributor hinted at the opposite. It seemed to Ava that he was going to be on the offensive, and her worry was that they weren't ready for it.

"May, I didn't have a chance to tell you that Mo, the chairman of the China Movie Syndicate, is in Cannes. He could be at the premiere tonight," Ava blurted out.

"Is that the guy who gave you and Fai such a hard time?" May said.

"He is. I just want to make sure that you're comfortable walking the red carpet with us. He knows Fai and I are together, but I can't imagine he knows that you are connected in any way to this film. It might be prudent to keep it that way."

"You and I have gone through hell together. Why would I worry about someone like Mo?"

Ava reached for May's hand. "I love you," she said.

"I love you too," May said.

Traffic thickened and the stoplights became more frequent. Ava looked at her watch and realized they weren't going to be that early.

Henri turned towards the back seat. "We'll go directly to the theatre. When we arrive, I'll get out of the car and open the doors for you. Then I'll lead you onto the red carpet and walk slightly ahead at a slow, measured pace that I would like you to match. Ms. Pang, you should feel free to stop to sign a few things or pose for some pictures for fans, but don't spend too much time in one spot. We do have to keep moving."

The car came to a sudden stop at a roadblock, and Ava wondered if there was a problem. A police officer walked to the car accompanied by a man dressed in a tuxedo. Henri rolled down his window so they could see him.

"*Bon soir, Henri, vous etes arrive exactement a l'heure*," the man said, then spoke to the police officer. "*Mademoiselle Pang est le vedette du film ce soir.*"

The officer looked at Fai. "I was so happy to draw this assignment. I think you are *merveilleuse* — marvellous. Could you sign this for me, please," he said, showing her the DVD cover for the film *Mao's Daughter.*

"You are very kind, and I'll be pleased to sign it," Fai said.

"Could you make it out to Roger, from Pang Fai?"

"Of course."

"You're going to get a lot of that tonight," Henri said as the car moved past the blockade and away from the happy police officer. "So many movie lovers are excited you're here, Ms. Pang, and of course Lau Lau's return and your reunion with him have also created tremendous anticipation for the film."

The car turned a corner and suddenly they were facing a wall of people.

"Good grief," May said.

"Even more people than I imagined," Henri said. "But not to worry, we'll manage."

The limo with Lau Lau, Chen, and Silvana had already arrived, and Ava saw they were halfway up the first flight of stairs.

Their limo inched forward until it came to a stop at the curb where the red carpet began. Henri got out and went to Fai's door. She exited and then waited for Ava and May. When Fai turned to face the crowd and took her first step onto the carpet, a chorus of voices shouted "Pang Fai" and "Come this way."

"Are we ready to have some fun?" Henri asked.

"Let's do it," Fai said, waving at the people who were yelling at her.

Ava stayed several steps behind Fai as they slowly made their way to the stairs. The noise was almost deafening as fans implored Fai to acknowledge them with an autograph, a word, or a smile as they took photos. Ahead of them, Ava saw Lau Lau signing a movie poster. She smiled when she saw he was wearing a black bow tie.

It took them a full ten minutes to make their way to the platform where the festival president and other officials waited. It would have taken longer if Henri hadn't pressed them. "They love you," he said to Fai, "but we have to keep moving."

Ava saw May's eyes flitting in all directions. She seemed excited and nervous at the same time as people shouted at them as well.

"This is crazy," May said. "They seem to think we're in the film."

"Smile and wave," Ava said. "There haven't been many times in my life when I've been so popular — and I haven't had to do anything to earn it so I'm going to enjoy this, and so should you."

May nodded, and waved at a small group of Chinese women screaming at them.

"Look, you're the main attraction," Henri said to May, pointing up at an immense screen that overhung the steps and featured May and Ava.

"That's the closest I'll ever come to being in a movie," Ava said. "I do have to say that my dress looks nice."

As they reached the platform, Lau Lau, Chen, and Silvana were leaving it. Lau Lau was grinning, and that caught Ava by surprise because she couldn't remember ever seeing him look happy.

Henri started to introduce Ava, May, and Fai to the festival officials, but he had barely gotten their names out of his mouth before the festival director reached for Fai's hand and bent over to kiss it. "This is such a thrill. I have long admired your work, and I was delighted when *Tiananmen* was submitted for consideration at this year's festival," he said, and then lowered his voice. "I want you to know that I think it is a wonderful film, and your performance is magnificent. I am confident it will secure your reputation as one of the finest actors of any generation — and by that I mean your worldwide reputation, not just in Asia."

"You are very kind," Fai said, her hand still resting in his as hundreds of cameras caught the director's show of homage.

"Over here," several voices shouted.

Fai turned to face the cameras on the other side of the platform. She waved and smiled.

"Who are you wearing?" someone yelled.

"Clark Po," she said loudly, then motioned at Ava and May. "We are all wearing PÖ. He is the best young designer in Asia."

"We should leave now, Ms. Pang, if we are to get to the theatre on schedule," Henri said softly.

"Of course," Fai said, but instead she walked closer to the cameras. She turned sideways so she was in profile and her leg was fully exposed by the slit in the cheongsam. She posed for several seconds, and then went to the other side of the platform, repeated it, and said to Henri, "I'm ready to go now."

They made it to the lobby with only a few minutes to spare before the scheduled screening. Chen and the others in his group were there drinking water. Bottles were being offered to the arrivals, and Fai and Ava took one.

"We are a little tight for time," a young woman wearing a festival badge that read *guest relations* said. "But if any of you ladies need to visit the washroom, please feel free to do so."

They all shook their heads.

"Then follow me, please, to your seats."

"Where am I sitting?" Lau Lau asked.

Ava noticed that the grin she had seen outside had been replaced by a look of worry. And when he put down his bottle of water, she saw his hand was shaking.

"You are seated in the middle of the row," the woman said.

"I want to sit between Fai and Ava. I don't want to sit anywhere else."

"That may not be the current seating plan, but it should be simple enough to adjust," said the woman.

"Don't worry, we'll sort it out," Chen said.

"Yes, we will, and now let's enter the theatre," the woman said.

As intimidating as the red carpet had been, the walk into the theatre and to their seats was even more intense. Ava imagined two thousand sets of eyes fixed on them, and she felt her face flush as self-consciousness took over any other thought or emotion she might have had. It was a relief when they reached their assigned seats. Accommodating Lau Lau's request simply meant him switching seats with Chen. As soon as they sat, Lau Lau reached for Fai and Ava's hands. Ava took his and felt it tremble.

During the walk to their seats, she had been oblivious to anything but the thought of being watched. But as they sat with their backs to the audience, she heard a steady buzz of noise from indistinct voices. Ava lowered her head. She had given up Catholicism in her teens because of the church's stance on homosexuality, but she hadn't forsaken everything connected to it. One thing she had retained was the occasional need to pray. During difficult times in her work and personal life, she had often prayed to St. Jude, the patron saint of lost causes, and invariably the difficulties were conquered. Perhaps the Cannes Film Festival was an unusual place to reach out to St. Jude, but she did it anyway.

"St. Jude," she said under her breath, "help us this evening. I want the film to be a success, but not for any financial gain. My friend Lau Lau was in a private hell with little hope of escaping. Let this film affirm his return to his craft, and give him the confidence and support he needs to continue to work and be happy... And, lastly, please ensure that Chen gets the recognition he deserves for being brave enough to take on this challenge, and that Fai and Silvana are also properly acknowledged. Amen."

The lights dimmed, the voices went silent, and the word *Tiananmen* filled the screen in English and Chinese.

4

AVA HADN'T SEEN THE FINAL VERSION OF THE FILM. SHE had seen bits and pieces in rough-cut form in Taipei, where a lot of it was shot, but had decided to keep it at a distance until she could see it as the viewing public would. And Cannes was the first opportunity.

"I want to see it the way Lau Lau intended people to see it," she had said when Fai urged her to look at the copy Chen had emailed for her to download. "I don't want a small screen. I want a full screen. I want to be surrounded by film lovers."

Within ten minutes of the start of *Tiananmen* in all of its full-screen glory, she knew she had made the right decision.

Ava found the opening of the film to be slow, but knew from reading the script that Lau Lau's aim was to build understanding, empathy, and tension in two separate story-lines. The first had Silvana as the mother of a young man, a university student, who left their apartment every day starting in mid-April to join the democracy demonstrations at the square. The other had Fai as a general who was part of the military hierarchy providing advice to the Chinese government, as the demonstrations and protests persisted through April, all of May, and into June.

As the weeks passed, the mother became more and more concerned about her son's safety, but he refused to abandon what had become a cause with a large student following. He went to the square every day, even after the government declared martial law on May 20th and moved 300,000 troops from various divisions into Beijing. The last time she saw him was the morning of June 3rd. That evening and into the next morning, tanks and troops moved into the square and the attacks on protestors began. He didn't come home. She heard about events in the square and went there to try to locate him.

The female general was a member of a military committee that reported directly to the Communist Party's most senior leaders. That committee had been charged with finding the right way to deal with the protestors. One faction supported a more open society, while another wanted the demonstrations shut down by any means necessary. Lau Lau's representations of the discussions held within the committee showed a shift in policy that became increasingly hardline as the protests continued. The female general believed the non-violent protests should be allowed to continue, but her opinions became marginalized and excluded. By the time martial law was declared, she had been removed from the committee, temporarily relieved of her command, and told to stay silent. Her reaction was to go — dressed as a civilian — to the square, as a witness to what she feared would transpire. Her worst fears were realized, and she wept as she watched soldiers shoot and tanks run over defenceless citizens.

The two women met on a street that ran off the square

early the following morning. They were cautious with each other, neither willing initially to talk about their reason for being there. Ava remembered Fai talking about filming those scenes. Lau Lau had wanted her and Silvana to inch towards sharing their truths. Not knowing who or how much to trust, it was a slow and careful process. When their truths were finally revealed, Fai agreed to help Silvana find her son.

Once again in uniform, Fai visited the scene of the worst of the violence, and attempted to pry information out of the officers who were overseeing the removal of bodies and the injured and placing others under arrest. She managed to get access to some records and found the name of Silvana's son on a list of the dead. It shook her, and she was shaken even more when she told Silvana about her son and saw her distraught reaction.

After the imposition of martial law, all news coverage about what was going on in the square had been quashed, so there was no mention of the military action. As far as the PLA and the government were concerned, nothing had happened. But Fai's general decided the truth needed to be told, and through some friends she made contact with foreign media. She provided them with an eyewitness account of the attack on civilians, and passed them copies of the lists of the dead, injured, and arrested she had been able to obtain. Stories about the massacre ran in newspapers and on major media outlets around the world. China was the exception.

The government was irate, and believed someone inside the system had leaked the information. Two days later, Fai was arrested, interrogated, and charged with treason.

The movie ended with her sitting alone on the floor of a cell. The cell door opened. She looked up and stared defiantly at her captors before lowering her head in acceptance of an unknown fate.

As the credits began to roll, the theatre was deathly quiet. Lau Lau squeezed Ava's hand so tightly that it hurt. "That was magnificent, even better than I'd imagined," she whispered to him. And then, confused by the audience's lack of reaction, she thought, *What is going on?*

"Lau Lau," a single voice shouted from behind as the theatre lights came on. Ava turned and saw a man in the balcony standing and clapping. Others around him began to stand. They started clapping as well, and yelling "Lau Lau."

Then, almost as one, the crowd sitting on the ground level rose to their feet.

"*Magnifique, magnifique,*" someone shouted.

But that was overtaken by more cries of "Lau Lau," until it seemed everyone in the theatre was chanting his name.

Ava turned and looked at him. His shoulders were shaking and tears were streaming down his cheeks. Fai was crying too, but not as loudly as Silvana, who was sobbing.

"Lau Lau, you should stand to acknowledge the cheers," Chen said.

Lau Lau pressed his hand on the armrest, started to rise, and then sat again. "Fai and Ava, help me, please," he said.

They each took an arm and pulled him gently to his feet. He stiffened his back, turned, bowed his head, then put his fists together and moved them up and down to signify his thanks and respect.

Ava and Fai stood by his side. Fai, several inches taller than him even without heels, towered over him. As small and thin and vulnerable as he looked now, all Ava had to do was think of the first time she'd met him in Beijing to realize how far he had come. *It's a miracle he escaped that life*, she thought. And how else could she describe two thousand people standing on their feet shouting his name, but as proof that it was indeed a miracle?

5

THE SHOUTING AND CLAPPING DIDN'T ABATE, BUT after a minute Henri came to them. "We should leave now. We can go by a side exit. There are festival officials and some special guests waiting for you there," he said.

As they filed towards the door Henri had indicated, some of the people they passed reached out to touch Lau Lau, Fai, and Silvana. Ava saw it made Lau Lau uneasy and moved to his side. "They love you, but I understand it can be unnerving."

"It has been such a long time…" he said.

The door opened into a hallway. Ava saw the festival director and president, and several other people with festival name tags.

"My name is Jean Belisle," a man said, stepping forward with his hand extended to Lau Lau. "I am the assistant program director. I was the first person Harris Jones spoke to about this film, and I was the first person in our organization to see it. I have to admit that when I saw it ran for more than three hours I had some reservations, but those vanished almost immediately, and the three hours seemed like one. Congratulations, I think you've made a masterpiece."

"What a grand success," the president said.

"I second those sentiments," the festival director said. "I trust you'll be staying in Cannes until the awards ceremony?"

"That was our plan," Chen said.

"I think it could be worth your while," Harris Jones said over the festival director's shoulder.

"My friend, we can't thank you enough for your support," said Chen.

"It is easy to support work like this," Jones said. "Now, do you have any late evening plans?"

"We were going back to our hotel in Cap Ferrat. I wanted to plan a big celebratory dinner, but Fai wouldn't let me. She was afraid it might jinx us," said Chen with a smile.

"Well, there has to be some kind of celebration. Some critic colleagues and I have reserved several tables at La Palme d'Or in the Hôtel Martinez," Jones said, and smiled. "By the way, we didn't choose it because of its name. It is very good. We invited some of the festival officials to join us and some of them accepted. Most of them are there already. We would love to have all of you as our guests."

"What do you think?" Chen asked the others.

"That's very kind of Mr. Jones," said Silvana. "Maybe we could join them for at least a drink."

"Sure, let's go," Fai said. "But I'm not sure one drink will be enough."

"We have two limos. I'm sure we can fit everyone into them," Chen said.

After a prolonged series of thanks and goodbyes, Henri led the group through a maze of hallways to a door that opened onto a side street. The limos were there waiting for them.

"Harris can come with us," said Chen. "I'm sure Mr. Belisle won't object to riding with the ladies."

"Not at all," Belisle said, smiling at Fai. "Although I have to admit I am somewhat overwhelmed. I have seen all of your films, Ms. Pang, and you are one of my screen goddesses. And if you don't mind me saying, you are even more formidable in person."

"Please don't go on like that," Fai said good-naturedly. "I am not displeased by flattery, but this is Lau Lau's night. He's the one you should be celebrating."

They got into the limo. Henri pulled a jump seat down for Belisle so he sat facing the three women. The car left the side street and immediately hit heavy vehicular and foot traffic. As it inched forward, faces appeared on the other side of the tinted glass windows; some people knocking and waving.

"What a night," May said. "I'll never forget it."

"Excuse me, but we haven't been introduced," said Belisle. "I know your names from the guest list, but that's all."

"I'm Ava Lee, and this is my friend and business partner May Ling Wong," said Ava.

"Chen speaks very highly of both of you. He hinted that you, Ms. Lee, had a great deal to do with the resurrection of Lau Lau. On behalf of the entire international film community, you have my thanks."

"I'm just a fan who was pleased to do what I could. Chen deserves most of the credit."

"I suspect you are more than a fan, but what matters is that, after a rather difficult day, we had a wonderful evening."

"If you don't me asking, what was so difficult? Are you referring to something that relates to the film?" Ava asked.

"Yes, but it passed. It is water under the bridge," he said.

"We would still like to know what it was," Ava said rather insistently.

"Very well, but you shouldn't make more of it than it was," he sighed. "I assume you know Mr. Mo from the China Movie Syndicate."

"Yes, we know him," said Ava.

"He and several members of his executive team paid us a visit this afternoon. He wanted to meet with the festival president, but he was busy so Mr. Mo had to make do with the director and me," said Belisle. "We've had dealings with him in the past, and they've usually been civil. The meeting today started that way, but rather quickly deteriorated."

"How so?"

"He wanted us to cancel the screening of *Tiananmen* this evening, and to withdraw the film from competition. We, of course, refused."

"What reason did Mo give for their request?" asked Ava.

"He said the film exaggerated, twisted, and distorted a minor event in recent Chinese history. He said it was massively insulting to the Chinese people and their government," said Belisle. "The director then said he hadn't noticed them at the critics' screening and asked when they had seen the film. Mo's answer was to repeat his claims about it being insulting."

"He doesn't have to see it to hate it. The title alone is enough," said Fai. "Our thanks to you for defending the film."

"We hardly deserve credit. The film is wonderful and needed to be seen. Besides, we've had to deal with bullies before and have learned how to handle them. In the case of Mr. Mo, he needs our support as much as we need his. So, despite his bluster, he won't do us any damage," Belisle said.

"I'm pleased you don't think he will present you any problem."

"As I said, it's water under the bridge, and now no more talk about the horrible Mr. Mo. This is an evening for celebration," said Belisle.

La Palme d'Or was on the first floor of the Hôtel Martinez, an art deco grand hotel that was almost one hundred years old with a balcony overlooking La Croisette. Belisle was the first person to leave the limo when it stopped in front of the hotel. The car with Chen and the others was close behind. Belisle looked up at the balcony and waved at a line of people watching them arrive.

"Those are some of my colleagues, and friends of Harris. I told them there was a chance you might join us," he said to Fai as she stepped out of the car.

They went into the hotel and followed Belisle towards La Palme d'Or. Ava saw the eyes of everyone in the lobby turn in their direction and lock in on Fai. She wasn't surprised. Even in the theatre amid a thousand or so well-dressed women Fai had stood out; in the more enclosed atmosphere of the hotel lobby, her presence was dominating.

When they entered the restaurant, heads turned in their direction once more. Though Ava knew that Fai was the target of their attention, she felt a mild level of discomfort at the idea of being even indirectly examined. She looked at Fai, who was smiling and nodding as if she were entering a room full of friends. It reminded Ava of the first time she'd met Fai, at a restaurant in Shanghai. At one point they'd walked to the washroom together and Ava had commented on the attention Fai drew.

"Being stared at is part of the price I pay for being an actor, and given that it is my job, being well-known is infinitely better than not being known at all," Fai had said.

"Doesn't it ever bother you, being examined like that?"

"Only if it goes beyond looking or if people are really rude. Truthfully, that doesn't happen very often."

There was no rudeness at La Palme d'Or, only smiles and waves. As Belisle led them to a group of tables, the people who were already there stood and began to gather more chairs and reconfigure the seating arrangements.

Before they reached the tables, a tall, thin man wearing jeans and a dark blue silk shirt took several steps towards them. His face was long and bony, but a full head of curly grey hair softened his appearance. He bowed in their direction, and when he straightened, he reached for Fai's hand. She looked at Belisle.

"Ms. Pang, I'd like to introduce Patrice Malle. He is one of our country's best directors, and the president of this year's eight-member Cannes jury."

"I can't speak Chinese, and I'm sure you don't understand French, so let me say in English that it is a privilege to meet you," Malle said.

"And for me to meet you," Fai said.

Malle lifted Fai's hand to his lips and kissed it. He smiled, and then something over her shoulder caught his attention. Ava looked in that direction and saw Chen, Silvana, Harris Jones, and Lau Lau entering the restaurant.

"Lau Lau," someone shouted, and there was an immediate ripple of applause.

"Ah, *le plus grand auteur Chinois*," Malle said, and turned to Fai. "Do you know what that means?"

"No."

"*Un auteur* isn't just a film director; he's an artist with a style that's all his own, and he imprints it on everything he makes. Without knowing in advance who made *Tiananmen*, I could have told you after watching ten minutes of it that it was Lau Lau. We French adore *auteurs*. There are so few of them, and they need to be treasured," he said. "Now, please excuse me, I must go and greet him."

When Malle left, Ava said to Belisle, "Is it appropriate for a jury member to be so public with his opinions?"

"Mr. Malle has the status to do whatever he pleases, but I will point out that he didn't actually tell you his opinion about the film," said Belisle. "Although I have to say that I don't think he would have introduced himself if he was harbouring any negative thoughts about it."

"Ladies, we have seats waiting for you," a man said.

Tables had been pushed together to make a long row. The chairs in the middle of both sides were vacant. Ava, May Ling, and Fai took seats next to each other, facing into the restaurant. Lau Lau, Silvana, and Chen sat across from them.

"If no one objects, I'm going to order champagne," Harris Jones said. "But first, some introductions."

It took several minutes for Jones to work his way around the table. Except for Patrice Malle and Belisle, Ava knew none of the people, but did recognize the names of several newspapers and magazines. When Jones finished and was speaking to a server, a smartly dressed middle-aged woman sitting next to Ava whispered, "I'm told that you are Pang Fai's lover."

"I beg your pardon?" Ava said, taken by surprise.

The woman placed her hand on Ava's. "Not to worry. You are with friends here. My girlfriend is in London and couldn't get away."

"Yes, we are lovers," Ava said after a slight hesitation.

"It is wonderful to be living in this day and age. There was a time —"

"That time hasn't passed in China," said Ava. "Maybe it has here and in London, but in Chinese society people still need to be discreet, to be careful, or risk losing their family and career."

"Is it still really like that?"

Before Ava could answer she saw a group approaching their table. They stared at her. Ava stared back.

"I guess I shouldn't be surprised to find you here with this gang," Mo said to Ava as he came to a stop behind Lau Lau's chair.

Lau Lau, Chen, and Silvana turned to look at him.

"We were preparing to leave when we saw you arriving," Mo said. "Do you remember my deputy, Mr. Fong, and my assistant, Ms. Hua?"

"Of course. I hope you all enjoyed your dinner," said Ava.

"I'm glad it was over by the time we saw you, Chen, and the others arrive, otherwise it would have been ruined."

"You ate so early? I heard you were going to the premiere," Ava said.

"We left halfway through. As a loyal Chinese citizen, there is only so much filth I can handle," he said. "And now, in addition to that, I have to look at you again."

"Are you still upset over our dealings in Beijing? I thought we had agreed to put all of that behind us," she said.

"You know very well this has nothing to do with Beijing," Mo said, and looked down at Lau Lau. "You are a disgrace to your country, and everyone who helped you make this work of lies is tarred with the same brush."

Lau Lau shrugged and turned away from him.

Hua's face became distorted. She leaned towards them. "Traitors. You'll pay for this," she hissed.

"I think you should leave before Ms. Hua gets any more excited," Ava said to Mo. "We don't want this to get out of control and cause anyone embarrassment."

Mo tapped Chen on the shoulder. "You'll hear from us. You are going to pay a price," he said, and then he stared at Lau Lau and Fai. "You are all going to pay a price."

"What was that about?" the woman next to Ava asked as Mo and his group stormed out.

"They wanted us to know that they didn't like the film," said Ava.

6

THE EVENING AT LA PALME D'OR WAS A LOVEFEST where Lau Lau and the film's cast were concerned. They were showered with compliments and repeatedly toasted. With the exception of Lau Lau, everyone was drinking, and as the drinks accumulated, the mood became festive — with Silvana becoming particularly ebullient. Ava saw Chen eyeing her, and wondered if he was concerned about her losing control. When Silvana left to go to the bathroom with Fai, Ava turned to Chen.

"Are you concerned about her? From what we've seen in Taiwan she can handle her liquor," she said.

"Do I look concerned?"

"A bit."

"Well, I am, but it doesn't have anything to do with Silvana," Chen said softly. "I keep thinking about Mo. His behaviour was extreme even for him."

"Maybe it was, but I can't say it surprised me."

"Still, it isn't something we can completely ignore."

"What are you suggesting?"

"Nothing specific, only that I don't think we should ignore

him," he said. "Perhaps we should have a meeting to talk it over."

"Sure, I think that's a good idea," said Ava. "When?"

"I would like to do it tonight, but most of us have had quite a bit to drink."

"And everyone is so happy it would be a shame to end the evening on a sour note," said Ava.

"Then we'll leave it until tomorrow night." Chen said. "We can't do it earlier than that because Fai, Silvana, and Lau Lau have a full day of interviews scheduled, and I have meetings with distributors."

"I don't think waiting a day will make any difference," she replied.

An hour later they left the restaurant and bundled into their limos. Ava, Fai, and May had a group cuddle. Then May yawned. "I'm really tired, and I can't remember the last time I drank so much," she said.

"Go straight to bed when we get to the hotel, but think about what you would like to do tomorrow," Ava said. "The rest of our team are going to be busy so we're on our own."

"Changxing told me I should visit the Picasso Museum in Antibes. I think he would be disappointed if I didn't," May said.

Changxing was May's husband and one of the wealthiest men in Hubei province. He had started collecting Western art many years before, and focused on paintings by the Fauvists, who had formed an early twentieth-century movement. That he would also like their contemporary Picasso wasn't a surprise to Ava. "How far is the museum from our hotel?" she asked.

"The hotel concierge said it was about thirty-five kilometres."

"That sounds fine, but let's not leave the hotel too early. I want to sleep without worrying about a wake-up call or an alarm," said Ava.

"That makes two of us," May said.

"Do you know how jealous that makes me?" said Fai.

"We aren't in demand, and you are — and for all the right reasons," May said.

Half an hour later, Ava and Fai lay in bed, nose to nose, body to body, but too tired to do anything but hug.

"I think this might have been the most satisfying night of my professional career," Fai mumbled.

"That makes me so happy to hear, and thank you for using the words 'professional career' to qualify it."

Fai laughed, but said nothing, and seconds later was gently snoring.

When Ava woke the next morning, the sun was already high in the sky, and she was the only person in the bed. Fai had left a note on her pillow. *Enjoy your day, I'll miss you, love Fai*, it read.

Ava checked the time and saw it was past ten. There were no messages from May, so she was either still sleeping or waiting for Ava to call. After a short debate, Ava phoned her room.

"I hope I'm not waking you," she said.

"I've been up for about ten minutes. I slept like a log."

"Me too. Do you want to have breakfast before we head out?"

"Actually, let's not eat right away. I just spoke to the concierge and asked him if there were any restaurants he would recommend for lunch near Antibes. He said there were a lot, but if we wanted to experience something special we should go to La Colombe d'Or in Saint-Paul-de-Vence. It will add an hour to our trip, but I booked a car so we don't have to worry about driving. He suggested we go there first, and see the museum on the way back."

"Whatever you want is fine by me," Ava said, pleased to leave the decision up to May.

"Great, the car will be here at eleven, and I'll make a lunch reservation for one."

"What are you going to wear?"

"Slacks and a blouse. I'm told the restaurant is casual but chic."

Ava knew that May's idea of casual still usually included designer wear. "I guess that means I can't wear my Adidas training pants and jacket."

"It certainly does," May said.

At eleven o'clock, Ava — wearing black linen slacks and a dark blue silk blouse — walked into the lobby to find May in deep conversation with the concierge. It ended when Ava entered her line of sight. May hurried towards her, they hugged and then headed for the hotel entrance.

"What were you talking to the concierge about?" Ava asked as they got into the back seat of the grey S-Class Mercedes.

"He was telling me about the restaurant. It turns out it is famous for more than its food," May said. "It's part of a small hotel that is about a hundred years old and was frequented by many of the artists who lived or vacationed in the south of France. Some of the artists bartered their work for food and lodging. According to him, there are paintings by Picasso, Matisse, Chagall, and Miró hanging on the walls, and an Alexander Calder mobile is outside by the pool."

"Changxing will be sorry he missed this."

"I'll take photos for him."

"That might make him sorrier."

"That's a good point. I'll skip the photos," said May.

Their conversation lulled as the car purred along. They were comfortable with each other and with silence. Ava looked absent-mindedly out of the window and thought about the night before. Financing the PÖ fashion line had given her a sense of what it was like to do something whose success was based on public opinion. But as stressful as launching PÖ had been, there had always been a backup plan if the line wasn't as well-received as they'd hoped. Making a film and putting it out into the world was, by comparison, doing a high wire act without a net. In retrospect, her reaction to the audience's and critics' responses was as much relief as joy, and perhaps Lau Lau's tears had reflected that as well.

Three Sisters, through BB Productions, had invested just under fourteen million dollars in the film. That was slightly more than they had originally budgeted, but as Chen had told them when he asked for more, "You can't budget for the unexpected." The unexpected was that Lau Lau's shoot was taking longer than planned, and using more extras and crew than Chen had counted on. And the thing was, as Chen explained, "Once the film is half-shot there is no backing out."

Three Sisters had not gone into the project to make money. But now, seeing how well it had been received, Ava hoped that at least they could break even, and she wondered what kind of distribution deal Chen would be able to land. They wanted as much money upfront as possible, of course, but he wanted to retain a percentage of the gross receipts for BB. The more money they asked for upfront, the lower the percentage would be. In their discussions with Chen, Ava and May had made it clear they preferred not to be extreme in either direction. But as he'd made clear to them, the distributors knew the game inside out, and even if one of them truly loved the film, there would be no easy negotiations.

When Ava saw a sign that indicated Saint-Paul-de-Vence was about half an hour away, she turned to say something to May, but then stopped when she realized her friend was napping.

May woke just as La Colombe d'Or came into view. It looked more like a grey-stone family mansion than a hotel. "Sorry for nodding off," she said.

"*Momentai*, I was just thinking about what we need in a distribution deal to make us as close to whole as possible."

"Well, even if we get what you want, and as much as I love the film, I can't help hoping that we don't make a habit of this kind of investment," May said with a sigh. "I understand trucking, warehousing, and logistics. They're predictable. Films aren't, and I sometimes find the uncertainty unsettling."

"But you also have to admit that the excitement last night was a once-in-a-lifetime experience."

"It was, and I'll never forget it or regret getting involved with the movie. It just isn't something I'm eager to repeat."

The Mercedes pulled to a stop, and the driver leapt out to open the back door. Ava and May stepped out. In front of them was a door that led into a reception area that had a small bar as an adjunct. Sitting on a bench at the bar was a familiar face.

"Henri, is that you?" Ava asked.

"Ah, Ms. Lee and Ms. Wong, how nice to see you again, and so soon," Henri said, and turned to a young woman sitting next to him. "Camille, Ms. Lee and Ms. Wong are affiliated with *Tiananmen*. And ladies, Camille works with me at the agency. We are here with some other clients."

"And we are simply here for lunch," said Ava.

"Oh, my goodness, what a pleasure to meet both of you," Camille said. "Your film was the talk of the office this morning. We'll be surprised if you don't win the Palme d'Or."

"That would be lovely, but it is enough for us that Lau Lau is appropriately recognized."

"He is a genius," said Camille. "Award or no award, he has made a magnificent film."

"I agree, but that doesn't stop him from feeling insecure," Ava said.

Camille smiled. "Henri said Lau Lau was supported by a tremendous team. I can see that's true."

"We are here to support our friends, but we are hardly part of their team," Ava said, and then attempted to switch topics. "We were told this restaurant is as famous for its artwork as it is for its food."

"That is true, but most of the paintings are in the dining room and it's closed for lunch this time of year," Henri said, and then pointed to a wall behind them. "But that's a Picasso hanging there, and when you go into the courtyard for lunch you'll see some wonderful sculptures."

May used her phone to take a picture of the Picasso.

"May I help you?" a woman asked as she entered the reception area.

"We have a lunch reservation in the name of Wong," May said.

The woman checked a book that sat on the bar. "Of course — follow me, please."

There were about twenty tables spread around the cobblestone courtyard. The woman led Ava and May to the only one that wasn't occupied. They sat, and that was the beginning of a sublime lunch that lasted close to two hours.

On the recommendation of their server, they ordered the restaurant's hors d'oeuvre platter and a bottle of rosé to start. The platter came loaded with plump sardines, candied onions and raisins, marinated peppers, tomatoes Provençal, and a side plate of vegetables and various sausages. They tried everything, but not to excess, because both of them wanted to leave room for a main fish course. May decided on Dover sole, while Ava opted for poached *loup de mer*. The wine went down so easily that they finished the bottle before the main course arrived at the table.

Before leaving, they went to the pool to see the Calder mobile. It looked like a tattered abstract windmill. May took several photos of it, and of her and Ava standing in front of it.

Ava checked her phone as they returned to the Mercedes. "I don't think we have time to visit the Picasso Museum. It's already three, and I'd like to be back at the hotel by five. Chen should be having his last meeting now, and I'm anxious to see how the day went."

"I was going to suggest the same thing, but for a different reason," said May.

"What reason is that?"

"I've had too much to drink again, and I'd rather nap in the car than walk around a museum."

Ava laughed. "That's good thinking. The festival awards are tomorrow night, and we should be rested just in case there's a lot more drinking to do."

Traffic was heavy, and the drive to Cap Ferrat took close

to two hours. Ava and May alternated between chatting and napping, and the time passed pleasantly enough. At four o'clock, Ava phoned Fai to let her know they were on their way, and then asked how her day had gone.

"The PR company did a terrific job. They have two suites at one of the big hotels and set up shop there. They ushered in camera crews and journalists almost non-stop. Lau Lau, Silvana, and I must have done at least ten interviews each," Fai said.

"And how did Chen's day go?"

"I'm not sure. He wasn't with us, and I haven't seen him since I got back to the hotel."

"I'll call him," said Ava. "Have any arrangements been made for dinner?"

"We're all tired and none of us want to leave the hotel. Silvana managed to book a table at Le Cap, so unless there are any objections, we'll eat here. The reservation is at seven thirty. so we were going to meet in the bar at six thirty."

"That all sounds entirely sensible."

"What's going on?" May asked when Ava ended the call. Ava repeated what Fai had said, and then phoned Chen.

"*Wei*," he answered briskly.

"Am I interrupting anything?" she asked.

"No, I just finished my last meeting. I should be at the hotel by six."

"I'm with May. We're on our way back from Saint-Paul-de-Vence and our eta is about the same as yours," she said. "How were your meetings?"

Chen hesitated, then said, "Encouraging."

"Then why do you sound less than encouraged?"

"I'm keeping my expectations in check until we actually

have a firm offer in hand. Two of the four companies I met with today indicated they might be putting one on the table, but we didn't get into any numbers and their focus — after saying how much they loved the film — was on telling me how difficult it would be to market."

"Was that simply a strategy so they can lowball us?"

"I'm sure that was part of it, but they did make some valid points," he said. "The film is a bit longer than most venues like these days. The fact it is in Mandarin with subtitles detracts from it. And finally, they all understand that the film will never be allowed to be shown in China, when theoretically that should be its biggest market."

"That still leaves the rest of the world."

"I know, and that includes the streaming services. I have two of them on my schedule for tomorrow morning."

"How much of a difference will it make if we win the Palme d'Or?"

"Not as much as you might think. In fact, the two firms who are interested in *Tiananmen* told me already that they think we have a great chance of winning."

"Ah, that's good and not so good to hear."

"There's something else that might be not good either."

"What's that?"

"I may be paranoid, but I felt I was being followed all day," Chen said slowly. "My meetings were all over Cannes, but no matter where I went there was someone Chinese hovering in the background."

"There are a lot of Chinese in this world. Why is it surprising to see them here?"

"I can't help but think they could be connected to Mo."

"In what way?"

"He might want to know who I'm meeting with," Chen said. "If he was willing to threaten the distributor I lunched with yesterday, I can't imagine he's going to hesitate to do the same with others."

"You told me yesterday that some of them won't give in to threats."

"That's true, but some of the largest — including everyone I met with today — make a great deal of money in the Chinese market. The superhero franchises are as popular there as they are in the United States. Deciding to buy the rights to *Tiananmen* knowing that the Syndicate might retaliate by shutting them and their other films out of the Chinese market wouldn't be an easy business decision to make."

"Surely not every distributor does a lot of business in China?"

"No, but while I don't mean to sound negative, I have to say that the biggest ones do."

"Then we'll have to find someone who is capable, but not quite so big."

"I do have hopes that we can interest one of the streamers. I also have meetings with two more distributors tomorrow, and I know for certain that one of them has no interest in the Chinese market."

"Chen, we'll find a way to make this work. The film will be seen."

"I'm not worried about that. My concern is getting back for BB the money that was put into the film."

"When I got into business I never thought I'd say what I'm about to say, but here it is anyway," Ava said. "If you can find a way to get us close to breaking even, we'll be happy. And now, no more talk about money. I know we were going to talk more about Mo tonight, but let's put it aside for now. Silvana has made a dinner reservation for us at Le Cap, and we have the awards ceremony tomorrow night to look forward to. This is a night for celebration and optimism."

7

FOR EVERYONE EXCEPT CHEN, SATURDAY WAS SPENT
relaxing until the public relations people arrived with the
makeup artists and hairstylists to get them ready for the
festival's award ceremony. This time, though, Ava decided to
do her hair and makeup herself, and then sat on the terrace
with a glass of Prosecco while she waited for Fai.

The ceremony began at seven, and they were scheduled
to leave the hotel at five. Ava had hoped to hear from Chen
before they left, but there was still no word by the time she,
Fai, and May slid into the Mercedes limousine.

The mood in the car was different than it had been two
nights previous. Then, they had all been full of doubt about
how the film would be received, and nervous about walking
the red carpet. Now, with no concerns about how an audience would respond, and the experience of the red carpet
behind them, it came down to what the eight jury members
thought of *Tiananmen*, and its director and cast, in comparison to the other festival entries.

"You ladies look marvellous again," Henri said to them
as they pulled away from the hotel. "We have great hopes
for this evening."

"As negative as it might seem, I'm preparing myself for us not to win," Fai said. "Many other films were also well-received and are probably as deserving. Besides, the reviews we got are almost recognition enough."

"I was looking at a list of the entries and I don't recognize the names of many of the directors or actors," May said. "I certainly saw no one who surpasses you or Lau Lau in terms of reputation."

"Reputation, popularity, and commercial potential typically don't matter to the festival jury," Henri said. "It focuses on artistic achievement, and that is why I believe that *Tiananmen* will do very well tonight."

"Are you trying to say that you think our film won't be commercially successful, and that Fai and Lau Lau don't have great reputations?" Ava asked.

"No, no, no," he said hurriedly, and then turned to look at them. "What I meant is that *Tiananmen* succeeds as a work of art. Ms. Pang's and Mr. Lau Lau's involvement are an added plus, of course, and I'm sure your film will do very well at the box office."

Ava saw his face was red. "I was teasing you," she said.

"And I appreciate your comment about the film's artistry," Fai said.

Before Henri could say anything more, Ava's phone rang and she saw Chen's name on the screen.

"Where are you?" she asked.

"I'm changing clothes in one of the PR company suites. I'll meet you at the theatre."

"How was your day?"

"I've had better. We have one offer which is so small it's laughable, and two of the larger distribution outfits told me they've decided to pass," Chen said.

"Did they tell you why they're passing?"

"They told me it was all about money. They had weighed what they thought they could make from *Tiananmen* against losing access to the Chinese market for their other films — it was an easy decision for them to make," Chen said. "Obviously they had also been contacted by the Syndicate."

"So Mo threatened them?"

"No, he had Fong do the dirty work."

"Is there anything we can do to persuade them otherwise?"

"They were apologetic, but very firm. I can't imagine them changing their minds."

"Where does that leave us?" Ava asked.

"Waiting to hear from a handful of other companies, but after what I was told today I can't say I'm very optimistic that any of the major streamers or distributors will want to risk taking on *Tiananmen*."

"But we do have that one offer — laughable or not — and we can hope that the smaller distributors won't be so easily scared off," she said.

"I'm sure we'll find one or two who won't be, but going with them will dramatically weaken any chance we have of breaking even on the film."

"I told you already, we didn't go into this project to make money, so we won't complain if we don't."

"Still . . ." Chen said gloomily.

"Hey, enough of that," Ava said. "We're all dressed up and ready for a good time tonight. Win or lose, you and Lau Lau made a great film, and win or lose we're going to celebrate after the awards presentation. We'll see you at the theatre."

"I don't like the sound of that conversation," May said as Ava put down her phone.

"Mo and his gang are threatening the major distributors, and it seems to be working."

"It is what we expected."

"I know, but that doesn't make it any more palatable."

"Ava," May said slowly, "if the Syndicate feels so strongly about the film, I have to believe there could be negative personal repercussions for Chen, Lau Lau, and even..."

"Me?" Fai said.

"I hate to say it, but yes."

"That's why Chen sold everything he owned in China and moved to Thailand, and why Lau Lau intends to go back to Taipei for at least a while, if not permanently."

"What about you?"

"Ava and I have decided that I'll live with her in Toronto until this passes."

"The Chinese government has a long memory," May said.

"Then I could be there for a long time, and frankly that idea makes me rather happy," said Fai. "Aside from being with Ava, I'm going to take another crack at making films in the West. The reality is that, after my last run-in with Mo, my career in China is as good as over — so this will give me a fresh start. Chen is helping me find an agent in Los Angeles, and I'm going to take English lessons again."

"I thought I had explained a lot of this to you?" Ava said to May.

"I know we talked about it a bit in Taipei, but I didn't remember the details. I apologize for that."

"There's no need to apologize," said Ava. "But tell me, May, are you also worried about the impact the film might have on us?"

"Not unless the government decides that being someone's

friend is a crime, and as crazy as they can be at times, that's a bit much even for them," May said.

"I agree, so as I said to Chen, let's not talk about it anymore and just enjoy our evening."

8

FOR THE SECOND CONSECUTIVE MORNING, AVA WOKE up in an empty bed, but this time there was no note on the pillow. She turned her head to look at the bedside clock and blinked unbelievingly when she saw it was almost noon. What time had they returned to the hotel? She knew it was somewhere between two and three, and if her memory wasn't playing tricks on her, she thought it was closer to three.

The awards ceremony had been as exciting and — if anything — more stressful than the premiere. They had walked the red carpet again, to more adoration for Fai and Lau Lau, and then settled into their seats for the awards ceremony, with Lau Lau again sitting between Ava and Fai.

When the best actress category was announced, Ava gripped one of Fai's hands, and saw Lau Lau was holding the other. "Please, St. Jude," Ava whispered.

The presenter, much to Ava's annoyance, paused for at least ten seconds after reading out the names of the nominees. It was, Ava thought, a cheap attempt at creating some drama. Finally, she looked out at the audience and said, "The winner is Pang Fai for her magnificent performance in *Tiananmen*."

"*Eiiii*," Silvana shouted, and the audience erupted into applause.

Fai reached across Lau Lau, grabbed Ava's hand, and squeezed it. Then she took a deep breath, got to her feet, and made her way to the steps that took her onto the stage. She took the award from the presenter and looked admiringly at it. In case she won, she'd had Ava write a speech and had memorized it. Now, in halting English, Fai thanked the festival, Chen, Lau Lau, Silvana, and the rest of the film's crew. When she was done, she paused, and added in Mandarin, "There is one person I need to thank more than any other, but it is something I'd rather do in private. I know she'll understand why."

Ten minutes later, Lau Lau won the award for best director. When his name was called, he turned to Ava. "Will you come on stage to translate into English for me?"

The request caught her by surprise, and she hesitated before saying, "Of course I will."

They held hands as they made their way to the stage. The presenter was Patrice Malle, and he was beaming as he hugged Lau Lau before giving him the award.

Ava had no idea what Lau Lau was going to say, but whatever it was she expected it to be short. She was wrong. He began by saying what an honour it was to receive the best director award from Malle, and then thanked at least ten members of the crew and cast by name. He saved Silvana and Fai for last, and spoke for about a minute about each of them. He then looked out at Chen, and said, "It took a brave man to produce this film, and an even braver man to take a chance on me to direct it. Chen and I have been friends for close to two decades, and he never failed me, and never abandoned me when others had. This award is as much for him as it is for me."

Finally, Lau Lau reached for Ava's arm and gently pulled her close. "I want to thank you more than anyone. You saved my life and not just my career," he whispered. "But I don't think it's wise to connect you to the film so directly, do you?"

"No, and thank you for being sensitive to that," she said.

They returned to their seats to a round of loud applause. "Now it's your turn," Lau Lau said to Chen. "We can't lose now."

They didn't, and when *Tiananmen* was named as the winner of the Palme d'Or, Ava felt a burst of pride that was outside any previous experience. "This must be how a parent feels when a child does something remarkable," she said to Fai.

"That's one reason I love acting," said Fai. "Every once in a while you get a role that takes you completely outside of yourself, to the point that when I watch the end product I don't recognize myself. That's when I know I did a good job, and that's when I feel proud."

After the awards ceremony, there was a question-and-answer session that Ava found anticlimactic and sometimes awkward as she continued to translate for Lau Lau. When it finished, the *Tiananmen* team and a large group including Patrice Malle, several other panel members, some festival staff, and Harris Jones and six other journalists descended on Shanghai Memory — a Chinese restaurant in Cannes — where the PR company had reserved a large private room in the event there was a reason to celebrate. They ate and drank for hours. When Ava, Fai, and May left the restaurant to walk to their limo, they did so with their arms linked for support.

Now, as Ava climbed out of bed, she felt the stirrings of a

hangover. She drank two glasses of water, and was making a coffee when the door that led out to the terrace opened.

"Finally, you're awake," Fai said.

"When did you get up?"

"An hour ago. There's coffee that's still warm and juice out here on the table. Come and get some."

After a trip to the bathroom, Ava slipped on a black Giordano T-shirt and a pair of shorts, and made her way to the terrace. The coffee and juice were on a table between two of the padded chairs, but Ava's eyes were immediately drawn to what was on the round table in front of them.

"I love the way it glows in the sun," she said, looking at the delicate gold branch adorned with slender gold leaves and set in a rock crystal base that glittered like an immense diamond.

"It is beautiful. I really didn't look at it that closely last night — maybe because I was so shocked to win," said Fai.

"It was shock after shock after shock in the most fantastic way. First you winning, then Lau Lau, and then the film," Ava said. "I know we fantasized about it, but for it to actually happen is bizarre. I almost felt as if I was in a dream."

"Lau Lau was so talkative I could hardly believe it."

"He certainly surprised me."

"And Chen handled it well, don't you think?" Fai asked.

"Yes, his first movie wins the Palme d'Or and he acted as if it was commonplace." Ava poured a cup of coffee and sat. "Have you heard from him or Lau Lau this morning?"

"No, but it is a wonder my phone didn't crash. I had text messages and voicemails from seemingly everyone I've ever worked with. Lau Lau must have had as many, if not more. I don't know how things could have turned out any better than this."

"We still don't have a distribution deal," Ava said.

"Winning the Palme d'Or has to help."

"I certainly hope it will." Ava looked up into a sun that was beaming down on them. "Anyway, deal or not, this has been a wonderful trip and experience and I'm almost sorry we have to leave. I really like this place."

"We can always come back."

"I think you can count on that."

"Do we have any plans for today?" Fai asked.

"Absolutely none other than saying goodbye to Lau Lau and May. They're flying out of here tonight. I think the plan is for us to have lunch before they leave for the airport. My head is a bit fuzzy about last night, but I think I'm remembering correctly."

"How about Silvana? When is she leaving?"

"She's going to Thailand with Chen, and he had planned to stay here for another few days," Ava said, and then heard her phone sound. She left the terrace, went to the bedroom to retrieve it, and saw she had missed a call from Chen. She phoned him as she walked back to rejoin Fai.

"Good morning," Chen answered.

"I was on the terrace with Fai and her award when you called."

Chen laughed. "I look at mine every few minutes or so. I can't believe it's real."

"That was quite the night."

"And if my hunch is correct, this is going to be a very interesting day."

"What's happened?" she asked, her interest immediately spiking.

"I received two phone calls this morning and now have two meetings scheduled — one this afternoon, and the other over dinner. The first is with a company I met two days ago. They weren't ready to make an offer then, but they are now. The second is with someone I haven't met. They called me an hour ago with the dinner invitation, and made it rather clear they want to acquire the distribution rights."

"That's terrific, Chen. Who are these companies?"

"The first is based in Paris and is very strong in the European market. They don't have a large presence in the U.S., but do have working arrangements with several American distributors," he said. "The second is Top of the Road Production and Distribution. They work out of Los Angeles and are relatively new, but from what I know they are well-financed and very aggressive."

"Do you have a preference?"

"Yes — the one that offers us the most money."

"Should money be the only consideration?"

"Of course not, we want maximum distribution, but my experience is that the more a company pays for the rights, the harder they will work to recoup their investment."

"Have either of them given you any idea what they are prepared to offer?"

"No, but it's great that we have two of them at the table. It should give us some room to play one off against the other," said Chen.

"That's in your hands," Ava said. "You know we'll go along with whatever you recommend."

"Actually, I was wondering if you would like to take part in the meetings," Chen said. "As much as I appreciate your faith in me, it would take some pressure off if you were involved in the process. Besides, I do know first-hand how well you negotiate and how well you read people."

It was an intriguing invitation, and for a few seconds Ava was tempted, but then common sense kicked in. "Aside from being seen with Fai a few times, and translating for Lau Lau, I've managed to stay completely in the background. Now isn't the time to signal, even indirectly, that I have any involvement in the film."

"I understand," Chen said, his disappointment evident. "But are you completely sure that if the Chinese government starts digging into BB Productions your name won't emerge?"

"There are so many lawyers and banks between the money and me that I would be shocked if that were the case," she said. "And the money's origin, believe it or not, is with a fundamentalist Christian organization that has a presence in China. It cannot be traced to me or any of the businesses I own with my partners."

"I knew you had been careful, I just wasn't sure to what extent."

"Now you know."

"Thank you for sharing that with me."

"When is your first meeting?" Ava said, not so subtly changing the subject.

"At two, and I should start getting organized for it."

"Does Silvana have any plans for this afternoon?"

"Her main priority seems to be to recover from last night."

"Well, tell her if she's up to it, she can join Fai and me for lunch with Lau Lau and May before they leave for the airport."

"Just a minute, I'll let her know right now," he said, and then came back on the line. "She'll be happy to join you."

"I'll call her when we're ready to go downstairs," Ava said before ending the call.

"What did Chen have to say that was so terrific?" Fai asked.

"He has two meetings today, and he's expecting to get offers for the distribution rights from both companies."

Fai closed her eyes, took a deep breath, tipped her head towards the sky, and said, "Thank you, God. We deserve this."

"Let's not get ahead of ourselves. We don't have any dollar amounts yet."

"At least one of the offers is going to be good. I just have that feeling."

"Actually, I feel the same way, but I'm always afraid of jinxing myself," Ava said, and then checked the time. "I'm starting to feel really hungry. I'll call May to see if she's going to join us. Why don't you phone Lau Lau?"

An hour later, Ava and Fai walked into La Véranda to find Lau Lau, May, and Silvana already sitting at a table.

"Silvana was just telling us that Chen is optimistic about his meetings today," May said as the newcomers joined them.

"Fingers crossed," said Ava.

"What time did you get up?" asked Silvana.

"Around noon."

"Me too. I can't remember the last time I drank so much."

"There was a lot to celebrate," said Ava, and turned to Lau Lau. "You must be feeling very proud this morning."

"I am. Winning the Palme d'Or was more than I could have ever imagined, but there is something else I'm quite proud of."

"And that is?" asked May.

"I didn't have anything to drink last night, and *Tiananmen* winning best picture was as big an excuse as I could have," he said. "I actually now believe I'm going to be able to stay dry."

"That is wonderful to hear," said Fai.

Lau Lau smiled. "I guess the next thing I'll have to do is come out of the closet, but I'm not brave enough yet, unlike you."

"I haven't actually spoken about it, but I've made it obvious enough," Fai said. "Certainly Mo and his group know, which means just about everyone else in the Chinese film industry does as well."

"In or out, it makes no difference as far as both of your talents are concerned," May said.

The server arriving at their table ended the conversation. They ordered lunch, Ava starting with a gazpacho with tuna, peppers and watermelon, followed by beef tartare and langoustines for her and Fai to share.

"I'm going on a diet when I get back to Wuhan," May said.

"I'm always on a diet," said Silvana.

Sparkling water and tea were all anyone drank, and the next two hours were spent eating and chatting. At three, May excused herself to go to her room to finish packing. And at three thirty the others met her in the lobby for a round of hugs and goodbyes. As Ava watched her friend and Lau Lau get into a taxi for the trip to the airport, she couldn't help but think how fortunate it was that Uncle had talked her into making peace with May all those years ago.

(9)

AFTER MAY AND LAU LAU'S DEPARTURE, SILVANA invited Ava and Fai to her terrace for drinks. They declined.

"I can't party like I used to. Last night took its toll. I think I'll take a nap," Fai said.

"And I'll join her," said Ava.

They undressed and got into bed as soon as they got to their suite, but any thoughts about sleeping were put on hold as soon as they wrapped their arms around each other. And by the time Ava did fall asleep, she had no idea what hour it was. When she woke it was to the sound of Fai whispering in her ear, "Chen is on the line. He sounds excited."

Ava sat upright and reached for the phone. "We were sleeping," she said.

"That's what Fai told me, so you should be rested."

"Why does that matter?"

"I'm downstairs in Le Bar with Silvana, and I've just had them open a bottle of vintage Bollinger. Come and join us."

"Is there a reason?" Ava asked.

"We have a deal, or at least a deal that I like. Before I say yes I want to go over it with you."

Ava bit back her own excitement. "Give us fifteen minutes."

At Le Bar you could sit at the bar, or in the library, or on the terrace. Chen and Silvana were on the terrace watching the sun creep close to the horizon when Ava and Fai arrived. Seeing them, Chen started to pour champagne before they were seated. "We've had two glasses already, and I've ordered another bottle," he said.

"This must be a *really* good offer," Ava said.

"*Ganbei*," Chen said raising his glass.

Ava and Fai sat and lifted theirs. "*Ganbei*," they both said and then drank.

"Don't tease us, what is the deal?" Ava asked.

Chen smiled, and Ava saw Silvana smile as well and knew that she knew. "As I hoped, we received two offers. The French production company, Bien Fait, is willing to pay five million euros, and give us fifteen per cent of the net proceeds for the distribution rights."

"Net proceeds in the film business usually amount to zero," Fai said quickly.

"Fai is correct, of course. Production companies always have creative accounting companies on their payroll," Chen said. "But our other suitor, Top of the Road, offered us cash and a gross proceeds deal that I think is damn good."

"How much?" Ava asked.

"Ten million U.S. dollars and five per cent of the gross. The cash will cover the majority of our costs. The proceeds should give us a profit."

"I like those numbers," Ava said. "But Top of the Road isn't concerned about blowback from the Chinese government?"

"They tell me they have virtually no business there, and what they do have they're prepared to risk."

"How much do you know about them?"

"The company is five years old, and was founded and is run by three men who were agents together at the TAW agency. Between their money and the support of an investment firm, they are financially rock-solid," Chen said. "I did my due diligence. They're for real."

"I wasn't suggesting that you hadn't, I was just curious," Ava said.

"I think you did a fantastic job with this," Fai said.

"Me too," Ava said. "Congratulations, and thank you."

"No, thank you. You made it all possible."

Ava gently shook her head. "You do need to stop saying that. I didn't contribute one iota of creativity."

"No, but you are the one who saw the faint spark of life still existing in Lau Lau."

"Okay, I'll take credit for that, but nothing more," Ava said. "Now...tell me, how long will it take to paper the distribution agreement?"

"At least two weeks, maybe even longer. We may have agreed on the basics, but it will have to be lawyered, and that's never simple in my business," he said. "Do you want to be involved — discreetly, of course?"

"Not particularly, I prefer leaving it entirely in your hands."

"Do you want me to use the Burgess and Bowlby legal firm?"

"Only if it makes sense."

"Well, actually, there is another firm in Hong Kong that specializes in entertainment law that I was thinking of engaging," Chen said.

"By all means use them."

"Then that leaves the question of what to do with the ten

million and our cut of the box office proceeds when we get them," Chen said as he refilled everyone's champagne glasses.

"Put everything into the BB Productions bank account. We'll have to figure out from our end what to do with it after that," said Ava. "May Ling isn't crazy about the idea of being in the film business, but if this turns out to be profitable enough, and if you can find projects that won't bring us into conflict with the Chinese government, she might change her mind."

"Are you saying there is a possibility you might maintain BB as a viable production company?" Chen asked.

"Are you interested in making more films?"

"Yes."

"Then I'll talk to May Ling and Amanda about that as an option."

"I can't tell you how much I would appreciate that," he said and raised his glass. "To a long friendship."

"Indeed," Ava said.

"When are you leaving France?" Silvana asked.

"Tomorrow morning. We fly from Nice to Zurich and connect there for a flight to Toronto."

"I've never been to Canada," she said.

"You're welcome to visit anytime."

"I may take you up on that, if Chen gets tired of me hanging around."

"Bring him with you," said Ava. "My condo is too small for you to stay, but my mother has a large house and is one of your fans. She would be thrilled to have you as a guest."

Fai leaned towards Chen. "Speaking of travelling, did the Top of the Road people give you any idea of how they intend to promote and release the film? If they go the film festival route, will they want the cast and Lau Lau involved?"

"I'm not sure yet about any of those details. They did speak generally about their promotional ideas and several festivals were mentioned, but there was nothing specific."

"Did they mention TIFF — the Toronto International Film Festival?" Ava asked.

"Actually, they did."

"Before it moved downtown to King Street, my neighbourhood was the headquarters for TIFF, and its main theatre was only a hundred metres from my condo building," Ava said. "During festival week I always saw three or four films."

"How far is it now?" Silvana asked.

"About a half-hour walk," said Ava, and then turned to Chen. "When you're talking to the Top of the Road people, please urge them to submit our film to TIFF. If it was shown there, it would be an almost out-of-body experience for me."

Lake Couchiching
August

DURING HER RECOVERY FROM A BULLET WOUND IN HER thigh several years before, Ava had rented a cottage on Lake Couchiching, near the small city of Orillia and about a two-hour drive north from her condo. The cottage was spacious, with three bedrooms and every modern convenience, had no visible neighbours, and the only thing separating it from its private beach on the lake was fifty metres of lawn. Although she was a city girl, Ava had enjoyed the peacefulness and tranquility of cottage life so much that, after that first stay, she had rented the cottage for a few weeks every year. This year she had paid a premium to get the last two weeks of August. Her mother, Jennie, usually accompanied her, but that still left Ava on her own most of the time, because Jennie's main reason for going was to visit the baccarat tables at the nearby Casino Rama every day.

Fai — who was even more of a city girl than Ava — had

looked slightly hesitant when Ava raised the subject of the cottage.

"We aren't exactly going to be roughing it," Ava said. "It's like a big, comfortable city house that just happens to be located on a lake."

"That sounds okay, but I'm not sure about your mother. You know I'm fond of her, but two weeks together in a cottage?"

"You'll hardly see her. She goes to the casino every afternoon, and doesn't usually get back until well after midnight."

Ava's prediction about her mother had proved to be accurate, and by the end of the first week Fai was as relaxed as Ava had ever seen her. They started each day by carrying their mugs of coffee over the dew-laden grass to the Muskoka chairs that sat on the edge of the lake. There they sat watching the sun slowly rise, listening to the water lapping gently on the shoreline and occasionally seeing loons power-diving for fish, and beavers swimming across the lake. They chatted about anything and everything, none of it urgent. The outside world was exactly that — outside.

They would swim or take a long walk in the afternoons, and then retreat to their bed for lovemaking and a nap. In the evenings, after a late dinner, they'd watch television or one of the films that Ava had brought.

During the first week, they'd driven twice to the casino with Jennie to eat at Rama's Chinese restaurant. The food was fine, but on the second visit Fai was recognized and pestered by some Chinese gamblers for autographs and pictures to such an extent that they decided not to go back. So they ate at home. They had brought food with them, but had to make a trip to a T&T store that specialized in Chinese groceries in the north end of Toronto to restock when they realized that eating out wasn't an easy option. It didn't matter to Ava, since Fai was an excellent cook.

Both Ava and Fai kept their phones off except to check messages once a day. Ava also spent some time — but as little as possible — responding to business emails, and fortunately there were no emergencies.

And so the first week had blended effortlessly into the second, but as its end neared, Ava found herself thinking about what their schedule was going to be like when they returned to Toronto. At the top of her list from a business viewpoint was trying to get an ownership stake for Three Sisters in the ginseng industry. Jack Yee, Amanda's father, had traded ginseng for decades, and when the Sisters bought his company the ginseng trading operation came with it. Once Amanda saw how much money was to be made, and where the major source of ginseng was, she proposed to Ava and May that they look into buying into several farming operations.

Initially, Ava wasn't enthusiastic about the idea, but when she learned that what was regarded as the best-quality ginseng in the world was grown in an area less than two hours by car from her condo, she agreed to look into it. Three trips to southwestern Ontario, a lot of online research, and many meetings later, she was now in agreement with Amanda that ginseng would be a good investment, and she had also identified a business she thought was acquirable. She was scheduled to meet with the owner the following Tuesday.

Their return to Toronto also meant a major change in Fai's lifestyle. The critical success of *Tiananmen* and her winning of the best actress award had not brought any offers of roles of substance to her door. The problem was her lack of fluency in English. She could understand bits and pieces of what she heard, and could make herself understood in casual conversation, but none of it came easy. If she wanted to keep acting — which she did — and with the Chinese market closed to her, that meant going after English-speaking roles. She could try reciting her lines phonetically, but as she explained to Ava, whenever she did, it totally distracted from her acting.

The solution, they had decided, was for Fai to become more fluent in English. Ava had found a Berlitz language school near the condo, and Fai had registered in a rigorous three-month-long daily program. In addition, they had agreed the two of them would try to speak and live only in English at home. This type of immersion, the Berlitz director informed them, was the quickest and most effective way for her to learn. So, after they left the lake, there would be no discussions in Mandarin for at least a while, and Chinese television and films would be replaced by English media.

There was, though, one exception to the English-only rule, and that was when they were in bed. Fai could be quite verbal during lovemaking, and that was something neither of them wanted to change.

"Three days to go before we head back to the city," Ava said to Fai as they drank their morning coffee by the lake.

"I didn't think I would have enjoyed the life here as much as I have. The first day or two went by slowly, but since then time has flown. I would stay here again, anytime."

"If we want the cottage for the same two weeks next year, I have to let the owner know by the end of September."

"I'm game if you are."

"Then I'll let her know that we'll be taking it again," said Ava.

"I think I'm going to enjoy life in Canada, although obviously I hope we can go back to China at some point."

"Are you looking forward to starting your English classes, or is the thought making you anxious?"

"Neither — it's something I know I have to do and this time I'm determined to do it well."

"It will be strange and maybe a bit difficult at home for the first while, but if we stick at it, it will start to become natural."

The sun was well above the horizon now, and Ava figured it was close to ten o'clock. That was when she usually checked her messages, since it was a good time to call Asia if that was necessary. She turned on her phone, and Fai did the same.

She had one voicemail. It was from Chen, and he sounded flustered, perhaps even distressed as he said, "Call me, please, we really need to talk."

Ava looked at Fai. "I have a strange message from Chen."

"Me too. When he couldn't reach you, he called me. He doesn't sound happy," said Fai.

Ava scrolled to his number, hit the call button, and switched to speakerphone so Fai could hear what was being said.

"Ava?" he answered.

"I'm here with Fai. What's going on?"

"I only wish I knew."

"What does that mean?" Ava asked.

"I am beginning to suspect that we might have a problem with Top of the Road."

"Why do you think that?"

"I've been trying to reach them for two days now. They aren't taking my phone calls or answering my emails."

"Why are you trying to get hold of them?"

"They promised to share their promotion and distribution plans with me two weeks ago, but I've seen nothing."

"Do we have any control or say in how they choose to promote or distribute the film?"

"No."

"And are they obligated to share their plans with us?"

"No."

"Then I don't understand what the problem is."

"It is a common courtesy, almost standard procedure, to consult on those matters with the production company. In fact, when we talked in Cannes, Top of the Road went out of their way to stress how much they would value our input," Chen said. "I touched base with them several times during June and July, and was told by their CEO, Larry Christensen, that the plans were coming along and that they would forward them to me by mid-August. That's the last I heard from him, and none of my emails or voice messages have been answered."

"Perhaps they haven't quite finalized the plans and want to hold off until they have."

"Then they should just tell me that, and not ignore me."

"I agree it is rude," she said. "Do you have any other way of contacting them? Do you know anyone in Los Angeles who could act on your behalf? Maybe visit their offices?"

"I know a few agents, but I would look rather stupid asking an outsider to talk to our distributor."

"That's a good point, so what other options do you have? Have you thought about flying to Los Angeles?"

"I was trying to avoid doing that, but now I think it makes the most sense," Chen said. "I apologize for bothering you with this. I just wasn't sure what to do. We've already missed out on most of the submission deadlines for the festivals — including TIFF, which I know you wanted — and now I'm worried about scheduling premieres and other promotions. I don't know what commitments Fai has for the next six months, but Lau Lau and Silvana are going to be busy and need as much notice as possible if they're to fit promoting *Tiananmen* into their schedules."

"What does Lau Lau have on his plate?" Fai asked.

"He's directing a kung fu movie in Taiwan. It really isn't his kind of thing, but his stock has soared after winning the Palme d'Or and the producers are paying him a small fortune."

"When you speak to him next, tell him we're really happy for him," said Fai.

"And let us know how it goes in Los Angeles. We're always available for you," Ava said as she ended the call.

"That sounded a bit odd, although truthfully I've never concerned myself with that part of the business," Fai said.

"It did, didn't it? But whatever is going on, I'm sure Chen can sort it out."

11

THEY LEFT THE LAKE ON SUNDAY MORNING TO DRIVE back to Toronto. Traffic was heavy on Highway 400 heading south, but only a fraction of what it would be later in the day when traffic jams were the norm. Ava had always found it contradictory that weekend cottagers were so prepared to endure heavy traffic going north on Fridays and south on Sundays in order to escape the city traffic they put up with during weekdays.

It was a quiet ride. Jennie hadn't returned from the casino until three a.m. and now was sleeping in the back seat of the car, so when Ava and Fai said anything to each other, it was whispered. But the silence was broken when Ava's phone rang as they entered the city of Vaughan, just north of Toronto. Ava thought about not answering until she saw the Hong Kong country code.

"Hello," she said, activating Bluetooth.

"Ava, this is Silvana."

Ava blinked in surprise, and saw that Fai shared her reaction. Despite the time they'd spent together making *Tiananmen*, Silvana wasn't in the habit of phoning them.

"Silvana, where are you?" Ava asked.

"I'm in Bangkok. I've been here with Chen, but I'm alone right now. He left to go to Los Angeles."

"Did he go there to meet with Top of the Road?"

"Yes, they still weren't answering his calls or emails so he thought going to their offices was the only way to get the information he wanted."

Ava could feel the tension in Silvana's voice, and tried to moderate her own tone. "When I didn't hear from him after our discussion about the distribution company, I thought he had resolved his problems with them."

"He didn't resolve anything, but he didn't want to bother you about it anymore. Truthfully, he regretted telling you about it in the first place. After he did, he thought he had made himself look unprofessional, and maybe even incompetent."

"That's absurd. I have nothing but respect for him."

"I believe you, but he's still insecure in this new role as producer and I think he wanted to prove — to himself as much as anyone — that he could manage every aspect of it."

"So he went to L.A. to do that?"

"That was his plan."

"And how did it go?" Ava asked, wondering if Chen was using Silvana as the bearer of bad news.

"I don't know, and that's only part of the problem," Silvana said, her voice breaking.

Ava felt immediately guilty at having thought Silvana was fronting for Chen. "What's the problem?" she asked.

"I can't find him."

"What do you mean?"

"He left here two days ago. He was supposed to call me

when he landed in Los Angeles, and he hasn't. I've tried calling his phone and it goes directly to voicemail."

"Could his flight have been delayed or rerouted?"

"No, I've checked. It left Bangkok on time, and it arrived in Los Angeles on schedule."

"Could he have changed his flight plans at the last minute?"

"Ava, that's totally unlike Chen. He is super organized. Besides, I know he had a tough time getting a business class seat and was really happy when he finally landed one."

"On which airline?" Ava asked.

"He was supposed to take ANA's early morning flight to Tokyo, where he would connect to a flight to L.A."

"Have you checked with the airline to see if he actually got on the flight?"

"I tried and I got nowhere. They wouldn't even confirm that he had a reservation with them."

"Yes, airlines are sticky when it comes to sharing that kind of information," Ava said, and then grasped at an unlikely straw. "Maybe he's having a problem with his phone."

"Then he could buy a new one, or he could have called me from his hotel," Silvana said, and started to sob. "I've even called the hotel four times now. They've confirmed he had a reservation, but he hasn't checked in."

"Which hotel?"

"The Four Seasons in Beverly Hills."

"Well, I have to say that this is decidedly odd," said Ava, and then glanced at Fai who looked distressed.

"Ava, help me, please help me," Silvana cried.

"I'm not sure I can do more than you've already done."

"Please, Ava," Silvana said, her sobbing increasing.

"Okay, let me think about what else I could do. In the

meantime, try to calm down a little. There might be a perfectly logical explanation why he hasn't been in touch. Let's not jump to negative conclusions. I know that's easy to say, but I've often found our worst expectations are sometimes as unrealistic as our rosiest."

"I keep trying to tell myself that."

"Then don't stop," said Ava. "I'm in the car with Fai heading back to our condo. I won't be there for about another hour so there's nothing I can attempt until then. What's the time where you are right now?"

"It's almost eleven, but you can call me anytime. There's no way I'll be able to sleep."

"Well, regardless if I find out something or not, I will phone you later."

"Thank you, I'll be waiting," said Silvana.

Ava ended the call. "What do you think of that?" she asked Fai.

"Is it possible that this is Chen's way of dumping Silvana?" Fai asked. "Maybe he's had enough of her and didn't have the nerve to tell her to her face."

"You've known Chen far longer than I have," said Ava. "Do you really believe that he is capable of doing that?"

"He was an agent, and I've never met one who could be direct with a client. Chen was a master of packaging bad news and making it seem like it was the best thing that could have happened for the client."

"He never struck me as being that cynical or manipulative."

"He was never your agent."

"That's true enough, but I like to think I'm a decent judge of character."

Fai sighed. "And you are, and my comments about Chen

are simply *me* being cynical. The fact is, I'm rather afraid of what might have happened to him, and dumping Silvana is the most optimistic theory I can think of."

"What is this about Silvana getting dumped?" Jennie Lee asked from the back seat in a drowsy voice.

"Nothing, Mummy," Ava said. "But you should start pulling yourself together. We'll be at the house in about fifteen minutes."

When they reached the house, Ava declined Jennie's invitation to come in for noodles, and then her offer to treat them to dim sum at a nearby restaurant. With each passing minute, she found herself becoming more concerned about Silvana's phone call. If Chen was actually missing, there weren't a lot of possible explanations that made sense.

"I can tell you're really worried about Chen," Fai said as they left Jennie's and made their way to the Don Valley Parkway.

"I am."

"What are you going to do?"

"A lot of what Silvana has already done. Call the hotel and the airline, and I might try to track down someone at Top of the Road to see if he contacted them, although it is a Sunday and I doubt anyone will be working at the office."

"It might be a waste of time, but I'll phone some of his former agency colleagues and some of the actors he's close to. You never know, someone might have heard from him," said Fai.

"That's a good idea."

They were halfway down the parkway before either of them spoke again, and it was Fai who did. "One other thing that is really puzzling me is Chen's relationship with Top of the Road," she said. "Why would a company pay ten million dollars for the distribution rights to a film and then refuse to speak to the producer?"

12

AVA DID NOT START MAKING PHONE CALLS AS SOON as she got to the apartment in Yorkville. She preferred doing things in an orderly manner, so bags were unpacked, laundry was organized, and the almost empty fridge was replenished with a quick trip to the nearby Whole Foods store on Avenue Road. It was early afternoon by the time she sat down at the kitchen table with her phone and a notepad and pen.

The Four Seasons in Beverly Hills was co-operative and confirmed that Chen had made a reservation but had never checked in. Ava asked if he had cancelled the reservation or simply not shown up, and was told he was a no-show.

Dealing with ANA was more complicated. There was no Toronto reservation office, but Ava was able to contact an agent at its North American headquarters in California, and then another in an international office in an unspecified site. She had identified the flight that Silvana said Chen was supposed to take, and concocted a story about Chen being her ailing grandfather. He hadn't arrived in Los Angeles as planned, she told the agents, and the family was worried to death about him. Could the airline confirm that he had actually gotten on that flight? Despite what Ava thought was fine acting on her part, neither agent would. It went against company policy, they stressed. Could they at least confirm that he'd had a reservation on that flight? They were equally unyielding.

"You look frustrated," Fai said to her from the living room, where she had been phoning Chen's acquaintances in China.

"I can't get anywhere with ANA."

"And I'm not getting anything useful from the people I've been talking to. None of them have heard from Chen in ages," Fai said. "I have a few more on my list but it's getting far too late to call."

"Let me see if I can reach someone at Top of the Road," Ava said, opening her laptop.

She quickly found the company's website and phoned the office. When no one answered the main line or any of the extensions she was directed to try, she searched the site for the names of the principals. As Chen had told her in Cannes, there were three of them. Larry Christensen was chairman and CEO; Justin Black, COO and vice-chairman; and Marc Shiner, CFO and vice-chairman. Their bios were brief, there was no contact information for any of them, and aside from the general phone number there was only the generic email address, info@topoftheroad.com.

"Fai, what is that website that has a ton of information about people in the movie business?" she called across the room.

"IMDb," Fai answered.

Ava entered that site. Christensen, Black, Shiner, and Top of the Road were all listed, but there wasn't any information that Ava thought she could use. Frustrated, she stood and walked over to the window. She knew Silvana would be waiting for her to phone, and the idea of calling with absolutely nothing to report ate at her. She thought of possible options and two came to mind. One was a contact she had in Bangkok, but it was the middle of the night there and she didn't know him well enough to impose at that hour. She also wasn't sure he was still in a position where he could provide help. The other option was more obvious, and Ava chided herself for not having thought of it sooner. She returned to the kitchen table to phone Silvana.

"*Wei*," Silvana answered in a shaky voice.

"Hey, this is Ava. I'm calling back as promised."

"What have you found out?" blurted Silvana.

"So far, nothing more than you did, but I have a few ideas I want to pursue," said Ava. "I have to wait four or five hours before I can start on one, but the other is something we can work on right away — that is if you're up to it."

"If I'm 'up to it'?"

"Yes. Am I right to assume that Chen keeps his work files at the apartment?"

"Yes, he does."

"And does he use a desktop computer as well as his laptop?"

"Yes."

"Do you know the password for the computer?"

"No."

"I'd like you to look for it. If he is as organized as you said earlier, then he might have all his passwords written down somewhere — probably in a notebook, or at least a piece of paper. Check any drawers in his office, or anywhere else you think he might have kept them."

"And if find a password?"

"Do you have a pen and paper at hand?"

"Just a second, I'll get them," Silvana said, and then seconds later she returned. "I'm back."

"Write down these names — Larry Christensen, Justin Black, Marc Shiner. If you find the passwords, get into the computer and look for correspondence between Chen and any of those men or Top of the Road Distribution. Go back as far as you can. Forward whatever you find to me."

"Okay, but what if I don't find any passwords?"

"Then go through his paper files. I'm trying to find contact information for the men I mentioned, and copies of any communication between him and them. They run Top of the Road, so look for anything with that name or their personal names attached."

"Do you think they have something to do with Chen's disappearance?"

"Silvana, it's a bit premature to say he's disappeared when we don't know what's happened. It could be something that's innocent and easily explained," said Ava, trying to keep her calm. "And my interest in these men is just me being logical because I can't think of anyone else who might know he was headed to Los Angeles. Can you think of anyone else he might have told, besides yourself of course?"

"No."

"Then focus on them and see what you can come up with."

"What if I can't find anything?"

"Then I'll just have to wait until tomorrow, when Top of the Road should be open for business," Ava said.

"What about that other idea you mentioned?"

"It's a long shot, and I don't feel comfortable talking about it."

Silvana became quiet, and Ava wondered if she was offended. But even if she was, it wouldn't change Ava's mind.

"But you'll stay in touch with me?" Silvana finally said.

"Of course I will. Now go and see what you can find."

Ava ended the conversation with a sense of disquiet. Her fear was that Silvana's use of the word *disappearance* was far more accurate than not.

Fai had abandoned the living room for the bedroom. Ava found her there watching a movie on television, and to her surprise it was *An Affair to Remember* with Deborah Kerr and Cary Grant.

"This is a change," Ava said.

"I thought I'd start my English immersion early, and speaking it half as well as Deborah Kerr does would make me very happy," she said, and then took on a more serious tone. "How did it go with Silvana?"

"Not that well, but I've given her a project which should keep her busy and maybe contribute to finding out what the hell is going on."

"Is there anything else we can do?"

"I have an acquaintance in Bangkok who, if he remembers me — and if he is still in the same job — might be able to help. But I can't call him at three in the morning," said Ava. "I think I'll go for a run. Maybe we could go for an early dinner at Blu when I get back. After dinner I'll phone Bangkok."

During the summer months, Ava normally ran early in the morning to avoid the worst of the heat and humidity, but running at anytime helped reduce her stress levels. She left the condo building and turned right towards Avenue Road, and then turned right again to go north. This was her favourite route since it had the fewest stoplights, and the route from her condo to Eglinton Avenue was almost exactly four kilometres — a lot of it uphill, which made the return journey easier.

As she eased into the run, her mind began to turn over thoughts about Chen, and that inevitably led to her wondering if Arthon, her contact in Bangkok, would remember her. He was a lieutenant on the Bangkok police force, a fourth-generation Chaozhou Chinese, and somehow connected to the triads. She wasn't sure what the connection actually was — only that he had been assigned by his father, an old friend of Uncle's, to help her on a job several years before, in the city. The word *triad* hadn't been said by either of them, but he had spoken at length about how highly regarded Uncle was by his family — so she'd made the assumption that they had triad ties.

The job had been complicated with the potential to become violent. Arthon had helped steer her through the local culture, and had contributed some hands-on support when it was needed. The fact he couldn't speak Chinese and her Thai was non-existent wasn't an issue, because he had attended university in Liverpool and his English was excellent.

When she wasn't thinking about Arthon during her run, Top of the Road occupied her. She knew little about the film business, but it struck her as more than odd that the company wouldn't share their distribution plans with Chen. Had he offended them in some way? Was it a reluctance to discuss plans that weren't finalized? Then a picture of their website popped into her head, and it hit her so suddenly that she almost came to a halt.

On the right side of the page there had been a list of current and upcoming Top of the Road releases. She was sure that *Tiananmen* wasn't included, or at least she didn't think she'd seen the name. Maybe if she had scrolled down, it would have been there — but maybe not. She was still a kilometre away from Eglinton when she turned and began to run back down Avenue Road.

"That was a very quick run," Fai said when Ava burst into the apartment twenty minutes later.

"I thought of something that I need to check," Ava said and went directly to her laptop.

"What is it?" Fai said, standing behind her and looking over her shoulder.

Ava accessed the Top of the Road website. "Look, there's no mention of *Tiananmen* in the list of current and upcoming releases."

"My god, you're right. How weird is that?"

Ava shook her head. "I am beginning to feel very uncomfortable that we're doing business with this outfit."

"But Chen looked into them, didn't he?"

"He said he did, and I have no reason to disbelieve him. He told me they were relatively new but a well-financed and solid company."

"There might be an explanation why our film isn't on their upcoming release list," said Fai.

"If there is, I certainly want to hear it — and it had better be good," Ava said.

"What are you going to do?"

Before Ava could answer, her phone rang and she saw Silvana's number.

"This is Ava."

"I can't find his passwords. I've looked everywhere I can think of," Silvana said, sounding stressed.

"That's okay, it was a long shot anyway," said Ava, disguising her disappointment.

"But I did find a copy of the distribution agreement."

"I saw the final version before Chen signed it, but I can't remember all the details. Could you scan it and email it to me?"

"Yes, I'll do that right away," said Silvana. "There are also some of Chen's handwritten notes in the same file. It has the home and mobile phone numbers and an email address for Larry Christensen. That's one of the names you told me to look for."

Ava reached for a piece of paper and a pen. "It is indeed, and that is very well done on your part, Silvana. Could you read them to me, please?"

Silvana did, and then said, "I'll scan the agreement right away."

"Thank you, and after you've sent it to me, do me a favour and go to bed. There's nothing more you can do tonight, and if I need you tomorrow I would like you to be rested."

"I don't know if I can sleep, but I'll try."

"That's a good start. I'll be in touch with you later."

After hanging up, Ava pointed at the numbers Silvana had provided. "Those are the contact numbers for the guy who is chairman of Top of the Road," she said to Fai.

"Are you going to call him?"

"Of course, but I have to decide what approach I'm going to take. I need to shower. I'll think it over while I do."

The showerhead had variable settings that Ava adjusted depending on her mood. When she was angry or depressed she liked the strongest setting, but this was a time to think so she turned it to a fine mist. Assuming she could reach Christensen, she had a lot of questions to ask. The issue was, why would he provide answers to any of them for someone who was a complete stranger? She knew she needed a cover story, and decided she'd tell him she was a close personal friend of Chen who had been expecting his arrival in Los Angeles. Not only had he not arrived, he hadn't told her about any change in plans, and that was completely unlike him. She'd say Chen had told her he was coming to meet with Top of the Road, and she was reaching out to see if anyone in the company had heard from him.

Christensen might not take the "close personal friend" description at face value, she realized, and would probably ask for her name. That gave her pause. After all the work she had done to stay anonymous, there was no way she was going to directly connect her name to Chen professionally, and indirectly to *Tiananmen*. Jennie Kwong was going to have to handle the conversation. That was a pseudonym Ava had used several times in the past, and she actually had a Hong Kong passport and ID card, complete with photos, in the name.

Assuming she did reach Christensen and he was the least bit helpful when it came to Chen's whereabouts, should she — subtly of course — ask him about the release dates for *Tiananmen*? She might have to characterize herself as a business associate as well as friend of Chen, but that wasn't a huge stretch.

First things first, she thought as she stepped out of the shower and reached for a large, thick towel.

She entered the kitchen with a smaller towel wrapped

around her head, wearing a black Giordano T-shirt and Adidas training pants. She sat at the table, reached for her phone, and called Christensen's mobile number.

"Yeah," he answered.

"Mr. Christensen, my name is Jennie Kwong. I'm a good friend of Chen Jie."

The line went dead.

She stared at the phone, scarcely believing he had hung up on her so quickly. But maybe it was a bad connection, she thought as she dialled the number again. It went directly to voicemail and she knew he had turned off the phone. She took a deep breath and said, "Mr. Christensen. My name is Jennie Kwong and I am indeed a good friend of Chen Jie. I am visiting L.A. and was expecting him to arrive here two days ago. He didn't make it, I haven't heard from him, and since he told me he was coming to meet with your company, I'm wondering if you know what has happened to him?"

She sat back in the chair and called Christensen's landline. When she was directed to his answerphone, she left an identical message and her phone number.

"That doesn't sound very encouraging," Fai said from the living room.

Ava shook her head. "I have a hunch that I might have to go to Los Angeles, but I won't make that decision right now. I want to have dinner and I want to speak to Bangkok. And I want to see if that asshole Christensen calls me back."

13

IT WAS SEVEN THIRTY WHEN AVA AND FAI RETURNED to the condo after dinner at Blu Ristorante, a wonderful Italian eatery only two blocks from the apartment. They had shared ahi tuna tartare and beef carpaccio appetizers, and had both opted for the wood-fired rack of lamb that came with a mushroom veal jus. They'd drunk a bottle of Chablis with the meal, and the combination of fine food and good wine normally left Ava in the best of moods, but the question of what was going on with Chen hung over her head like a dark cloud.

She had kept her phone in sight during dinner in the hope that Christensen would call, and the first thing she did when she got back to the apartment was to try his numbers again. His cellphone rang twice before it cut out and went to voicemail. Frustrated and starting to get angry, she said, "This is Jennie Kwong again. I need to speak to you about Chen and I'll keep calling until I do."

"It certainly seems like he's avoiding you," Fai said.

"He can't do it forever," said Ava as she opened her laptop. She went into her contacts and found Arthon's email address and phone number. The way things were going, she wouldn't be surprised if neither of them was still active, she thought as she called his phone.

It rang only once before she heard a man say, "*Sa wat dee krap.*"

"Arthon, is that you?" she asked.

"Yes, this is Arthon. Who are you?"

"Ava Lee. I don't know if you remember me. I worked with Uncle in Hong Kong, and you helped us out on a job a few years ago," she said. "I'm calling you from my home in Toronto, and I apologize if it's too early."

"Of course I remember you, how could I not? And I've been awake for some time now," he said, and then paused. "I also heard about Uncle's passing. It saddened my father and many other people here a great deal. He was a highly respected man."

"He was, and I miss him terribly."

"But you aren't calling me to talk about Uncle, are you?" he said rather gently.

"No — I have a problem that I'm hoping you can help me with," she said. "Are you still a police lieutenant?"

"I'm still with the police, but I'm a captain now."

"Congratulations."

"There are days when it would be more appropriate to say 'condolences.' Things are difficult in Thailand right now. We have lost our democracy — as flawed as it was — and the military are basically running the country. The public is divided into two opposing camps and they don't hesitate to take to the streets to express their views and clash with each other. When we intervene to impose some measure of law and order we are vilified by one or the other side — and sometimes both."

"Yes, I've read about the yellow shirts and the red shirts, although I don't pretend to understand their significance."

"The red shirts support Thaksin, the former prime minister who is in exile, and they portray themselves as pro-democracy. The yellows think Thaksin was the devil incarnate, whose main objective was to undermine the royal family. Most of the power-brokers in the Bangkok region, including our military, support the royals, and thus the yellows."

"And you have a new king."

"I . . ." Arthon began, then stopped and said quietly: "It isn't wise to discuss the king, even on a phone that I think is secure. Why don't you tell me about the problem you have."

Ava knew Thailand had draconian lèse-majesté laws, and that even a faintly critical Facebook posting about the king could result in a jail term, but she was still surprised at Arthon's reaction to the mere mention of him.

"Yes — my problem is that a friend has gone missing. He was scheduled to leave Bangkok three days ago now on an early morning ANA flight to Tokyo, where he was to make a connection for Los Angeles. We don't think he arrived in L.A. because he didn't check into his hotel, he hasn't contacted his girlfriend as he was supposed to, and he has been unreachable."

"Three days ago?"

"Yes."

"Could he have changed his plans? Could he have stayed in Tokyo, or caught a flight to a different destination?"

"I am convinced that he did none of those things. He is a careful, organized, thorough, and considerate man. If he had made any changes he would have let his girlfriend know.

He didn't, and the fact she hasn't heard from him at all since then is more than strange."

"What is his name?"

"Chen Jie."

"He's Chinese?"

"Yes, but he lives in Bangkok."

"Have you spoken to ANA to see if he got on the flight here?"

"The girlfriend and I both have. They won't tell us anything. Sharing that information evidently runs contrary to company policy. I'm hoping you can be more persuasive," Ava said. "Simply knowing whether or not he got on the flight would be a starting point."

"I'll make some calls," Arthon said. "One positive thing about our current political climate is that civilians are more inclined than ever to co-operate with the authorities."

"That's wonderful, thank you."

"I assume I should phone you back on the number that's on my screen?"

"Yes, please."

"I'm leaving for my office in about half an hour. I'll make those calls as soon as I get there."

During Ava's conversation with Arthon, Fai had gone into the bedroom. After ending the call, Ava went in there and found her sitting in bed watching a Hong Kong–set soap opera on one of OMNI Television's Chinese channels.

"My mother watches this all the time. I didn't know you were into soaps," said Ava.

"I'm not, but Silvana is one of the stars."

"I had forgotten that she was," Ava said, sliding onto the bed.

"She can cry on cue. That's harder to do than it might

seem," said Fai, resting her cheek on Ava's shoulder. "How was your chat with Bangkok?"

"As good as I could have hoped for."

They sat quietly as they watched the drama, and despite knowing it was Silvana who was acting, Ava found herself getting drawn into her character. They were watching a scene where she was about to confront the cheating husband of her daughter when Ava's phone rang. For the briefest second, Ava thought about not answering, but then she saw Larry Christensen's number.

"Hello," she said as calmly as she could.

"Are you Jennie Kwong?"

"I am."

"This is Larry Christensen. Why have you been harassing me, and harassing me especially on a Sunday, which is my family day?"

"I apologize for my timing, Mr. Christensen, but I'm very worried about my friend Chen Jie."

"So you made clear in your messages, but what does that have to do with me or my company?"

"He was coming to Los Angeles to meet with you."

"That's news to me."

"Are you saying that he didn't have an appointment, that he didn't tell you he was coming?"

"That's exactly what I'm saying."

"He told me that he had been trying to contact you for weeks and that you weren't returning his phone calls or answering his emails," Ava said.

"I run a very busy company and I have to set priorities. Communicating with Mr. Chen wasn't anywhere near the top of my list."

"But you did buy the world distribution rights to the film *Tiananmen* from his production company."

"I don't understand what point you're trying to make, or indeed what your relationship is to Chen or the film."

"As I said, I'm a good friend of Chen's, and I've seen and really admire the film," said Ava. "My point is that all Chen wanted from you was information about your distribution plans, and he seemed to be having difficulty obtaining it. My understanding is that you paid ten million dollars for the rights. Surely you have a plan to recoup it."

"And if we do, why should I share it with you?"

"I don't expect you to, and that's not what I'm asking. What I want to know is why you wouldn't discuss the plan with Chen," Ava said. "He told me that when he met with you in Cannes you were very open and that he expected a lot of co-operation moving forward."

"Ms. Kwong, what do you know about the film business?" Christensen said, sounding exasperated.

"Virtually nothing."

"Then I will keep this simple. We wanted to acquire the rights to *Tiananmen*. Within the company it fell to me to persuade Mr. Chen to sell them to us, and so I told him what I thought he wanted to hear. Please believe me when I say we never had any intention of involving him in our planning process."

"But he also said that as recently as a month ago you promised to show him your plans."

"We never promised him anything of the kind. He either made that assumption based our Cannes conversations, or he was misinterpreting our recent communications. You would have thought that a man with that much experience in the business would have read between the lines and understood that we weren't interested in sharing anything with him."

Ava slid from the bed and walked towards the kitchen. "And you're certain that he didn't tell you that he was coming to L.A.?"

"I am absolutely sure, although to be perfectly honest, I stopped paying attention to his emails and listening to his messages some time ago."

"Could you go back and check on those that are more recent?"

Christensen hesitated, and then said, "No, I won't do that. I don't want to involve myself in whatever mess Chen may have fallen into. I can't take responsibility for someone I barely know."

Ava sat at the kitchen table and opened her laptop. "I guess that's understandable, but what I don't understand is why it seems your company has no intention of releasing *Tiananmen* in the near future, or if you are going to release it, why you have no intention of putting any promotional muscle behind it."

"What are you talking about?" Christensen snapped.

"I'm looking at your website. There isn't a single mention of *Tiananmen* on it, and that includes in the new and upcoming releases section."

"Ms. Kwong, I returned your calls because of your obvious concern about Chen. But I did it as a courtesy and that does not give you the licence to poke your nose into how my company runs its business," Christensen said abruptly. "This conversation is about to end, but I do want to say that I hope you locate Chen and that he's well. I must also ask you to refrain from trying to contact me again. Goodbye."

Ava put down her phone and stared at the website. She could see nothing she might have missed or misconstrued. She thought about Chen's experience as an agent. It was true it had all been in Asia, but was the movie business any different there than it was in the West? Were the players any less dissembling? She couldn't imagine that they were, and she couldn't accept that Chen would be so gullible — as Christensen had implied — as to believe everything he was being told if he didn't have grounds. She was now convinced that something had happened between Cannes in May and L.A. in July that had caused Top of the Road to change its mind about the film and Chen. She could only think of one thing — the China Movie Syndicate — and this prompted a groan and several shakes of her head. Had Mo gotten to Top of the Road?

"Was that Christensen from Top of the Road?" Fai asked from the bedroom doorway.

"It was."

"How did it go?"

"He swears that they didn't know Chen was going to L.A., and I have no way of disproving it. Even if I could, what would it actually mean other than they didn't want to talk to him."

"What about *Tiananmen*? Did you ask him why there's no release date?"

"I did, and he brushed me off and then hung up."

"Well, realistically that is something Chen has to sort out with them — unless you're willing to step forward and take official ownership of the film, which we know you can't do."

"Yes, there's no need to worry about that happening."

Fai walked behind Ava and wrapped her arms around

her. "I have a feeling that Chen is going to show up in the next day or two and everything is going to turn out better than it looks right now."

"I wish I had your confidence."

Fai kissed the top of Ava's head. "Do you have anything else you need to do tonight?"

"I'm waiting to hear from Bangkok, but other than that, no."

"Then why don't we get a glass of wine, get into bed, and watch another episode of Silvana's soap?" Fai asked. "The synopsis says that her love life is turned upside down when a mysterious stranger appears from her past."

"Well, at least that's better than a lover disappearing from her present life," said Ava.

UNCLE CAME TO AVA IN HER DREAMS THAT NIGHT. HE most often did when she was stressed and confused, and that accurately described her state of mind when she finally fell asleep.

He was sitting in the Kit Kat Koffee House on the arrivals level of Chep Lap Kok international airport in Hong Kong. Ava wasn't sure why she was in Hong Kong, but any concern she felt disappeared when she saw him. There were no other customers or servers, only Uncle with a cigarette dangling from his lips and the racing form open on a black and white tiled table. He looked up as she approached, smiled broadly, closed the form, and said, "It is so good to see you, and I'm so glad you came. I've been thinking a lot about you."

Ava took a seat next to him and somehow a cup of black coffee materialized in front of her. She took a sip. "I am involved in something that is turning out to be more complicated than it should be," she said.

"I sense you are feeling frustrated by it."

"If I am it is because I feel forced to operate behind the

scenes. You know I prefer being direct. I like meeting things head-on. This is a situation where I can't afford to act like that without putting other lives and Three Sisters at risk. So I have been restraining myself, and that isn't easy."

"You are speaking about the film business, and Chen's disappearance," he said.

"Yes."

Uncle took a deep drag on his cigarette, blew the smoke away from her, and leaned across the table to take her hand in his. "You need to simplify things."

"How?"

"Focus on Chen. Forget everything else until you do. If you can locate him then you'll have someone who can put the other pieces of the puzzle in place. Without him, there is nothing to be gained and much to lose from trying to do it yourself."

"When you refer to a puzzle, you mean *Tiananmen*?"

"Yes. If you don't have Chen then you need to start thinking about letting it go. With him, it will still be a challenge. Without him — even as Jennie Kwong — it would be reckless."

"But that film…"

"Ava, what more do you want from it? Hasn't it met your expectations in terms of Lau Lau's resurrection? Hasn't it already been publicly acknowledged as a fine piece of work? What difference will it make to your life if another ten thousand or ten million people see it in a few months? Whether they do or not, it is going to exist in one form or another for future generations."

"Even if I agree with you, how do I explain that to Lau Lau, Fai, and Silvana?"

"Tell them it is foolish and dangerous to keep poking the

dragon. My fear is that Chen may have already discovered that," said Uncle.

Before she could respond, Ava heard a phone ring. She looked towards Kit Kat's entrance, but there was no one there. She turned back to Uncle and he was gone. Then she felt her shoulder being shaken and heard Fai saying, "There's a call for you. He says it's urgent."

Ava sat up, rubbed her eyes, and took the phone from Fai. "Yes."

"This is Arthon. It is my turn to apologize for calling at this hour, but I thought you would want to know about your friend Chen."

Ava glanced at the bedside clock and saw it was almost three a.m. "Have you found him? Is he all right?"

"I don't know about all right, but I have located him," said Arthon. "He checked in for his flight but never made it onto the plane. He is currently being held in a cell at Suvarnabhumi Airport."

"Held by whom?" she asked, trying not to sound panicked.

"The Immigration Bureau, but that is only temporary until negotiations are concluded," said Arthon. "Ava, your friend is in great demand. There are at least three of our intelligence agencies who want to get their hands on him. Immigration is taking bids from them."

Ava took a deep breath as she tried to process what she had just been told. "Could you excuse me for one minute? I need to get a glass of water," she said, glancing at Fai, who had closed her eyes and seemed to have fallen back to sleep.

"Take your time," said Arthon.

Ava went into the kitchen, poured a large glass, and downed half of it. Then she sat at the table, put the phone on speaker mode, picked up a pen, and opened a notebook. "I'm back," she said. "But before giving me details on who is trying to do what to whom, maybe you could tell me how you know all of this?"

"I called ANA after speaking to you, asked them about Chen as official police business, and they told me that he had checked in but not boarded the flight. I assumed he'd either left the airport — which didn't make sense — or had run into an issue when he tried to clear immigration or security. I called an old police colleague who now works in the Immigration Bureau, and he confirmed that they had taken Chen into custody."

"Under what pretext?"

"He didn't know. The order to detain him had come from Immigration Bureau headquarters, but he thought he heard the National Intelligence Agency being cited so he assumed that's where the request originated. The NIA is headquartered in Paruskavan Palace, as is the Metropolitan Police Bureau, to which I am currently assigned," said Arthon. "I spent more than an hour at the NIA going from office to office until I found someone who would explain to me what was going on with Chen. It turns out he is being held at the request of the Chinese government, but this is where it gets tricky because it wasn't a formal diplomatic request. It came through security channels."

"The Chinese government made the request?" Ava asked, hoping she didn't sound as panicked as she felt.

"Yes — unfortunately that isn't uncommon these days."

"And what is the difference between a diplomatic request and a security one?"

"The diplomatic request normally comes accompanied

by a valid reason for an extradition — something like fraud, kidnapping, or even murder. The one for Chen came from the Chinese Ministry of State Security and had only his name and no mention of any crime. Chinese security contacted people in various Thai intelligence agencies and told them Chen was in Bangkok and would be flying out. They asked that he be detained and shipped to China. And Ava, they said they were willing to pay for him, and that is an offer our agencies are willing to accept."

Ava's breath caught in her throat. "Are you seriously saying that Chen could be sold to the Chinese?"

"Yes."

Ava stopped making notes and looked at what she had just written. Arthon had triggered an avalanche of questions. Where to start? As close to the beginning as possible, she decided, and asked, "When you say 'detained,' are you implying that the Chinese knew what his schedule was, what flight he was meant to be on?"

"They knew."

Who could have told them, she wondered? Could his email or phone have been hacked? Was he being tracked in Bangkok? And then a name popped into her head. "Christensen, was it you, you son of a bitch?" she muttered under her breath, before saying forcefully to Arthon, "And when you mentioned intelligence agencies, did you really mean that in the plural sense?"

"Unfortunately, I did. We have the NIA, which is theoretically the master agency, but there are six other intelligence agencies connected to the army, navy, air force, the special branch, supreme command headquarters, and the national security command headquarters, and frankly there isn't a lot of co-operation among them. The Chinese, according to my source at the NIA, went to them, the agencies at special branch and the army, and made the same request to have Chen detained and returned to China. Those agencies in turn all contacted the Immigration Bureau to request he be taken into custody at the airport."

"Would the Bureau have known there was a price attached to him?"

"There is no doubt in my mind that if they didn't figure that out immediately then they would have been told. The Chinese have made a practice of paying for people they want repatriated for several years now, and sadly we've co-operated."

"So now what — the Bureau is taking bids from the agencies?"

"More or less, and where your friend has been lucky is that there are three agencies involved so it hasn't been a quick process. The Bureau will be playing one off against the other to maximize the price, and I'm quite sure the three of them have been going back and forth with the Chinese trying to get more money to meet the Bureau's demands. The Chinese obviously overplayed their hand. They would have been smarter to focus on one agency. Though the fact they didn't does indicate how badly they want to get their hands on your friend."

"Has he been interrogated? Has he been hurt?"

"No — the Bureau won't let anyone get close to him until the price is settled."

"How much money are we talking about?"

"I have no idea."

"Can you find out?"

"Why?"

"What if my side is prepared to pay more? Do you think that the Immigration Bureau would turn Chen over to us?"

"It might have to be a lot more, and even then they might be reluctant to offend the agencies, and by proxy the Chinese."

"Enough money might eliminate any reluctance they have," she said. "But define 'a lot.'"

"I can't. I don't have a number, and truthfully I'm not comfortable trying to come up with one."

"Can you find a way to communicate with the Bureau, or better still could you find a way that we could speak directly to someone there?"

"Possibly," Arthon said after a slight hesitation. "But Ava, I won't be the middle man in any negotiations with them. I can't involve the police, even indirectly, in this. I'll try to find you someone you can talk to, but you'll have to manage it from there. I don't object to being a sounding board for you, but that's as far as I want to go."

"I understand, and I hope you didn't think I was suggesting you be our frontman," she said. "As you can tell, I simply don't understand how things work in Thailand these days."

"How things work are power and money — and usually you can't have one without the other," he said. "I'll make some calls."

"One thing more — can you keep my name out of your conversations until we know where we stand?"

"Sure, and I should know that soon enough."

It wasn't until Ava put down the phone that she realized she had been sweating. She took a paper towel from the counter and dabbed her brow and upper lip. At least Chen was alive and she knew where he was, but otherwise his situation was a mess, and if he was sent to China it would only get messier for everyone, because as brave a man as Chen might be, she couldn't imagine him holding up if the Chinese decided to interrogate him about who was behind BB Productions. There might not be a paper trail, but all it would take was for Chen to mention Ava, May Ling, and Three Sisters by name to unleash a witch hunt that could destroy everything they'd built.

This is not the time to imagine the worst or get overly dramatic, she thought. As Uncle had said, she should focus on Chen. If she could free him, then any imminent danger was at least averted. "I should call May Ling and Amanda to tell them about Chen," she whispered, the idea catching her by surprise. And then, just as quickly, she pushed it aside. What was there to gain by alarming her friends? There was nothing that she could think of that they could do to help. Given that fact, telling them was almost cruel. No, she decided, she would wait until the situation was clear one way or another, or if she thought of some way they could assist.

She poured a second glass of water and sat at the table. After seeing Mo's reaction to *Tiananmen* in Cannes, it was no surprise that the Chinese government wanted to get their hands on Chen and were willing to reach into Thailand to get him. They had done it before to others. There were often news reports about people being picked up off the street in places like Macau, Vietnam, Hong Kong, and Thailand, and simply shipped to China without a hearing or trial to face criminal or civil charges. Many of those people were citizens of other countries, but the Chinese government's position was that if someone was born in China, they were Chinese forever. Dual citizenship wasn't permitted, a foreign passport was irrelevant, and Chen didn't even have either of those to fall back on.

Where she might get lucky was that there was a price attached to him, and despite saying to Arthon that she didn't know how things worked in Thailand these days, she had a good idea that they hadn't changed much since her previous trips. Government, military, and police officials had always been on the take, and the only threat to their flow of illegal income was the competition among themselves to decide who got what from where. Traditionally, the government officials took a bite out of every contract that was issued; the military shared in contracts for weaponry, but had sole control over the massive drug trade in the Golden Triangle; while the police ran things like local drug dealers, gambling, car theft, and the allocation of spots for beggars. Occasionally, though, one group would trespass on another's turf and there would be trouble. Ava remembered on one trip to Bangkok the newspapers had been full of stories about the military raiding local illegal casinos. The casinos fell under the purview of the police, but the police had been trying to encroach on the drug importation trade, and the military responded by closing the casinos. Eventually it got sorted and everyone returned to their traditional sources of outside income.

Ava's hope was that the Immigration Bureau was independent enough from the security agencies to be able to say no to them and do a deal with her. She made a note to ask Arthon how independent the Bureau was, because if it wasn't then she could imagine being strung along, bled of a bit of money, and tossed aside.

She thought about going back to bed but knew she'd never sleep, and she didn't want to disturb Fai so she opened her laptop with the idea of streaming a film or television show. When she did, she saw she had received twenty emails overnight, which was a surprisingly large number. She smiled grimly when she saw they were nearly all emails from Chen to Christensen and Top of the Road that Silvana had forwarded. She opened the most recent. It read: I'll be flying out of Bangkok on the 25th and will arrive in L.A. mid-afternoon on the same date. I will come directly to your offices. I have no intention of leaving L.A. until we have talked, so don't think about putting me off. Yours, Chen Jie.

Christensen had not replied, but Ava didn't doubt for a second that he had read it and knew about Chen's travel plans. But was he the one who had passed them on to the Chinese? She quickly scanned the other emails and they reflected everything that Chen had told her. At the beginning of June and into the next month they were friendly and professional, but towards the end of July, Christensen's responses to Chen started to get vague and non-committal while Chen's became increasingly more questioning, terser, and even angry. By early August, Christensen had stopped answering altogether.

Ava reached for her phone and called Silvana.

"*Wei*," she answered.

"I got the emails, thank you."

"I kept searching for his passwords and finally found them taped to the bottom of a laptop he doesn't use anymore, about an hour ago. I thought it was too early to call you so I just sent everything along."

"Great work."

"Do you have any news about Chen?" Silvana asked in a voice full of anxiety.

"No, but I have spoken to a contact in Bangkok who is very well-connected. He is talking to all kinds of people. I promise that I'll phone you if he comes up with anything."

"I'm so scared something horrible has happened to him."

"Don't let your imagination run away with you," said Ava. "I'll be in touch sooner rather than later."

As she ended the call, Ava felt a touch of guilt for not telling Silvana the truth about Chen, but her knowing about the reality of his situation might be devastating. Not knowing at least left room for some optimism.

She turned back to the emails between Chen and Christensen. It was obvious the relationship had gone off the rails, and she had a strong hunch about what had caused this to happen but no way of proving it. Besides, Uncle had told her to focus on Chen, and that's what she was going to do. If she somehow, some way, could extricate him from the cell in Bangkok, then she could turn her attention to Christensen.

15

AVA GOT BACK INTO BED AT FOUR, TOSSED AND TURNED
for what seemed like an eternity, and finally fell into dream-
less sleep. When she woke, the bed was empty and the clock
read eight fifteen. She found Fai dressed in jeans and a blue
silk blouse, drinking a cup of coffee in the kitchen.

"You shouldn't have let me sleep so late," Ava said.

"I was going to wake you at eight-thirty. What time did
you get to bed?"

"Around four," Ava said, pouring herself a coffee.

"Where was that late-night call from?"

"Bangkok. We've located Chen."

"So it was good news?"

"Not exactly, but it wasn't entirely bad either. I'll have a
better idea how to classify it if my friend Arthon can find
me a solid contact in the Thai Immigration Bureau."

"That sounds complicated."

"Actually, it is, but I'm hoping it's something that money
can fix," Ava said and smiled. "I should put on some clothes
so I can walk with you to your first day of English school."

"You know that isn't necessary," Fai said, looking pleased
all the same.

"I know, but I want to."

Ten minutes later they left the condo and wound their way to the building that housed Berlitz, near the corner of Bay and Bloor Streets. They hugged outside the door. "I'm very excited for you," Ava said.

"I'm so nervous. What if nothing sinks in?"

"It will take time and perseverance, and you have to be patient," said Ava. "I promise you, if you work as hard as you can in class, and we only speak and listen to things in English at home, you'll start to feel comfortable in no time."

"And I promise you that I'll do the very best I can."

They kissed goodbye, and then Ava turned and started to make her way back to the condo, Bangkok now dominating her thoughts. She had checked her phone before she left, but there hadn't been any calls or texts, and she knew it was going to be a long morning until she heard from Arthon.

When Ava got home, she contemplated going for a run, but she didn't like taking her phone with her and decided to wait. Instead, she downed a coffee and went to shower. She left the phone on the bathroom counter, and it rang just as she began to wash her hair. She stepped out of the shower, dripping wet and with a head full of shampoo.

"Hello," she answered, trying to wrap a towel around her head with her free hand.

"This is Arthon."

"I've been hoping to hear from you," she said, putting down the toilet seat, laying a towel on it, and then sitting.

"I couldn't do what I wanted by phone. I had to meet my contact in person."

"And how did it go?" she asked, trying to mask her apprehension.

"I don't know other than that he's agreed to talk to you."

"He understands that my interest is in Chen?"

"I made that very clear. He was surprised, but didn't react negatively."

"So the Immigration Bureau hasn't done a deal yet with one of the security agencies?" she asked.

"That's how it seems."

"What else did you tell him, besides that I'm interested in Chen?"

"I stressed that it might be worth his time to talk to you," said Arthon. "He asked who you were, and I told him I thought it would be best if you introduced yourself to him."

"Does he know I'm a woman?"

"No."

"What's his name?"

"I won't give you his full Thai name; it's too long and complicated. You can call him Viroj," said Arthon. "This is his phone number . . ."

"Please hold on for a minute. I got out of the shower to take your call and I need to get a pen and a piece of paper."

Ava went into the bedroom and took paper and pen from a bedside drawer. "Okay, I'm ready."

Arthon relayed the number, paused, and then did it again more slowly.

"Thank you," she said. "Is this Viroj expecting me to phone him tonight?"

"I told him that there was urgency in this matter, so he won't be surprised if you do."

"I'll call him as soon as we're finished."

"There are some things you need to know about him that I don't want you to repeat, and that I don't want him to know I've told you."

"I'm listening."

"He works at the Immigration Bureau. He isn't in one of the top senior positions yet, although it shouldn't take long for that to happen because, even though he's young, he's incredibly intelligent and is the nephew of the under-secretary of the Ministry of the Interior. One of the under-secretary's most important responsibilities is his role as chairman of the Immigration Council. The Council oversees the activities of the Bureau, and no one has more power than the chairman, so you can assume that he ordered or approved your friend's detention. You can also assume that if Viroj isn't handling the negotiations for his uncle, he is being briefed. The two of them are incredibly close."

"I get the picture, and I'll be appropriately discreet."

"Good — now when you call him, you are to say that you've been told he has a motorcycle to sell and that you are wondering what the model is. If he answers 'Honda,' then it is safe to start a conversation with him. If he says 'Kawasaki,' you should tell him that model doesn't interest you, thank him for his time, and hang up. Then wait exactly two hours and call him again. If he can talk, he'll answer. If he can't, he won't, and you'll have to keep trying every hour on the hour after that."

"That is quite the process," she said.

"The phone number I gave you is for a safe phone, but even with that precaution Viroj is wary. Remember, there are three security agencies trying to do a deal with the Immigration Bureau. They all could be spying on him, and each other."

"I will follow those instructions to the letter."

"Then I will leave you to it."

"Before you go, there is one thing I have to tell you," she said. "I won't be using my real name when I speak to Viroj. For reasons too complicated to get into, I'm going to identify myself as Jennie Kwong. I have a Hong Kong passport and ID card in that name. If challenged, I have some proof. So if Viroj comes back to you after he and I speak, I would appreciate it if you could support my deception."

"That won't be a problem, although one day you need to explain what reasons could be that complicated."

"Let's hope that day comes," she said. "As for the present, would you like me to keep you updated?"

"Yes, do that. I'm curious to see how this turns out."

As Ava put down the phone she caught a glimpse of herself in the bedroom mirror. The towel she had wrapped around her head had come undone and was draped over her shoulders, and her hair looked like clumps of black seaweed. Her body was still lean and firm, but the older she got the more she noticed the scars that years of debt-collecting had earned her. The most striking was one that made it seem like a long, pink worm had attached itself to her upper thigh. It was the result of the work of a surgeon in Macau who had extracted a bullet lodged deep in her leg. Ava sighed. When Uncle died and the debt-collecting business closed, she had thought her life would be more peaceful and less violent. It hadn't turned out that way, and she didn't know if that was karma or if her personality was such that she was drawn to strife and danger. Either way, her life was rarely dull.

She turned away from the mirror and looked at the phone number she had written down. Arthon had opened a door, and now it was up to her to find a way through it. But, she thought with smile, she wasn't going to do it naked.

Twenty minutes later, wearing a black Giordano T-shirt and Adidas training pants, and with her hair rinsed and blown dry, she sat at the kitchen and called the number in Bangkok.

"*Sa wat dee krap*," a man answered.

Ava took a deep breath and said, "I understand that you have a motorcycle to sell, and I'm wondering if you can tell me what model it is."

"It is a Honda…and you are a woman. Arthon didn't tell me you are a woman."

"I hope that doesn't disappoint you, or is a problem."

"I went to university in Australia but I didn't adopt any of the Aussie men's worst attitudes towards women."

"That is good to hear, and may I say your English is superb."

"Before university in Australia I went to a private school — or as the English call it, a public school — just outside of London."

Ava had been nervous to make the call, but started to relax as Viroj didn't seem to be the least bit guarded or suspicious and was behaving unlike anything she had anticipated.

"But here I am going on about myself when I know absolutely nothing about you," Viroj said. "To begin with, can you give me a name?"

"Jennie Kwong," Ava said.

"You are Chinese?"

"Hong Kong born, but raised in Canada from the time I was two. Still, I speak Cantonese and Mandarin, and like to think that I have been blessed with the best that both cultures have to offer."

"My family, like our mutual friend Arthon's, has its roots in China, and although they go back more than two hundred years they haven't been forgotten."

"But, also like Arthon, you have a Thai name."

"One has to blend in. Even in a country as supposedly tolerant as Thailand, there is a fair amount of xenophobia," Viroj said, and then continued. "Well, now that we know a bit more about each other, why don't you tell me about your interest in Chen Jie."

"He is a very good friend. One who we value to a great extent," she said, with an emphasis on the word *value*.

"What was he doing in Thailand?"

"Living."

"Don't you mean hiding?" Viroj asked.

"No, because he has no reason to hide from anyone. He had a distinguished career as an agent and talent manager in China, and is now in the film production business."

"My understanding is that he produced a film about Tiananmen Square."

"He did, and it is a magnificent work. Good enough, in fact, to win the Palme d'Or award at the Cannes Film Festival."

"Evidently the Chinese don't share your view about its quality."

"There is nothing you can say, write, film, or paint about what happened in Tiananmen Square that wouldn't upset them."

"So then why would he do it if he knew it would get that kind of reaction?" Viroj asked.

"The director, Lau Lau, was a client, is his friend, and is one of the finest film directors in the world," Ava said. "Chen felt compelled to support his vision."

"Even if it meant spitting in the face of the Chinese government?"

"That was never his intention. He simply wanted to help a friend make a great film."

"And you simply want to help that friend get out of a very complicated situation."

"Yes."

"Why shouldn't we send him back to China?"

"The real question is why would you?" Ava asked. "He has committed no crime that anyone is aware of. What reason has the Chinese government given you for him to be handed over?"

"I can't discuss that."

Ava was about to say "because there is nothing to discuss," and then bit it back. "I think we both understand how complex the situation is, and all I want to know is what can we do to make it simpler?"

"By 'make it simpler,' you mean what can you do to get Chen released?"

"I mean more than that. What can we do to get him released and ensure he is sent to a safe port of call?"

"The Chinese seem quite determined to get him."

"This may seem presumptuous of me, and I apologize in advance if I've misread the situation, but we are prepared to outbid them or anyone else, and you wouldn't have to concern yourself with various security agencies acting as middlemen. It would be strictly between you and us, and we know how to protect the people we're doing business with."

"That actually is presumptuous, but I admire your directness," Viroj said.

"I didn't see any point in trying to tiptoe around the

subject. Either you're prepared to take money for Chen or you're not. If you are, as I said, we'll pay whatever is necessary to get him back."

"Who is 'we'?"

"Friends and business associates who have money."

Viroj became quiet, and Ava wondered if she had offended him. Then he said, "I don't think I am prepared to discuss this any further on the phone right now."

"If you need me to come to Bangkok, I will."

"Ms. Kwong, you need to slow down."

"I'm sorry. We are obviously very worried about Chen's well-being."

"You should have no concerns about his current situation," said Viroj. "As for his future, there are people I need to speak to, and until I do there isn't much more I'm prepared to say to you."

"How long will that take? And when can we speak again?"

"There you go, rushing again."

"Sorry."

"Give me two hours and then call me back. When you do, and if I say 'Kawasaki,' hang up and don't phone me again. If I say 'Honda' then you can start looking for a flight to Bangkok."

16

AVA HAD NO REAL IDEA ABOUT HOW WELL HER CON-
versation with Viroj had gone. Perhaps she shouldn't have
been so direct about knowing Chen was for sale, but it had
made her position clear and he hadn't disputed it. Her hope
was that it would come down to money. If it did, how much
was she willing to pay? Whatever it took, she knew, but no
more than was necessary. Her problem was that she had no
idea what the Chinese were offering, and her next challenge
was to find out what that number was otherwise she'd be
forced to bid blindly, and possibly against herself.

Arthon might be able to help, she thought. Although he
had been reluctant to get involved when she'd mentioned
money before, maybe she could convince him otherwise. It
was worth a try at least. She phoned him.

"I thought I would hear from you," he answered. "How
did it go with Viroj?"

"He heard me out, was non-committal but not negative,
and told me he had to speak to some other people — which
I assume includes his uncle. I'm to call him back in two
hours."

"You couldn't expect much more from an initial conversation."

"I guess not. He made it clear, though, that if we're to discuss a deal it will take place in Bangkok."

"Would you go as Jennie Kwong?"

"Definitely, and I told him a bit about her. Naturally, her background is similar to mine," she said. "Rather oddly, he also spoke about himself. Chinese heritage, a private school in England, a university in Australia — is all of that true?"

"Yes, thanks to his uncle. Viroj's parents died when he was young and his uncle, who has no children, raised him."

"That explains their closeness."

"Out of curiosity, did Viroj give you any clue as to how much money was attached to your friend?"

"No, and that is a problem, because I have no idea how much it will take to do a deal," Ava said. "A great starting point would be to find out what the agencies are offering the Bureau."

"Are you asking me if I know?"

"I am."

"I told you before that I don't. That hasn't changed."

"Can you find out?" she asked. Then, sensing she might be too pushy, continued with, "I think I phrased all of that rather badly. I know you said you don't want to get involved, but all I need is some rough idea. Otherwise I'm pulling figures out of mid-air that could be ridiculously high or stupidly low."

Arthon sighed as if he was annoyed, and Ava braced herself for disappointment.

"I will make some indirect, casual inquiries, nothing more than that."

"I would appreciate it, and I apologize for having to ask, but I have no one else to turn to," she said. "Whatever you come up with is better than what I have right now."

"It isn't something I'm going to do tonight or on the phone. Tomorrow I'll drop in and see my friend at the NIA for a coffee and see what I can ease out of him," he said. "That is assuming, of course, there is still a reason to do it. I hate to say it, but we can't discount the possibility that Viroj won't want to play ball with you and the Bureau will turn Chen over to one of the agencies."

"We should know that within the next two hours," Ava said.

"Call me back when you do know, and best of luck with him."

Ava knew time was going to drag until she could phone Viroj, and even though she had showered, she decided that a run would kill about an hour of it. Five minutes later she left the condo and started along her usual route.

As she ran she replayed her conversations with Viroj and Arthon and felt a growing sense of unease. Her most immediate problem was getting Viroj to agree to meet and negotiate with her. She dreaded the thought of hearing the word *Kawasaki*, but knew if she did she would have to ignore it and still try to engage him because she had no Plan B. When was the last time she had been in that situation? The only occasion in her memory was when she was abducted and held for ransom by a gang of thugs in Kota Kinabalu. She had been powerless, much like Chen was now, and completely dependent on outside assistance. Miraculously it had appeared in the form of a small army of men sent by Xu, the triad Mountain Master in Shanghai and a mentee of

Uncle. After Uncle's death, he and Ava had bonded, and had been there for each other through some challenging times. They were close enough, in fact, that he often referred to her as *mei mei* — little sister — and she called him *ge ge* — big brother. But Xu's intervention had been in Borneo, and the thugs had been no match for his men. What could she do to save Chen if Arthon turned her down and her friend was shipped to China? Nothing came immediately to mind, and that scared her.

Not so frightening a prospect, but still a worry, was if Viroj agreed to parlay and Arthon was unable to come up with even a rough estimate of what the agencies were offering. She couldn't imagine it could be more than a million dollars U.S., if that much. But if it was, how much higher would she have to go, and how aggressive should she be at the outset? There was nothing to be gained, and a lot to potentially lose, by trying to be conservative. If it was a million dollars, she thought, she would offer two million, or maybe even three. The objective was to offer a sum that the other side would have trouble immediately matching, so she could exploit their hesitation and strengthen her positon. She had ten million dollars in the BB account, she reminded herself, to which neither she nor Three Sisters had any traceable attachment. If she had to use it all to free Chen, she would. In fact, if it took more than that, she would find a way to do it. But it was too soon to start that kind of conjecture. The first priority was getting Viroj to agree to meet with her.

Ava heard a car horn, and came to an abrupt stop at a red light at the intersection of Davenport and Avenue roads. To her surprise, she had become so absorbed in the machinations surrounding Viroj and Arthon that she had almost completed her run without being aware of turning around at the halfway point. When the light changed, she continued going south, and a few minutes later was back at the condo. She checked for messages, had none, and went into the bathroom for her second shower of the day.

By the time she sat in the kitchen, she had ten minutes to organize her approach before she called Viroj. She opened her notebook, made a list of the points she had thought of during her run, and underlined the words *be aggressive*. With that, she took several deep breaths, picked up her phone and dialled Viroj.

"Yes," he answered.

"This is Jennie Kwong."

"Honda," he said.

"That's a word I'm very glad to hear."

"You called right on time," he said.

"I was raised to respect punctuality. My mother thought that lateness was a sign of rudeness."

"And what else did she teach you?"

"To be direct without being impolite."

"My upbringing was full of similar lessons."

"Then I hope you don't mind me asking for the result of the conversations you had with the people you wanted to consult?"

He hesitated, and she began to fear that his use of the word *Honda* didn't mean they were going to co-operate.

"There is some interest in your proposal, but that has to be weighed against the importance of some relationships that need to be amicably maintained. And I'm afraid that, at this moment, those relationships are probably more important," he said finally.

Ava felt an initial wave of disappointment, but as she carefully parsed his words she saw a glimmer of hope. He had started to close the door, but his use of the word *probably* left it at least still partially open. "I'm pleased there is an interest, now surely all we have to do is find some way to do business that won't put those relationships at risk," she said, finding the most positive response she could.

"You make that sound rather easier than I fear it is."

"I apologize if I'm not attaching enough importance to the political delicacy of your position, but another thing I was taught was that there isn't a problem for which there isn't a solution. I can't give you one off the top of my head, but given a day or two — say the time it will take me to travel to Bangkok — I'm sure I might be able to come up with something."

"Is that another of your mother's lessons?"

"No, I learned that from my former business partner, a man I called Uncle."

"Arthon mentioned someone named Uncle in your past. He said his father and your uncle did some very successful things together over the years. I assume that is how you and he are connected."

"It is."

"Arthon's father was a triad."

"As was my partner."

"I'm sure if I go back far enough in my family's history I might find a triad or two as well," Viroj laughed, and then quickly became more serious. "Jennie, let's say you're right and there is a solution of one kind or another to our problem. We still need some clarification on what you meant when you said you would outbid anyone."

"What is there to clarify? My statement is clear enough."

"We haven't mentioned what's on offer."

"I would love to know."

"I'm sure you would, but you must know I'm not going to tell you."

"Yes, I do, and I had assumed you would wait until I got to Bangkok," she said, deciding to act as if a meeting there was inevitable.

"I'm not sure we are ever going to give you a number, but if we do are you prepared to take our word for it?"

"Through Uncle's contacts in Hong Kong, Macau, and Vietnam, I have some knowledge of what the Chinese have been willing to pay for the extradition of people they've wanted to get their hands on. If I think your request is totally out of line, I'll tell you," she said. "But let me be clear — given that we are late to the party, and given our relationship to Chen, we are prepared to pay a very healthy premium over anything you have been offered."

He hesitated again, and she wondered if he was going to call her bluff about her knowledge of how much the Chinese paid for extraditions. Instead he asked, "And what about the value of the relationships that you want us to turn our backs on here?"

"I'll factor that in as well, and I'll try to come up with a solution that will make them less aggravated about losing Chen."

"Your banking is secure?"

"Completely. We can put money anywhere you want under any name you want," she said. "And dealing with us will keep the transaction totally private. Unlike your security agencies, we will have zero leverage over you."

"That last remark wasn't necessary. We trust the people we are doing business with here."

"I wasn't suggesting that you didn't or shouldn't, only that the politics in your country appear from the outside to be quite volatile, and who knows what can happen when politics change and loyalties change with them."

"There is a kernel of truth in that."

Ava began to feel they were circling the only question that needed to be asked and answered, and decided this was as good a time as any. "So, should I go ahead and book a flight to Bangkok? I can leave here tonight."

"Yes, go ahead, but I have to make clear that this is only a commitment for us to meet, and nothing more."

"I understand. I have made no other assumptions," she said. "Is there a specific hotel you would prefer I book? In the past, I usually stayed at the Grand Hyatt Erawan."

"It makes no difference to me."

"Where will we meet?"

"Wherever you are staying, call me after you've arrived."

"That will be close to forty-eight hours from now."

"You have my word that nothing is going to happen in the interim."

"That wasn't a concern," she said, but she was happy to hear him say it all the same.

17

AVA LEFT CANADA AT MIDNIGHT ON THE SAME DAY SHE
spoke to Viroj. She caught a Cathay Pacific flight to Hong
Kong, and then connected to another Cathay flight that
landed her at Bangkok's Suvarnabhumi Airport at noon,
twenty-four hours and an eleven-hour time change later.
She had been through the airport several times before, but
this was different, because as she cleared immigration she
couldn't shake foreboding thoughts about Chen locked in a
cell somewhere close at hand.

After making the decision to go, her day had been busy but
not frantic. She had booked her flights and a suite at the Grand
Hyatt Erawan, and then packed her bags. She'd phoned her
mother and a couple of her friends to let them know she was
leaving and wasn't sure about her return. She also cancelled
the meeting she had scheduled for the following day with
the ginseng company, but assured them she was still interested in discussing a partnership when she returned from an
unplanned trip. It was too late to call May Ling or Amanda,
so she emailed them to say she was going to Bangkok to meet
with Chen to discuss distribution plans and that she'd phone

them from there. She hated lying to them, but it was better than having them worrying about something they couldn't affect. Despite the hour, Ava did call Silvana, and wasn't surprised when she answered sounding wide awake.

"Are you still having trouble sleeping?" Ava asked after they shared greetings.

"I try, but then I get thoughts in my head that I can't get rid of. I've never experienced anything like this before."

"Hopefully you won't have to go through it much longer. I'm coming to Bangkok to meet with the contact I mentioned to you before. He hasn't stopped looking for information and I'm optimistic he might have something for us."

"When do you arrive?" Silvana asked, brightening. "Do you want to stay in our apartment? We have a spare bedroom."

"I'll be there in a couple of days, and I'm going to stay at a hotel — it's a better environment for meetings."

"But you will see me?"

"Of course I will, but I would prefer to wait until I have something concrete to share."

Silvana went quiet, and Ava, suspecting she might have offended her, added, "Hang tight. I promise you I will be in touch."

Ava's longest conversation was with Fai, who arrived at the condo after Berlitz eager to try out some of her new-found English. After a few moments discussing the class, Ava tried to tell her about her day in English, but quickly saw Fai was having problems understanding and switched to Mandarin.

"I know we promised to speak English, but this is too complicated to explain that way," said Ava, and proceeded to detail her conversations with Arthon and Viroj.

"So you're leaving tonight?" Fai asked when she finished.

"I have no choice. I need to get Chen released, and that means I have to go to Bangkok."

"I understand, and I wasn't complaining," Fai said. "In fact, I'm really pleased you're going, because I think without you, Chen is going to be bundled off to China and suffer God knows what kind of treatment."

"And if that happens, then Three Sisters' businesses in China and perhaps May Ling's and Amanda's safety are also at risk."

"I know you think that would be likely, but even if the Chinese take Chen isn't it possible that he might not tell them anything?"

"No," Ava said with as much finality as she could muster.

Fai had wanted to accompany her to the airport, but Ava hated airport goodbyes and discouraged her.

All day she had been anxious to call Arthon, but it wasn't until she got to the airport at ten that the time difference made sense. He answered with a brusque "Arthon."

"This is Ava —"

"I haven't had a chance to go over to the NIA yet," he interrupted.

"That's okay, there's no immediate rush," she said. "I spoke again with Viroj and we've agreed to meet in Bangkok. I'm at the airport in Toronto and I'll be leaving soon. I arrive in Bangkok around noon the day after tomorrow on a Cathay Pacific flight from Hong Kong."

"That makes it easier for me. I'll try to have some information by the time you arrive," he said. "Do you want me to meet you at the airport?"

Ava was surprised by the offer and said, "I don't want to inconvenience you."

"You mean inconvenience me more than you already have?" he said lightly.

"Yes, I know I've been a pest, but it is all for a good cause."

"I'm doing it more to honour my father and Uncle's relationship, but I guess that's a good cause in its own right," he said. "So, do you want me to meet you?"

"Very much so."

"Contact me if there's any change in your schedule, otherwise I'll see you in Bangkok at noon."

On her last trip to Bangkok, he'd met her at the airport wearing jeans and a T-shirt and carrying a sign with her name on it. As she walked through the arrivals door this time there was no sign, and Arthon's wardrobe had been upgraded to jeans, a polo shirt, and a blue linen jacket that was stylish despite being rumpled.

They exchanged a brief hug, and then he took her Shanghai Tang Double Happiness bag, "I'm parked just outside," he said.

She followed him through the terminal, fighting to contain her curiosity about what he'd learned. They got into a red Toyota Corolla with a piece of cardboard with a police insignia on the dashboard that was parked immediately outside the exit door.

"Where are you staying?" he asked as the car pulled away from the curb.

"The Grand Hyatt Erawan."

"And when is your meeting with Viroj?"

"I have to call him to set a time and place."

Arthon glanced at her. "He phoned me to ask about you, or I should say to ask about Jennie Kwong."

"What did he want to know?"

"What kind of business are you in? Do I know any of your associates? What is your real connection to Chen Jie? What is your financial situation, and if you aren't wealthy, who is backing you and what access do you have to money?"

"How did you answer?"

"I told him the truth — at least, what I know to be true about Ava Lee," he said. "I told him that you were and probably still are in the debt collection business; that Uncle was the only associate I am aware of; that I know zero about how you and Chen are connected; and my understanding is that you are exceedingly wealthy in your own right."

"All of that is true."

"But I'm not sure it made him any less suspicious."

"That can't be helped. For better or worse, I'm Jennie Kwong."

The Toyota reached the main highway, and Ava waited for Arthon to manoeuvre it onto the road before saying as casually as she could manage, "But, speaking of money, did you manage to find out how much the Chinese are willing to pay for Chen?"

"I was wondering how long it would take before you asked that question," he said. "The answer is I don't know."

Ava closed her eyes in disappointment. When she opened them, she saw Arthon was smiling.

"But I did manage to learn that the agencies have offered the Immigration Bureau amounts that keep edging upwards. My understanding is that the first number on the table was one hundred thousand, but that didn't take long to rise to four hundred thousand when it became apparent there was more than one bidder. That was the operative number for at least a full day, and then it began to go up again. I was told there are now two bids of eight hundred thousand U.S. dollars," he said.

"You shouldn't tease me like that," she said.

"I couldn't resist."

"I forgive you. Now, please tell me what you think those numbers equate to in terms of how much money the Chinese are prepared to pay the agencies."

"Assuming that the agencies are trying to keep at least twenty percent for themselves, I'd guess the Chinese started at half a million and have now upped it to one million," he said. "That is a big number for this kind of deal, and indicates just how badly they want to get their hands on your friend. It also makes it difficult for people on this side to say no to them."

"What makes it the most difficult — the amount of money, or not wanting to displease the Chinese?

"Probably a bit of both."

"If you had to choose one, what would it be?"

"The money."

"Then I have a chance."

"Are you really prepared to pay that much for your friend?"

"I am willing to pay whatever it takes."

Arthon shook his head. "Friends like you are rare."

"I do think of myself as a good friend to Chen, but there is also some self-interest at play here — I'm not exactly Mother Teresa," she said.

Traffic was moving well and she figured they'd be at the hotel within half an hour, though travel times could never be taken for granted into the city. Before the new airport opened, trips from the old — and still functioning — Don Mueang Airport had taken anywhere from an hour to four hours, and traffic jams in the city were so common that a 24-hour-a-day radio station was devoted strictly to traffic reports. New highways, like the one from Suvarnabhumi, and improved public transportation had made getting around considerably easier, but there was always congestion, and a horrific traffic jam was only an accident away.

Ava's estimate of when they would reach the hotel was off by ten minutes on the positive side, and it wasn't quite one o'clock when Arthon turned into the Grand Hyatt's driveway. She got out of the car, waved off a bellman who was rushing to take her bags, and spoke to Arthon through his rolled-down window.

"I can't thank you enough for all your help," she said.

"I hope your trip turns out to be worthwhile."

"You have at least made that a possibility," she said. "Do you want me to keep you updated on my progress, or lack of it?"

"I don't need blow-by-blow descriptions of how you and Viroj get along, but since I bear some responsibility for bringing you together I would appreciate knowing what the final outcome is."

"Then you will hear from me."

"Good luck," he said.

Ava walked through the towering glass front doors into the hotel and saw nothing had noticeably changed since her last stay, years before. A straight path from the door to a bank of elevators split the lobby in two, and both sides had sofas, chairs, and tables spread across their entire expanse. If she went left, she would eventually reach a restaurant that served marvellous buffets. The right side of the lobby led to a small shopping promenade. She went to the counter that was on the right just before the elevators, and within a few minutes was checked into her suite on the twenty-second floor under the name Jennie Kwong.

The suite, like just about everything else at the hotel, was classy in an understated way. Ava unpacked her bags in the bedroom, and then carried her laptop to the business desk in the living room. She turned it on, signed in, and accessed her emails. There were a few from May Ling and Amanda concerning some business issues, but nothing that was pressing. May had said to give her best wishes to Silvana and Chen. Ava hoped she'd get the chance. She wrote to both of them to say she had arrived and would be in touch after she had acclimatized. Next, she emailed Fai and her mother to let them know she was in Bangkok and all was well.

With that done, Ava reached for her phone and, feeling a touch nervous, called Viroj. She didn't actually expect that he would go back on his word, but she had been out of circulation for about thirty-six hours and she couldn't assume that nothing had happened.

"Is this Jennie Kwong?" he answered.

"It is. I have arrived in Bangkok and I have just checked into the Grand Hyatt," she said. "When do you want to meet?"

"As direct as ever, and it is a trait I am slowly beginning to appreciate," he said. "This afternoon is impossible, but I will be available from seven o'clock on."

"Then let's make it seven. Are you okay meeting at the hotel?"

"Yes, but not in the main lobby, that's far too public. There is a noodle house in the lower lobby called You&Mee, or a wine bar called Bar@494 in the same lobby. Which do you prefer?"

"The wine bar."

"Excellent, I'll see you there at seven."

"Just a second, how will I recognize you?"

"You didn't do a search for me on Facebook or any of the other social media platforms?"

"No," Ava said. "I'm not into social media."

"That's obvious, because when I searched for you I couldn't find a trace."

"As I said, I'm not into social media."

Viroj paused, and then said, "I am six feet two inches, and today I am wearing a blue pinstripe suit and a purple tie."

"I don't think I'll miss you."

"See you at seven," he said.

Ava put down her phone. There had been nothing in Viroj's manner or words to suggest he wasn't prepared to listen to her, and that was all that mattered. Now it was up to her to craft an offer that would bring him onto her side. She reached into her Louis Vuitton bag and took out a Moleskine notebook and a Pelikan ink pen. During the flight she had tried to outline various scenarios, but her conversation with Arthon and the introduction of real numbers had provided a different perspective. She had just started to write when a massive yawn overtook her. She had slept sporadically on the plane but didn't feel particularly rested. Now the problem was whether to nap and be jet-lagged for days, or find a way to fight through the fatigue and still be alert for the meeting with Viroj.

Fifteen minutes later she left the Hyatt in her running gear, made a left, and headed towards Lumphini Park. One of the reasons she liked the Hyatt was its proximity to the park. Like Victoria Park in Hong Kong, Lumphini was an oasis of greenery in the middle of a concrete desert. Running past other five-star hotels and dodging stray dogs, she made her way to the monument of the Thai king that marked the entrance to the park. Given the heat and humidity at that time of day, it wasn't as busy as it would have been in the morning, but it was still active enough and Ava had to manoeuvre around people walking on the two-and-half-kilometre path that went around the park's perimeter.

Ava had tucked a face cloth from the hotel into the waistband of her shorts, and she hadn't gone more than a kilometre on the path before she was reaching for it. A kilometre later she realized that if her hope had been that a run would re-energize her, the steamy hot air was killing any chance of that because her legs felt like lead and she was having trouble breathing. Deciding she'd had enough, she veered off the path and cut diagonally across the park towards the exit.

Back at the Hyatt, she drank two bottles of water, wrapped herself in a bathrobe, and sat sweating for half an hour before getting into the shower. Then, in a T-shirt and underwear, she slid under a white duvet that was so light it could have been filled with cotton balls. She lay on her back staring up at the ceiling and thought about Viroj. How much should she offer? How should the offer be constructed? How should Chen's release be managed?

She found herself struggling to find answers, and knew her mind was not operating at full capacity. She let the questions go and drifted into sleep, trusting that she would feel sharper when she woke.

18

AVA'S PHONE AND ROOM CLOCK ALARMS WENT OFF almost simultaneously at five. She turned them off and then lay quietly for a few minutes, already feeling far more alert than she had a few hours before. When she climbed out of bed, she made a black coffee, and then went directly to the desk, opened her notebook, and wrote down the same questions she had been thinking about before falling asleep.

If Arthon was correct that Chen's release was tied to money, then she had to offer enough not only to outbid the Chinese, but also to ensure that the Thais would be willing to incur their displeasure and maybe even their anger. How much above a million would it take?

What needed to be in the offer? There were two main considerations that came immediately to mind. The first was that she needed the Thais to make a quick decision. If there was no tight deadline it would leave the door open for them to go back to the Chinese, and that might result in her getting into a bidding war with them. Second, any offer would have to be twofold: a payment upfront to secure the deal, and a later payment when Chen was released. Ideally she would have liked to backload the money, but she couldn't imagine Viroj agreeing to that. In fact, she imagined he would want it all upfront, which she would resist and then try to find a proper balance. That second payment had to be large enough to discourage the Thais from reneging on the deal. If that was the case, she was going to have to go a hell of a long way above a million.

As she played with the numbers, a third factor popped into her head. She hadn't given much thought to Viroj's comment about maintaining amicable relationships with the agencies. If she paid him enough he might not care about that, but if he raised the topic again she needed to have some kind of answer. Would getting paid something, regardless of the source, satisfy them? She sighed. It was the only option she could think of, and with that the potential cost of Chen's release went even higher.

She finished her coffee, made another, and resumed sitting at the desk. She looked down at her notebook and saw the page was full of circles and question marks. Despite Arthon's help, she still felt like she was walking on a tightrope without a net. She eyed the last question on the page — how Chen's release would be managed — and knew she had an answer for it, but had no idea how receptive Viroj would be. Everything else, including agreeing on money, wouldn't matter unless she could get Chen on a plane headed for someplace safe.

At six, Ava closed the notebook and went into the bathroom. She took a quick shower to refresh herself, and began to get ready to meet Viroj. She brushed her hair back and secured it with an ivory chignon pin she had bought in an antique shop in Kowloon after her first successful job, and which she thought of as a lucky charm. She put on mascara, red lipstick, and dabbed her wrists with Annick Goutal Passion perfume before going into the bedroom to dress.

She debated between skirt and slacks, opted for a black pencil skirt, and chose a snug white silk blouse to go with it. There was no downside, she knew from experience, to looking as attractive as possible. Next she slid on her Cartier Tank Française watch, and then stepped into a pair of black leather pumps. She looked at herself in the mirror and thought she didn't look bad — not bad at all.

Back in the living room, Ava turned to her laptop instead of the notebook. The world was waking up in the West and both Fai and her mother had emailed. Her mother's message was matter-of-fact, but she asked Ava to be sure to call her father if she was going to be in Hong Kong. In her reply, Ava promised she would.

Fai's was full of concern for both Ava's and Chen's well-being, and urged her to be careful.

Don't worry, I have no intention of putting myself in harm's way. This is more a business transaction than anything else, and I think I have a way forward. In any event, I'll know soon enough. This is not going to be a protracted negotiation. I'll be in touch soon. Love you, Ava.

Yes, she thought as she sent the email to Fai, the one thing she was sure of was that it was not going to be protracted.

At ten to seven, Ava left the suite and took the elevator down to the lower lobby. In addition to You&Mee and Bar@494, the lobby housed Spasso, which was an Italian restaurant until ten p.m., when it became one of the best clubs and pick-up spots in Bangkok. Ava knew that many downtown working girls and university students made extra money by frequenting Spasso and befriending Western men for at least one night. Ava had only gone once, and after fending off three men had made a getaway. She didn't think poorly of the women who were regulars because — as Uncle often said — you should never judge what people need to do to survive.

At this hour, Spasso was quiet, but Bar@494 was busy, and as Ava stood in the doorway she couldn't see many vacant tables. The host nodded at her. "Do you have a reservation?" he asked.

"No, but I'm meeting a colleague, a man by the name of Viroj. He might have made one."

The host grinned. "Mr. Viroj did. He's not here yet, but can I take you to the table?"

"Please," said Ava.

She didn't remember Bar@494 from previous visits, and she guessed from its sleek, minimalist, ultra-modern look that it was a relatively new addition. The tables had frosted glass tops supported by thin steel legs and were surrounded by black leather chairs. Above many of the tables were platforms suspended from the ceiling by metal rods. On the platforms were blown glass forms surrounding dolls or sculptures of Thai human figures. The host led her through almost the entire bar to a table for two set in a corner that could not have been more private.

"Would you like something to drink while you wait?" he asked.

"Do you have a white wine you can recommend?"

"We are featuring a William Hardy Australian Chardonnay tonight."

"I'll have a glass."

"I'll tell your server," the host said.

Ava surveyed the restaurant. There was no one who didn't

look like a professional, and that included the large man who was walking directly towards her in his blue pinstripe suit and purple tie. Viroj had described himself accurately in terms of height and dress, but what he hadn't mentioned was how large he was. He wasn't round, just close to it, and for a man who appeared to be in his late twenties or early thirties he had an impressive set of jowls.

"Don't get up," he said to her as he neared.

"You're right on time," she said.

"I believe I told you we share a passion for punctuality," he said as he sat and offered his hand to her.

They shook.

"How was your flight?"

"Uneventful."

"Isn't that always preferable?" he said.

"It is indeed," she said as a server appeared with her glass of wine.

Viroj smiled at him. "I'm going to have a glass of the Attitude Pinot Noir."

"Certainly, Mr. Viroj," he said.

"I'm a regular," Viroj said to Ava once the server had left.

"So I see."

He stared across the table at her, and made no pretence that he wasn't examining her. "You are an incredibly beautiful woman. Are you in the film business?"

"No."

"Then how is it that you know Chen?"

"Through a friend of a friend — you know how that kind of thing works in Chinese society."

"To a certain extent, but I think what you are trying to do goes beyond any knowledge or experience I have."

"What can I say? Chen is valued by a great many people who would prefer to remain anonymous."

"How valued?"

Ava smiled. "That is what we are here to discuss."

Viroj nodded as if he was really thinking about her last remark, and then said, "I'm hungry. The menu here is limited, but the food is quite good. I'm going to eat. Will you join me?"

"Sure, why not?" she said.

"The menu is on the back of the wine list," Viroj said, sliding it towards her.

She read it, all the while feeling Viroj's attention focused on her, until the server arrived with his wine.

"Do you know what you want to eat?" he asked her.

"I'll have the steamed fish balls with lime and chili sauce."

Viroj turned to the server. "Angus beef sliders for me."

When the server had left, Viroj picked up his glass and extended it towards Ava. "Good health."

"The same to you," she said.

They both sipped from their glasses, and then almost reflexively sat back in their chairs as if waiting for the other person to start the conversation. It was Viroj who did. "It has been an extremely interesting past thirty-six hours," he said.

"I'm not sure I'm pleased to hear that," Ava said as lightly as she could.

Viroj shrugged. "I didn't go back on my word, although I have to say there was some temptation."

"Thank you for not succumbing."

"I like the way you don't dive right in and ask me what tempted us."

"I figure you will tell me sooner or later."

"Are you always this calm?"

"Yes," she said, taking another sip of wine. "Tell me about the last thirty-six hours."

"The NIA increased their bid for your friend Chen."

"By how much?"

"I don't recall telling you what their initial bid was."

"Based on what I know the Chinese have paid in Vietnam and Macau for high-profile targets, I would guess they started at half a million, moved it up to a million when they didn't get the response they wanted, and now may be at a million and a half," she said. "Figuring that the NIA would want to pocket at least twenty per cent of that, I'd say they offered you one million two or three."

Viroj lifted his glass to his lips, peered at her over the rim, and she knew in that instant that her numbers were close.

"Whatever it was, I'm prepared to beat it," she continued.

"What number are you talking about?" he asked.

She hesitated, and then said, "One million five hundred."

"That's hardly enough to justify—" he quickly began.

"Wait one second, I'm not finished," Ava said abruptly. "I'm willing to pay one million five to seal the deal, and another one million five when Chen is released and on his way out of Thailand."

Viroj didn't overreact, but he pursed his lips, and that was enough for Ava to push ahead.

"So, we'll pay you three million to let Chen — who is innocent, after all — get on a plane to a country where the Chinese can't get their hands on him," she said, and then decided to go one step further. "And I've thought about your wish to maintain cordial relations with the various other Thai players. To help you with that, I'm prepared to offer an extra seven hundred and fifty thousand that you can allocate any way you see fit, to compensate them for their troubles."

Viroj looked startled, but before he could speak the server arrived with their food. Viroj waited for him to go before he picked up a slider, looked at it, and then put it down. "You have caught me off guard. That doesn't happen very often. Are you always so full of surprises?"

"I have made what I think is more than a fair offer, so I don't know what is so surprising?"

"The fact that you have just put almost four million dollars on the table is a good place to start."

"What did you expect?" Ava said. "This is a serious matter; a man's life is at stake."

"From everything I've been told, I think that is a bit of an exaggeration."

"When for whatever reason someone disappears to a Chinese jail, you can never assume they will come out alive, or if they do come out, that they will be the same person," she said, and then motioned with her pinkie in the direction of his plate. "Your sliders are getting cold."

"I've lost my appetite, but I could use another glass of wine."

"Me too," she said.

Viroj turned, and when he raised a hand in the air, the server rushed to their table. "There is nothing wrong with the food; we've just decided that we're not that hungry. So please take our plates away and bring us each another glass of wine."

When they were alone, Ava said, "You haven't told me what you think about my offer other than that it surprised you."

"It is competitive."

Ava shook her head. "C'mon, it's more than twice what anyone else has offered, and if you think that the other side will match it, you're going to have to wait for a while without any guarantee that they will. Now, Viroj, are you in a position to make a decision about my offer, or are there others you need to speak to?"

"There are others, but they are easy enough to reach if I choose to."

Ava ignored his last few words. "There are some details we still need to discuss, but after that's done I would appreciate it if you could contact them, and among you make a decision."

"You're trying to rush me again."

"I want to leave Bangkok tomorrow morning with Chen, so yes, I am in a rush."

19

AVA WATCHED VIROJ'S EYES FLIT BETWEEN HER AND the wall behind her, and she knew she had rattled him. If he had thought he was in control of their conversation, that idea was now at least shaken.

"I don't want to pursue that last remark of yours until the server has brought our wine," he said after a short, uncomfortable silence.

That took several minutes, during which Ava debated how quickly and how hard she should push her position. By the time the server returned, her decision was made.

"Again to your health," Viroj said, raising his new glass.

"To everyone's health," said Ava.

Viroj took several sips of wine and then leaned forward. "When you mentioned leaving Bangkok tomorrow with Chen, was that your way of giving us a deadline? If it was, my people won't react positively to it."

"I have made you a serious and substantial offer, but unfortunately there is a time limit attached to it. Given the nature of the situation and the disposition of the people on the other side, we can't risk getting into a protracted negotiation."

"What is the time limit?"

"We want an answer by midnight tonight."

"What — yes or no?"

"Exactly."

"That is *really* not going to be well-received."

"Apologize for us — and look, to sweeten the pot a little, we'll add another two hundred and fifty thousand. So that will be three million for you, and a million for you to distribute among the others or keep for yourselves. It makes no difference to us what you do with it."

Viroj lifted his glass to his lips and held it there for several seconds. Ava stared at him, gauging his reaction and wondering if her strategy would backfire. She couldn't discount the possibility that it might, but were he and his uncle capable of walking away from four million dollars? She thought not, although if she was wrong she'd have to mend some fences — and that would end up costing more than four million.

He put down his glass, and leaned back with his hands clasped across his chest. Ava knew he was trying to look relaxed, but the fingers pressed into his knuckles suggested he was anything but. "Even if we reach an agreement — and I'm not suggesting we will — I still find your idea of leaving Bangkok tomorrow morning to be quite fanciful. How could it be executed that quickly?" he asked, sidestepping the issue of a deadline.

"I can have half of the money in any bank account you name within an hour of reaching a deal, and I can have the other half confirmed and ready to transfer the moment the plane that Chen and I are on takes off," she said. "And all you have to do is make a phone call to the Immigration Bureau's office at the airport to tell them to release Chen, give him his passport, and escort him to the departure gate. I will provide you with the airline and flight number."

Viroj raised an eyebrow. "You make it sound so simple."

"That's because it is."

"Except what is to prevent you from getting on the plane and not sending the second tranche of money?"

"And what is to stop you from promising to release Chen and then simply pocketing the first tranche and doing nothing of the sort?" asked Ava. "There is plenty of room for mistrust on either side."

"That is an understatement, and I have to tell you that when I speak with my associates I expect they will want all of the money upfront."

"Let me be clear, there is absolutely no way we are going to send you four million dollars in the hope that you will honour your word. In fact, my associates will be unhappy with me for promising you two upfront, but I am prepared to withstand that criticism if you agree to my proposal," Ava said.

"So in addition to setting a time limit, you want me to also tell my people that asking for the four million upfront is a deal-breaker?"

Ava hesitated, but she had made the decision before he asked the question. "I'm afraid that is our position, but I like to think there has to be a way to make that not so extreme — a way that satisfies both of our needs."

"By your tone, I'm guessing you have thought of something."

"It would have been irresponsible of me not to anticipate there would be resistance to some aspects of our proposal," she said, pleased that the conversation seemed to have settled on money rather than timing.

"I'm listening."

"What if we offered a form of guarantee for the second payment?"

"What do you have in mind?"

"Well, I was thinking, what if we sent the money to a middleman, someone we both trust, with instructions to release it to you the moment our plane departs. You would have the assurance of knowing that the money is being held for you, and we would have the comfort of knowing you won't get it unless we are in the air."

"That might actually work," said Viroj. "But there's the problem of finding someone we both trust."

"I was going to suggest Arthon," she said.

"Obviously I knew the two of you were acquainted, but I wasn't sure to what extent."

"We aren't close, if that's what you are asking, but we do share a common bond from our pasts. From my experience with him I think he is honourable, and a man of his word. If he agreed to take this on, I have no doubt he would do it to both of our satisfactions."

"Are you saying he knows you're here?"

"He does, and he knows why I'm here."

"I suspected as much."

"So, how about it, do you trust him enough?"

Viroj looked thoughtful. "I trust him well enough," he finally said.

"Then we should talk to him. I have put his name into our conversation without his knowledge, and without any idea if he'll agree to do it. There is no point in you suggesting it to your people unless we know Arthon is on side."

"I agree."

"Then let's talk to him right now," Ava said, taking her phone from her bag. "I'll put him on speaker."

"Are you serious? You would do that here?"

"Why not? Who is going to hear us over the noise?"

Viroj glanced at the nearby tables, where people were engaged in animated conversations. "Okay, but keep it down."

Ava smiled, and thought *please answer your phone* as she dialled Arthon's number.

"Hello," he answered.

"This is Jennie Kwong," she said quickly, afraid he'd call her Ava. "I'm sitting at the Hyatt with Viroj, and I have my phone on speaker mode so we both can hear you...Viroj, say hello to Arthon so he knows I'm not pulling his leg."

"Yes, this is Viroj," he said.

"Arthon, we're calling you to discuss a possible solution to the situation that brought me to Bangkok. Without speaking for Viroj, I believe we've agreed on many of the details, but there is an outstanding issue that that we would both appreciate you helping us out with."

"I can't even begin to imagine what I could do to help."

"I know you have said you are reluctant to act as a middleman, but this does not involve any real active involvement on your part," Ava said. "All we need is someone to facilitate a financial transaction. Specifically, my team has agreed to pay for the release of Chen Jie and we've offered to do it in two tranches. The first will be when the final deal is struck, and the second will be when Chen and I are on a plane that's in the air heading out of Bangkok. The second payment is the sticking point. Viroj would prefer it upfront, and I don't want to pay until I know Chen and I are safe."

Viroj leaned forward. "She has suggested sending the

money to you to hold until she's gone. Are you okay with doing that?"

"I'm a bit confused. Has an agreement been reached and this is the last sticking point?"

"No, I haven't presented her proposals to my people yet," Viroj said. "But I want to make sure we've agreed on the details before I do, and you agreeing to facilitate the transaction is the last one."

Arthon hesitated, and then said, "Truthfully, I am very reluctant to take part in this."

"You are my only option. If you don't agree, then I'm not sure where that leaves us," Ava said. "I hate to put it like that, but that's where we are."

Arthon didn't respond right away, and Ava began to prepare for the worst. Then he said, "Viroj, if I do agree to help, can you keep a lid on the fact that I did?"

"Yes, and I would expect the same in return. It is obviously in both of our interests to keep this as private an arrangement as possible."

"Then in that case I will help."

"Thank you," said Ava.

"How much money are we talking about?"

"Two million U.S. dollars," Ava said.

"Good grief... so you'll be sending me half of that?"

"No, the offer I've made is four million. I'll be putting two million into whatever bank account you specify."

"I am trying to act cool, but that is a lot of money," said Arthon. "When would you plan to do it?"

"Immediately after my offer is accepted," Ava said, staying determinedly confident.

"And how soon do you think that might be?"

"I am hoping to close the deal tonight and to leave Bangkok with Chen tomorrow morning."

"Even if you can move that quickly, I think you'll have to hold off sending me money until mid-morning tomorrow," said Arthon. "I would want to give my bank manager a heads-up that the money will be going into my account and then will be transferred out of it. None of us want him getting so surprised that he puts a hold on the money or starts asking uncomfortable questions."

"And you can't leave until Arthon confirms he has it," Viroj said to her.

Ava noticed that now Viroj was acting as if they already had an agreement. She nodded. "I wouldn't dream of doing that, so I'll start looking at flights leaving later in the day."

"Okay, is that all?" Arthon asked.

"I need your banking information," Ava said.

"I'll text it to you in a few minutes."

Ava looked at Viroj. "Are you all right with this? I know we're jumping the gun a bit, but there's no harm in being prepared."

"Yes, go ahead and send her your banking information," he said to Arthon.

"And I will need yours."

"I'll send it to you after I get the go-ahead from my associates. I'll be calling them as soon as we finish."

"Do you expect any opposition?" Arthon asked.

"I don't want to predict how they will react," said Viroj.

"Then I'll wait to hear from you."

The connection to Arthon went dead. Ava looked at Viroj. "Where do you want to make your call? If you want to do it from here, I'll leave."

"I think you should."

"I'll go upstairs and wait in the main lobby. Either call me or come to get me when you're finished."

20

AVA FELT THE LAST OF HER ENERGY DRAIN FROM HER body the moment she stepped out of the bar. She knew jet lag played a part, but the wine and the effort of trying to stay calm and in control while she was speaking to Viroj and then Arthon had also taken a toll. As she made her way upstairs to the main lobby, she wished she had told Viroj she was going to her room and for him to call her when he was ready to talk again. But she wasn't about to bother him with that now.

She found an unoccupied sofa in the lobby, settled into it, took her phone from her bag and placed it on the table next to the sofa. When a server approached, she ordered sparkling water. Her phone pinged as the server left, and Ava saw she had a text from Arthon. She opened it.

My compliments on making the progress you have. I attach my bank information. Let's hope you are able to put it to good use. Keep me posted. Regards, Arthon.

No one hopes that more than me, she thought, and then immediately wondered if she had done enough. Well, if Viroj and his uncle kept all the money, they would have almost four times what anyone else had offered, and she had kept things as simple as she could. What more could she have done? Nothing she could think of offhand unless she had been prepared to give them all the money at once, and that would have been beyond irresponsible and, for all intents and purposes, an act of desperation.

The server brought Ava her water, and fifteen minutes later a second glass. There was a recent *Economist* magazine on the table, and Ava read it between sips and frequent glances in the direction of the stairway that led to the lower lobby. She tried not to think too much about the conversation that might be taking place one level below, but it was impossible to stop these thoughts from intruding. Was Viroj supporting her proposal, or had she misread him? Would her deadline be a problem? Could they possibly ask for more money? Of anything they might ask of her, she knew more money would be the easiest to agree to.

At one point, a tall, willowy Thai woman entered the hotel with a Westerner who was about three inches shorter and at least twenty years older than her. When they neared the elevators, Ava watched hotel security speak to them and then the woman moved to one side and opened her purse. She handed security what looked like an identification card. The guard she gave it to nodded, made a note of it, and handed it back to her. *A working girl*, Ava thought. In the morning, if he had any class, the Westerner would walk her to the front doors of the hotel and see her safely into a taxi. Most mornings there was a parade of men leading women to taxis. It was called the 'walk of shame' and, appropriately, locals attributed the shame to the men and not the women.

The brunette slightly reminded Ava of Fai, and for a few seconds she thought about calling Toronto, where Fai would be getting ready to leave for school. But as unlikely as missing a call from Viroj was, she didn't want to risk it.

Ava had finished reading the magazine, and was considering ordering a third glass of water when her phone finally rang. She reached for it and saw Silvana's name. She groaned and didn't pick up. Seconds later, her phone signalled she had a voice message. She was certain it was from Silvana but knew she had to listen to it just in case it wasn't.

"Ava, this is Silvana. I don't mean to bother you, but I thought you would want to know that Christensen from Top of the Road sent Chen an email earlier today. I didn't check Chen's account until a few minutes ago, which is why I've been slow to tell you. Call me if you can."

Ava was slightly annoyed that Silvana didn't tell her what was in the email, but guessed it was her way of enticing Ava to phone her. If it was, it had certainly worked, Ava thought as she dialled Silvana's number.

"Hi Ava," she answered.

"Hey Silvana, I got your message. Could you read that email to me? I don't mean to be abrupt but I'm waiting for someone to call me with news about Chen."

"Have you heard something?"

Ava could hear the anguish in her voice, and felt almost guilty for fobbing her off. "No, I've heard nothing, but my contact was following up on a lead and sounded like he was making progress the last time I spoke to him. His call is the one I'm expecting," Ava said.

"I keep thinking he's dead. I know that's dramatic, but I can't help thinking it."

"Silvana, the one thing my contact is sure of is that Chen is not dead. So let go of that notion," Ava said, and then decided that wasn't providing enough comfort. "What he believes is that Chen has run into a problem of sorts with some local authorities. And, if he has, we'll sort it out."

"What kind of problem?"

"I won't know until I talk to the contact. Once I know — and that may not be tonight — I promise you that you will hear from me," said Ava. "Now, could you read the email from Christensen?"

Silvana hesitated, and then said, "It reads, 'I got your email expressing your determination to come to our offices, but I have heard nothing since. My hope is that you've had a change of mind because, to be clear, while we might have met with you, it would have been out of politeness. So if you are still thinking of coming to L.A., I suggest you adjust your plans accordingly. Yours sincerely, Larry Christensen.' What do you think that means?"

"He obviously doesn't want to talk to Chen, but other than that I don't know," said Ava, while thinking that if Christensen was trying to cover his ass, he wasn't being subtle about it. "Now, Silvana, I'm sorry but I really have to go. I'll be in touch the moment I know anything."

Even without that email, she had thought that it might have been Christensen who told the Chinese that Chen was preparing to leave Bangkok to fly to Los Angeles. Now in her mind it was confirmed. She was also convinced that the China Movie Syndicate was involved in some way with Top of the Road. She wasn't sure whether the two sides had struck a deal before or after Top of the Road cut one with Chen, but it didn't make any real difference. She was sure Top of the Road had sold out the film, and then — perhaps for more money — had sold out Chen. Ava clenched her jaw as she tried to bite back an anger that made her want to scream.

She saw the server passing by, and stopped her. "Another water, please," she said.

Okay, she told herself, *get back in control and take one thing at a time* — and that started with getting Chen released. When that was done she could use his input to figure out how to handle Top of the Road. Then, as the server put the glass of water on the table, Ava's phone rang. "Yes," she answered.

"This is Viroj. I'm coming upstairs to see you," he said and hung up.

Ava found him slightly abrupt, but hadn't detected anything out of the ordinary in his tone. She returned to watching the stairs. When he appeared, she stood and waved in his direction. He walked towards her, his face impassive. He had a choice between sitting next to her on the sofa or in a chair that was to her left. He chose the chair.

"Do you want something to drink?" she asked. "I switched to sparkling water."

"No, let's just get down to business," he said.

They aren't going to accept my offer as is, she thought. *I just hope they don't put my back against the wall.*

"That's why we're here," she said with a smile.

Viroj turned sideways so he was looking directly at her. "As I predicted, my associates weren't pleased with the deadline you imposed, and would prefer to get all of the money upfront," he said.

"I thought I had addressed that, and we had resolved both of those issues."

"I explained what we had discussed, but that didn't prevent them from being displeased."

"Of course not, but I'm sure at the end of the day they are practical people."

"Well, I did represent your side as well as I could, and I believe they are prepared to be reasonable."

"Thank you for that, Viroj, but tell me what will it take for your associates to move from being prepared to be reasonable to actually *being* reasonable?"

He shrugged and pursed his lips as if he had been asked a question that required some thought. "An additional million dollars, and they want it all upfront," he finally said.

Ava had to stop herself from smiling. If she had known they were going to ask for more money, she would have expected them to demand a larger sum — maybe even as much as another four million. It was her turn to look thoughtful, and truthfully there was something she needed to clarify before responding to their request. "When you say you want it all upfront, do you mean the additional million, or do you mean what would now amount to five million?"

"The million, plus of course the other two million we agreed would be paid that way."

"So three million upfront, and two million after Chen and I have left Bangkok?"

"Exactly."

"That rather tips the scales in your favour."

"We are not about to sacrifice two million dollars."

"Actually, if you took a million from one of Chen's other suitors, then you'd only be giving up one million," Ava said. "I'm sure you can understand why that makes me nervous."

"You talk about a million dollars as if it is chicken feed," he said.

"I don't think it is, but there is the need to maintain

amicable relations with the sister agencies that you mentioned. I'm sure your associates are weighing that as well, and a million dollars may be a small price to pay to keep those relationships nicely balanced."

"You have that backwards," Viroj said.

"How so?"

He leaned closer to her and lowered his voice. "The more they've thought about it, the more my associates like the idea of doing business with a neutral third party. If they cut a deal with one local outfit, they are going to offend several others, so if the price is right, why not offend them all? They also like the fact that the details of the agreement won't be the subject of gossip within a bureaucracy that loves gossip. The less anyone knows about our financial situation, the happier my associates are. And I assured them that you wouldn't be sharing that information with anyone, and that Arthon had already agreed to do the same."

"I can certainly see the logic in that," Ava said, not surprised at the revelation that they intended to keep all the money. "Still, I can't help but be a little bit nervous."

"Jennie," Viroj said, putting a hand on her knee. "I give you my solemn word that you have nothing to worry about. Follow through on your commitments, and we'll follow through on ours."

Ava shifted her leg until his hand slid off. "Okay, I will accept at your word," she said, after a slight hesitation. "Tell your associates that we have an agreement."

He smiled, and nodded.

"How soon can I get your banking information?" she asked.

"Within an hour."

"I already have Arthon's," she said, looking at her watch. "It is almost half past eight. If you get me yours by nine-thirty, I'll have the money in your account by ten."

"You'll have it."

"And I'll forward your banking information to Arthon."

"Excellent."

"One last thing — how do I contact you to tell you when Chen should be released?"

"You can use the number you called me on earlier today."

"I'll do it in the morning, after Arthon confirms he has the second tranche of money."

"Yes, there's no point in doing it before."

"And just to be clear, after Chen is released you will make sure that he is escorted to his gate. I'll be there with his ticket, but we might need help to check him in."

"We'll look after all of that."

"I would feel a lot more comfortable knowing that you were going to take care of it in person, so I would appreciate it if you came to the gate with him."

"Then I will be there."

Ava stood, and watched as Viroj got awkwardly to his feet. She held out her hand. "We've done well here tonight."

21

AVA COULDN'T HAVE IMAGINED THAT BEING IN ESSENCE blackmailed out of five million dollars would make her anything but miserable, but as she made her way to the twenty-second floor all she felt was a guarded sense of relief. She hadn't been exaggerating when she told Viroj that they'd done well. The priority — the only priority — had been to get a deal done that she could live with. She thought she had accomplished that, and if everyone stayed true to their word, then the five million was irrelevant. Mind you, she thought as she entered the suite, the operative word was *if*, but for reasons that were more instinctive than cerebral she actually trusted Viroj. And following instincts when it came to granting trust was something that Uncle had practised and Ava had adopted.

As she rode the elevator, she started making a mental list of everything she needed to do, and that now included tying up some loose ends. Once in her suite, she went directly to the desk, opened her notebook, and wrote down the night's tasks. When that was complete, she went to the bathroom and then changed into a T-shirt and her Adidas training pants. She eyed the mini-bar on her way back to the desk, and decided that a small bottle of Chardonnay would help her get through the next few hours.

Her plan after Viroj's banking information arrived was to transfer three million to his account and organize the two million for Arthon. But before doing that, she needed to discuss the transaction with May Ling and Amanda. She had no doubt they would agree to it, but it was one thing not to tell them about Chen's situation and to negotiate a settlement, and quite another to transfer money that was collectively theirs without their knowledge and permission. She called Amanda first.

"*Wei*," Amanda answered.

"This is Ava. Are you somewhere you can speak freely?"

"I'm at home by myself."

"Great, could you phone May Ling and hook her into a conference call with us? I need to speak to the two of you."

"Sure, but you sound so serious you're making me nervous."

"There's no need to be nervous, but we do need to speak."

"Okay, I'll call you back when I have it set up."

Ava put her phone on the desk and poured a glass of wine. The phone pinged, and she saw she had a text from Viroj with his banking information. It was a numbered account at a bank in the Cayman Islands. She copied the details into her notebook and then opened Arthon's text and wrote down his Bangkok bank information. Just as she'd finished, the phone rang and she saw Amanda's number.

"Hey, is May Ling on the line as well?"

"I'm here."

"Good, I didn't want to have to go over this stuff twice. It will be depressing enough to do it once."

"Are you still in Bangkok?" May asked.

"Yes."

"There's been a problem with Chen, hasn't there?"

Yet again, Ava marvelled at how strong May's intuition was. "There has been a problem, a serious one, but we're on the verge of solving it."

"I guessed you had a reason for going there other than working on distribution plans with Chen."

"I apologize for not telling both of you right away, but I wanted to make sure I understood what was going on."

"And what was going on?" Amanda asked.

"The Chinese have been trying to get the Thais to extradite Chen to China. The Thais grabbed him at Bangkok airport almost a week ago, and the Immigration Bureau has been holding him in a cell there while various Thai government agencies negotiate with the Chinese."

"My God, I didn't think it would be that bad. And the Thais are negotiating for what?" asked May.

"Money. The Chinese were prepared to pay for Chen, but as of today a price hadn't been agreed to," said Ava.

"That is so awful, and I only wish it wasn't so believable. People here in Hong Kong are carted across the border against their will all the time, but I've never heard of one being sold like that," Amanda said.

"It isn't any stretch to figure he has been targeted because of *Tiananmen*," said Ava. "Fortunately, and the reason I'm calling you right now, I've worked out a deal with the Thais to get Chen released and flown out of Thailand, but I want you to sign off on it before I close."

"Whatever it is, I agree," said May.

"Me too," Amanda said.

"You still need to know that it is going to cost us five million dollars. I was going to take the money out of the BB Productions account."

"I wouldn't care if it was fifty million," said May. "If they managed to get Chen across the border and into China we might never see him alive again, and every one of our businesses in China would be at risk."

"That obviously was my thinking as well, but the number is five million."

"That is well done on your part," said May.

"When is all of this supposed to happen?" Amanda asked.

"My plan is to fly out of here with Chen as early as possible tomorrow. I think we'll be able to make a flight sometime around noon."

"And where will you go?" Amanda asked.

"Los Angeles — that is where Chen was trying to go before he was taken into custody at the airport. He was having issues with our distributor, Top of the Road, and was going there to sort them out."

"What kind of issues?" May asked.

"He couldn't get them to share their distribution plans for *Tiananmen*, and that might be because they have no plans and have no intention of distributing the film. I suspect they've been playing footsie with Mo, and that they were responsible for telling the Syndicate that Chen intended to fly from Bangkok to L.A."

"This is getting crazier and crazier," May said.

"You're right, so let me slow down and back up a little, and explain how all of this came about," said Ava.

Even condensing some of the story, it took Ava twenty minutes to recount Chen's concerns with the distributor,

Silvana's panicky phone calls, and Ava's interactions with Christensen, Arthon, and Viroj.

"So what's the plan?" May asked when she'd finished.

"I'm going to send three million to Viroj, book three tickets on a flight to L.A. and get ready for tomorrow. Job one in the morning will be to send Arthon's money to his bank, and job two will be to confirm it got there. Once that's done I'll head to the airport, praying that everything runs smoothly."

"Did you say three tickets?" May said.

"We can't leave Silvana here and risk her becoming collateral damage. After I do the banking tonight I'm going to call her and finally tell her the truth about what's been going on. I'll get her to come to my hotel and we'll go to the airport together. She can travel to L.A. with Chen and me."

"Will you confront Top of the Road?" Amanda asked.

"I'm not sure they'll let us in the door, but we'll try."

"And if you can't?"

"I trust that Chen will know what our legal rights are."

"We must have some. It is inconceivable that a company can acquire the rights to a film for the sole purpose of making sure it isn't shown."

"I hope we don't have to find out, but I suspect we might."

"Does Lau Lau know about any of this?" asked May.

"No, and now that you mention it I should give him a heads-up about Chen. He's working in Taiwan and we need to make sure he stays there."

"Will you tell him about Top of the Road?"

"Not until we can actually confirm what's going on. I'm sure he's still on cloud nine after Cannes, and there's no point in causing him worry."

"Handle it as you think best," said May. "I love the film

and I love Lau Lau, but I can't help wishing that this wasn't such an adventure."

"I agree," Ava said, only too mindful that it was her who had involved her partners in it.

"But then life with you is always an adventure and I wouldn't have it any other way," May continued.

"Well, let's hope that things calm down after tomorrow. There are times things get too much even for me."

"Ava . . ." Amanda said. "Please keep us updated on how things are going there. I won't be able to relax until I know you, Chen, and Silvana are safely out of Bangkok."

"I will, and now I had better start getting things organized so that can happen," Ava said. "Don't worry, things will be fine."

Ava ended the phone call thinking for maybe the hundredth time how fortunate she was to have friends like May and Amanda. The fact they were business partners and Amanda was her sister-in-law was incidental; it was their friendship that mattered most, and it was friendship that would continue to sustain their partnership.

She took a sip of wine, eyed her to-do list, opened her laptop, and ten minutes later had sent three million dollars from the BB Productions bank account to the account in the Caymans, and had another two million organized to send to Arthon. She then sent a text to Viroj that simply read: The money has just been wired to your account.

Next, she went online to search for flights from Bangkok to Los Angeles that didn't go through China or any other airport where the Chinese might be able to exert their influence. To her surprise, flying ANA to Tokyo, and from there to L.A., was still the best option. There was a flight leaving at one in the afternoon, and she booked three first-class seats. It would arrive in Tokyo at nine after a six-hour flight and a two-hour time adjustment, and Ava managed to find a connecting flight that left Tokyo at ten-thirty in the evening.

With that settled, she called Silvana.

"*Wei*," she answered in a scratchy voice.

"It's Ava, and I have some good news for you. Are you sitting down?"

"What has happened?"

"I am going to tell you, but do me a favour and don't interrupt until I'm finished. Can you manage that?"

"I'll try," Silvana said, her mood already seeming to brighten.

There were a few interruptions, but mainly Silvana did listen, and her first tear-filled question was "How did they know he was in Bangkok, and that he was planning to fly from here?"

"I don't know for sure, and there isn't much point in guessing."

"Was Chen hurt at all?"

"No, I'm told he was simply being held in a cell."

"Thank goodness," she said, sounding less distressed. "What time do you want me to meet you at the hotel?"

"Come at nine — I'd rather get to the airport early than risk being late."

"Where will we meet Chen?"

"They'll bring him to the gate."

"I hope I don't make a fool of myself. I know I'm going to cry, I just don't want to be out of control."

"We can all have a good cry," Ava said. "Now, you should

start packing, and don't forget your passport. I'll see you in the morning."

Lau Lau didn't answer his phone and Ava's call was directed to voicemail. "This is Ava, I would have preferred to speak to you directly, but this will have to do for now. I wanted you to know that the Chinese government tried to arrange to have Chen picked up in Thailand and sent back to China. They are obviously extremely angry about the film. I know you're in Taiwan, and I want to stress that you should stay there. Don't even consider returning to China for some time — and it could be a long time. The good news is that Chen should be leaving Thailand tomorrow for the U.S. I'll confirm that when it happens. Take care and I'll be in touch."

Ava's last call was to Arthon. There was a lot of noise and music in the background when he answered, and it sounded like he was in a bar.

"I hope I'm not disturbing you," she said.

"An hour from now you would have been, but I can talk."

"I reached an agreement with Viroj. It cost me another million, and he wanted it upfront. I've just sent it plus the two million I had already agreed to."

"That's quite a haul."

"I have also organized a wire transfer to your account. I want to send it as early as possible tomorrow. Do you have any idea when you can speak to your bank manager?"

"It opens for business at eight and he's normally there then. I'll call him first thing.

"I would appreciate that. The sooner I can get to the airport, the more comfortable I'm going to be."

"No problem, I'll contact you right after I've spoken to him."

"Viroj will want to know that I sent you the money. I'll copy him in on the transfer, but maybe you could call him as well to confirm."

Arthon sighed. "I can't imagine what you think about how things are run in this country. There are times when even I find myself getting embarrassed."

"Well, at least Viroj was a gentleman and no one put a gun to my head, and that's an improvement over some of your neighbours."

22

AVA THOUGHT SHE MIGHT HAVE TROUBLE SLEEPING, BUT the opposite was true, and when she woke at six, she barely remembered putting her head on the pillow. She did a quick check of her phone and laptop and was pleased there were no messages or emails that required her immediate attention. Lau Lau had called, and simply said, "Don't worry, I'm staying put. Let me know when Chen is safe."

She made a coffee and went to the window. The sun was rising, and only a sliver was visible as it peeked over the horizon — but the sky was clear, which was what she had hoped to see. She went into the bathroom and put on the running gear she had hung there to dry. Then she grabbed a face cloth and left the suite to make her way to Lumphini Park. Traffic was light and the only pedestrians on the street were vendors pushing their carts towards the park. Ava knew by the time she finished her run, the carts would be lining the sidewalk outside and selling a variety of drinks and snack foods. There were more dogs on the sidewalk than the day before, and she had to give a couple of aggressive ones a wide berth. Stray dogs were a presence on virtually every street in central Bangkok, and Ava couldn't understand why something wasn't done to help them or control them.

The park was already busy when she got there, but the running path was mainly occupied by joggers moving at a reasonable pace, and Ava fell in behind a group of four women. Like many of the parks in other urban Asian cities, Lumphini was a place to walk, run, practise tai chi, dance, bring birds in cages, and take part in group exercise classes. Normally, Ava enjoyed watching all of the activity around her, but this morning her mind was fixated on the day that lay ahead. She felt she had done everything she could to ensure it would be a success, but her mind kept turning over the possibility that things could go wrong. If they did, there could only be one reason for it, and that was Viroj reneging on their deal. She didn't think it was likely, but she couldn't discount the possibility. As sincere as he'd been, and as much trustworthiness as he'd exuded, she didn't really know him. The fact that Arthon had brought them together worked in Viroj's favour, but when it came right down to it, she didn't know Arthon that well either. What was to stop the two of them from doing a side deal and splitting the two million she had yet to send? If they did, Viroj still had the security agencies to fall back on and would end up pocketing more millions on top of that.

I'm going to make myself crazy with this, she thought as sweat poured down her face at the start of her second lap. *If things do go off the rails, I have absolutely nothing to fall back on. There is no Plan B — not even the germ of an idea for another option. So either my instincts are right, or I've made the biggest mistake of my life. But when have I misread anyone that badly? Never — and all I'm doing is overthinking this.* As she told herself this, she felt her anxiety begin to recede.

By the time Ava finished three laps of the park, the run had done its work. She felt more mentally and physically alert, and if not totally confident, then at least not beset with doubts. She made her way to the park exit, wrung out her face cloth, rued the fact she hadn't brought money to buy a drink, and then headed back to the Grand Hyatt.

It was just past seven when she entered the suite. Ava stripped, wrapped herself in a bathrobe, drank two glasses of water, then made a coffee and sat at the desk. She thought about calling Fai, and then decided to wait until she was at the airport and the situation was clearer. But she picked up her phone anyway with the intention of sending a reminder to Arthon to contact his bank manager as early as possible, and saw she had a message from Viroj. The money has reached our account. Thank you, it read.

That was good news, she thought, but couldn't he have added something like *see you later at the airport*? Still, one commitment had been fulfilled, and that prompted her to phone rather than text Arthon.

"Yeah," he answered, sounding sleepy or hungover, or a bit of both.

"It's Ava. Viroj just confirmed the three million has reached his account. Now I'm waiting for you to give me the green light."

He paused and said, "It isn't eight o'clock yet."

"I know, and I'm sorry to be a pest but the wait is killing me."

"Ava, *you* are killing me," he said. "But okay, I'll try to reach him now. If I don't call you back it is because I had no luck."

"Thank you."

She sat at the desk for a few minutes hoping to hear back. When she didn't, she carried the phone into the bathroom and placed it within reaching distance while she showered. Twenty minutes later, dressed in slacks and a blouse, Ava returned to the living room. She made another coffee and sat down again at the desk. She opened her laptop and had started to double-check the reservation codes for the flight to L.A. when the phone finally rang. She almost leapt at it.

"Hi."

"It's Arthon. I spoke to my bank manager and you can go ahead and send the money. I couldn't believe how matter-of-fact he was. He acted as if it was nothing out of the ordinary."

"That's great. I'll transfer it to your account in a few minutes. It won't take long to arrive."

"I'll let you and Viroj know when it gets there, and of course I'll wait to hear from you before I send it to his account."

Ava hesitated. "Arthon, I really owe you for all the help you've given me. I would like to make up for some of it financially. Would you mind if I sent you a token of my appreciation?"

"No — I've told you before, I won't take your money, but I do expect that if I ever need a favour from you, I only have to ask."

"You can count on that."

"Okay, then I'll wait to hear from you later. What time is your flight out of Bangkok?"

"We're on ANA, and we are scheduled to leave at one. I'll text you from the plane once we're airborne."

"Fingers crossed," he said.

"Indeed."

Ava put down the phone and turned to her laptop. She entered the BB Productions bank account, found the transfer she had drafted, confirmed it, and sent the money. She then texted Arthon and Viroj and told them it was done. Now she could pack and get ready to leave for the airport without feeling like she was getting ahead of herself.

At ten to nine she left the suite and made her way down to the lobby. She heard her name being called as soon as she exited the elevator, and saw Silvana waving to her from a sofa near the entrance. "You're right on time," Ava said when she reached her.

Silvana held out her arms, and they shared a long, intense hug. "I've actually been here since around eight o'clock," Silvana said, finally letting go of Ava.

"And it looks like you brought a lot of Chen's apartment with you," said Ava, pointing at the two huge suitcases and two smaller ones that sat on the floor.

"I don't travel light, and I doubt he'll be coming back here anytime soon, so I brought what I could of his things."

"That was smart. Let's get a bellboy to take them outside to the taxi stand."

Five minutes later, as the cab pulled away from the Hyatt, Silvana slipped her arm through Ava's and leaned her head against her shoulder. "I hardly slept last night, but for a change it was because I was excited instead of being terrified thinking about what might have happened to Chen."

"Have a rest," Ava said. "It could be hectic when we get to the airport."

Ava took her phone from her bag and laid it in her lap. She figured the two million going into Arthon's account would have arrived shortly after she sent it, and it was now just a matter of Arthon confirming that fact. She had expected him to do so by now, and hoped he hadn't gotten sidetracked. She thought about calling him, but decided she didn't want to bug him so soon. Let him phone her.

Traffic was heavy but started to ease as they left the city centre. Ava began to say something to Silvana, and then heard a soft snore.

It was just past ten o'clock when they reached the airport. Ava gently nudged Silvana as they pulled up to the departures area. Silvana woke with a start and said, "We're here already?"

They loaded Silvana's suitcases onto a baggage cart and made their way to the eastern concourse. Ava stopped just inside the doors.

"Is there a problem?" Silvana asked.

"I don't want to check in until I hear from my contact."

"You're making me nervous," said Silvana.

"I'm just being careful," Ava said, trying to hide her own growing discomfort about the fact she hadn't heard from Arthon.

"Okay, so what are we going to do?"

"We'll wait over there," Ava said, pointing in the direction of some empty seats.

"For how long?"

"I don't know, but please stop worrying, he will call," Ava said. "In the meantime, why don't you find a departure board and see what gate we'll be leaving from? It's ANA Flight 5606 to Tokyo at one o'clock."

"Sure," Silvana said.

Ava watched her walk away, and when she was certain Silvana was out of earshot, she phoned Arthon.

"Hey," he answered.

"You were supposed to call me," she said. "Is there some kind of problem?"

"No, I've just been crazy busy."

"Has the money reached your account?"

"Yeah, it's there. I was going to let you know in a few minutes."

"And have you notified Viroj?"

"I did," Arthon said, and then laughed. "The son of a bitch tried to talk me into transferring it right away to his account in the Caymans."

"What!"

"Relax, it was a lame effort, and when I reminded him of what the agreement was, he backed right off."

"Still . . ."

"Don't sweat it. He's the kind of guy who can't help trying to cut a corner, but his word is usually good. Even if I'd sent it, it doesn't mean he would have reneged," Arthon said. "And Ava, remember, I know what the deal is, and he knows we're close. I don't mean to make this about me, but if he tried to pull a fast one, he knows I'd be on his ass."

"I want to believe you're right, but do me a favour and stay close to your phone for a while. I'm going to call Viroj next, and if I suspect there's a problem, I might need you to intervene."

"Okay, I don't think it will come to that, but if it does, I'll do what's necessary."

"Thank you — and if you don't get a call then expect a text from the plane. We're scheduled to leave at one."

"And I'm sure that text will be the next time I hear from you," he said.

Ava shook her head in frustration as she ended the call. Thank goodness Arthon had some leverage over Viroj, because it was obvious she had none. *Be calm*, she thought as she hit Viroj's number.

"Good morning, where are you?" he answered.

"I'm at the airport, and Arthon just told me that he informed you that the two million is in his account," she said.

"That's correct."

"So when will I see Chen at the gate?"

"Have you checked in yet?"

"No."

"Between that, clearing immigration, and passing through security, it will take you about an hour," Viroj said.

"Then I'll see you and Chen in an hour."

"I'm not actually at the airport yet, and I have a few things I need to finish here at the office before heading there."

Ava felt her frustration begin to morph into anger, and she struggled to stay even-keeled as she said, "We have an agreement, and I've honoured my side of it to the letter. But I don't like how non-specific you're being when it comes to your side. Please don't make me regret trusting you."

He didn't respond at once, and Ava wondered — but didn't care — if she had offended him.

"Your friend Chen and I will see you at the airport," he said curtly. "It may not be exactly in an hour, but it won't be far off."

"We have seats on the one o'clock ANA flight to Tokyo. I don't have the gate number yet."

"I don't need it," he said and then hung up.

"Who were you speaking to?" Silvana asked.

Ava hadn't seen her approaching. "The contact. Everything is good to go. He will bring Chen to the gate."

"Doesn't he need the gate number?"

"Evidently not, but I do."

"It's gate thirty-nine."

Ava stood and grabbed the handle of the baggage cart. "Let's find the check-in counter," she said.

23

VIROJ HAD BEEN CORRECT WHEN HE SAID IT WOULD take them about an hour to work their way to the gate. It was a smooth process, though, with the exception of some anxious seconds when the immigration officer pored over the Jennie Kwong passport more intently than Ava thought normal. But he asked no questions, and all he said to her when he handed it back was "Have a good trip."

As they walked to the gate, Ava kept glancing in all directions looking for anything or anyone untoward. She knew she was being overly alert and self-conscious, but this was the airport where Chen had been plucked from a passenger line and put into a cell. What was to prevent Viroj from making a phone call to order the same treatment for her?

There was no sign of Viroj or Chen when they reached the gate, and Ava could see that Silvana was on edge. "It's only eleven o'clock. Relax, they'll be here soon enough," she said before Silvana could speak.

"It isn't that I don't believe you. I'm just so nervous about everything."

"I know the last few days have been rough, but the worst is over."

Fifteen minutes later, Ava wasn't as convinced that it was over. There was still no sign of Viroj and Chen, and she had to restrain herself from phoning the Thai. *I'll give him another fifteen minutes*, she thought. Silvana hadn't spoken again, but the head that kept swivelling in all directions, the hands she clenched and re-clenched, and the feet that were bouncing up and down told Ava all she needed to know about her state of mind.

They sat with their backs to the tarmac and directly facing a bookstore. Pedestrians went past them from the right and the left, many of them in groups and in a steady flow, making it difficult to pick out individual faces. Ava was looking for Viroj, thinking that he had the more distinctive height and frame, when Silvana leapt to her feet.

"There he is," she yelled, pointing to the right.

Ava looked in that direction and saw Chen walking between two men wearing uniforms. His face was gaunt and grim, and his steps were unsteady. She couldn't see Viroj and began to fear the worst. Before those thoughts went any further, Silvana left the seating area and ran towards Chen. The officers seemed alarmed, stepping in front of Chen and stretching out their arms to block her. To Ava's surprise, Silvana burst through them and threw her arms around Chen's neck. As he held on to Silvana, he looked over her shoulder and saw Ava. His face collapsed, and even from a distance she could see him start to cry, and then she heard Silvana loudly join him. The two officers — one of whom Ava now noticed was carrying a carry-on case that she thought was Chen's — looked uncomfortable and uncertain about what to do.

Ava walked towards the group. "Where is Mr. Viroj?" she asked the older officer. "He was supposed to be here."

"Are you Jennie Kwong?" the officer asked.

"I am."

"Can I see your ID please?"

Ava took the Jennie Kwong passport from her bag, and with some apprehension passed it to him.

He examined it, looked at her, and said, "Could you step to one side?"

"What's going on?" she asked.

"Just step to one side."

Ava fought back the urge to resist. This wasn't the time or place to start something that she knew she had no chance of winning. "Certainly," she said, moving several metres towards the bookstore.

The officer joined her. "Viroj sends his apologies. He meant to be here, but there were some issues at headquarters with colleagues from other organizations that he had to deal with. He said that he thought you would understand why it was important for him to make that his priority."

"Did he mention which organizations?"

"No, but he did say you could call him if you wished, although he also made it clear that there wasn't much more he could tell you."

"What about my friend Chen — is he free to get on our flight to Tokyo?"

"If that's where he wants to go. He has his passport and there is nothing keeping him here."

"Speaking of passports, can I get mine back?"

"Of course," he said, handing it to her.

Ava nodded her thanks. "One last thing — I would like

Chen to be able to check in for the flight here at the gate, but that means forgoing security and immigration. You might have to vouch for him with the airline."

"That won't be a problem. I'll speak to the gate agent right now," he said.

"Would you mind if I went with you?"

"No — let's go."

They had to walk past Chen, Silvana, and the other officer to reach the gate, and as they did so Ava saw their cheeks were still wet with tears. She stopped and said quickly, "Everything is fine. The officer is just going to tell ANA that Chen can board without going through security and immigration. I'll be right back."

Ava did not join the officer at the gate, staying a few metres behind him, but close enough to hear him emphatically — and almost forcefully — instruct the female agent that as long as Chen had a reservation he was to be allowed to board. The woman asked no questions, but kept nodding and saying, "Yes, sir."

"There — that should settle it," the officer said to Ava.

"Thank you. When I speak to Viroj, I will make a point of telling him how helpful you have been."

They walked back to the others. "Everything is set," she said to Chen, reaching into her bag and taking out a slip of paper. "Here is your reservation number. Why don't you check in now?"

"You'll need this," the other officer said, passing the carry-on case to him. Then he nodded at Ava, and he and his colleague left.

Chen didn't react at first, and Ava realized he was dazed and perhaps having difficulty understanding what was going on. "Silvana, maybe you could go with him to the gate and help with the check-in?"

"Sure," Silvana said, wiping at her eyes.

"That's it? Just like that, I'm allowed to leave?" Chen asked, his voice cracking.

"Yes. We're flying to Tokyo, and if you're up to it, I thought we'd go on from there to Los Angeles."

Chen shook his head. "Ava, why were the Thais holding me in that cell?"

She hesitated, not sure if this was the right time, and then decided there was no right time. "The Chinese government asked the Thais to repatriate you to China. Obviously they wanted to punish you in some way for producing *Tiananmen*. We were fortunate that several Thai government organizations were vying with each other for the money the Chinese were willing to pay for you. I was able to insert myself into the negotiations — and simply put, I paid a lot more than the Chinese were offering. Or, should I say, *we* paid more, because you are going to find that the BB Productions bank account has taken a major hit."

"Good god, I never thought they'd go to that kind of extreme," he said, and tears trickled down his cheeks again. "I don't know how to thank you for what you've done. You've probably saved my life."

"I wouldn't go that far, but now that you're safe we have to be extra careful in order to keep you, Silvana, Lau Lau, and Fai out of their reach."

"Ava thinks that prick Christensen from Top of the Road was the one who told them about your schedule. That's how they knew where to come after you," Silvana blurted.

"Are you sure about that?" he asked, regaining some of his composure.

"Silvana was able to access your emails, and from what we read it certainly seems that way," said Ava. "It also seems probable that Top of the Road has cut some kind of deal with the Chinese — most likely with the China Movie Syndicate — to deep-six our film, which is why Christensen was avoiding you."

"Yet another reason to go to L.A.," he said.

"So you're up for taking him on?"

"Oh, yes I am. Are you?"

"I can hardly wait to meet Mr. Larry Christensen," Ava said.

24

ALTHOUGH THEY BOARDED WITHOUT INCIDENT, AND took off on time, Ava didn't fully relax until the plane was over the Gulf of Thailand. The moment it was, she messaged Arthon and told him he could transfer the money to Viroj. She had phoned Fai earlier to update her on what was going on, and now she texted her to say they were on their way to L.A.

She was sitting two rows behind Chen and Silvana and noticed they were clinging to each other. She didn't want to disturb them, but when they reached cruising altitude and the flight attendant served champagne, she couldn't resist walking up to their seats.

Chen looked up at her with a blend of relief and joy.

Ava raised her glass. "*Chang ming bai sui*," she said.

"And a long life to you as well," he replied, raising his. "And thank you again for saving mine."

The three of them sipped their champagne, and then Ava said to him, "You look tired. You should get some sleep. I'll need you in peak form when we get to L.A."

"I'm exhausted. I don't think I slept for more than an hour

at a time with all the comings and goings in the cell. Who would have thought a cell at the airport would have been that busy?"

"Before you do sleep, I was going to make hotel reservations for us, but I've never been to L.A. and I'm not sure where we should be staying. You had a booking at the Four Seasons — do you still want to go there?"

"No, it's a five-star hotel, but I think you and Silvana would prefer the Peninsula. It's quieter, surrounded by some beautiful gardens, and looks a bit like a palace on the French Riviera," he said, and then turned to Silvana. "It's also no more than a few minutes from the shops on Rodeo Drive."

"And how far is it from Christensen's office?" Ava asked.

"His office is even closer. It's on Santa Monica Boulevard, a few buildings away from what used to be the headquarters of CAA, the largest talent agency in the world. That building was like Mecca to people in my business, and then CAA moved to Century City, another L.A. district. They are still the biggest, but I think they lost some lustre when they left that building."

"Then I'll see what I can find at the Peninsula," Ava said. "Now, get some sleep."

They landed twenty minutes early in L.A., but the lines of passengers at immigration were long and slow and it was an hour and a half later that they exited the airport.

"How long will it take for us to get to the Peninsula hotel?" Ava asked the driver as they got into the limo.

"It's a twelve-mile drive, and two hours ago it would have been a half-hour trip. Now we're in rush hour."

Ava checked her watch. "By the time we check in and get settled, it will be too late to pay Christensen a visit at his office, but that's not necessarily a bad thing. It will give us some time to talk through things. I've been so focused on getting you released that I haven't given any thought to how to deal with Top of the Road."

"Do you really believe that they've cut a deal with the China Movie Syndicate?" Chen asked.

"I can't come up with any other reason for the way they're behaving, can you?"

"No."

"And if we're right, then what options do we have?" asked Ava.

"We either need to force them to distribute the film or make them sell it back to us."

"In terms of those options, does the agreement you signed give us any leverage?" she asked.

"What do you mean?"

"Is there anything in it that requires them to distribute the film within a certain time period?"

"No."

"Does it specify any markets or level of distribution?"

"No," Chen said, then paused and looked intently at Ava. "But there is one thing we might be able to use. The agreement prohibits Top of the Road from reselling the rights, or assigning them to another partner in part or in whole, without our specific approval. So if they did cut a deal with the Syndicate..."

"Then they breached the agreement."

"Exactly, but how do we go about proving that?"

"You know how Mo and the Syndicate operate, do you think they would do a deal without papering it?" Ava asked.

"If it was something that cost them a few thousand dollars

they might, but Top of the Road paid us ten million for the rights, so the Syndicate would have to have paid them that plus at least another few million to do nothing with the film. Given that they're a government agency, they have a budget to work within and are also subject to legal and financial oversight. So yes, I'm sure if they did a deal, it would have been papered."

Ava nodded. "Is there anyone working for the Syndicate you're close to?"

"Are you asking if I know someone who could give me a copy of whatever deal was made?"

"Yes."

"I know a couple of people who would have access to that kind of document, but we aren't exactly on speaking terms anymore. After the battle with Mo over Fai's future they kept me at arm's length. And now with *Tiananmen* it would cost them their jobs, or worse, if it was known they were even having so much as a casual conversation with me. Within that organization I am decidedly the number-one persona non grata."

"Do you have any friends in the business who have their own contacts within the Syndicate that we could use?"

"Ava, I couldn't ask anyone to do that for me. It would be putting them into the line of fire."

"I understand," she said, not prepared to give up on that idea but putting it aside for now. "Then that leaves the banking avenue. How many banks does the Syndicate use?"

"I only know of one, and that's the Bank of China."

"Do you have an account number for them?"

"I have the one they used to pay my clients. I can get it for you from my laptop."

"Great, and I'll also want the name of the bank and the account number for Top of the Road that was on the wire they sent to BB."

"It was a branch of the Bank of the South in Beverly Hills — that's a name that's hard to forget. That account number is in a file on my laptop as well," Chen said. "What are you going to do with this information?"

"I want to know if money was exchanged between the Syndicate and Top of the Road after you closed the deal," she said. "If it was, we at least have a starting point in terms of putting pressure on Christensen and his partners."

"What kind of pressure?"

"Let's not talk about that until we can confirm money was exchanged," Ava said.

25

THE DRIVE TO THE PENINSULA TOOK ALMOST AN HOUR longer than the driver had predicted, and Ava noticed that however much sleep Chen and Silvana had gotten on the plane, it didn't seem to be enough because they kept nodding off.

When they finally reached the hotel, checked in, and were in the elevator going to their floors, Ava said, "Let's not even think about dinner or doing anything else tonight. A good night's rest will benefit all of us. But please send me the banking information as soon as you can."

"Do you still plan on us going to see Christensen tomorrow?" Chen asked.

"Oh yes, but it would be ideal if by then we had some information on his relationship with the Syndicate."

Chen nodded. "I'll send you the account information in a few minutes."

After a round of hugs, Chen and Silvana exited the elevator on the third floor, while Ava rode to the fourth. She had booked corner suites with balconies, and after putting her bags in the bedroom she went to inspect hers. To her delight it was as spacious and well-furnished as the one at the Grand-Hôtel du Cap-Ferrat, and although it didn't have an ocean view, it did look down on a beautiful garden. She returned to the suite, took her laptop and notebook from her bag, and sat at a desk that looked like it belonged in an English country manor. In fact, she thought, that was true of the entire suite, with its plush sofa, chairs, and multitude of cushions.

She turned on her phone for the first time since landing and saw Arthon had texted to tell her he'd sent the money to Viroj. She texted him back to thank him, and reminded him she owed him a favour whenever he chose to exercise it. Fai had left a voicemail. Ava chided herself for not contacting her as soon as she'd landed, and called her now.

"*Wei*," Fai answered.

"It's me," Ava said in English, and then switched to Mandarin. "I'm sorry for not calling earlier. We've landed safely, and I'm in my hotel room at the Peninsula Beverly Hills. You'd like this place."

"I care more that you are safe. How is Chen holding up?" Fai said.

"He's not quite one hundred percent but a good night's sleep will help."

"That is so good to hear. When will you be coming home?" Fai asked.

Ava smiled at Fai's use of the word *home*. It was starting to feel as if she thought she belonged in Toronto. "I don't know. We'll try to see the Top of the Road people tomorrow. I'll have a better idea depending on how that goes."

"What do you expect?"

"Nothing and everything, but I'm trying to connect them

to the China Movie Syndicate. If I can establish that they're partners in trying to kill our film, then I'll have some options."

"Do you believe they are connected?"

"I think that it's at least a strong possibility."

"That bastard Mo," Fai said.

"Yes, he is a bastard, but I'm certain he's been told by the Chinese government to make sure the film is never viewed again. If he fails, you know that they'd come down hard on him, so he'll do everything he can to succeed."

"God, I hope he fails. That would be doubly satisfying."

"I share that sentiment, but I have no idea what I have to do to make that a reality."

"You'll think of something, you always do," said Fai.

Ava paused, and then switched gears as subtly as she could. "This mess with Chen in Thailand has made me really nervous for you and Silvana. Lau Lau is in Taiwan and out of harm's way, but I think the two of you have to be super cautious about where and how you travel."

"Well, I have no plans to leave Toronto — but what about Silvana, is she going back to Hong Kong?"

"I don't know, but I'll certainly urge her not to. The Chinese have tightened their grip on the city and no one living there is beyond their reach."

"And I guess Chen won't be going back to Thailand anytime soon."

"I think not. A prolonged stay in California might be the best thing for both of them."

"Give them a hug for me."

"I will."

"Call me tomorrow after school. I'm anxious to hear how things go," Fai said. "Love you."

"Love you too," Ava said, and ended the call.

She sat at the desk, opened her laptop, accessed the hotel Wi-Fi, and saw that Chen had sent her bank account information that included branch addresses and phone numbers. She copied it all down in her notebook and then stared at it. It would be ideal if she could get into either account, but even with the help of her friend Derek — who had hacked his way into several accounts for her in the past — she didn't think it was likely; and even if there was a possibility, it was typically time-consuming. Besides, she thought, all she needed was for the Bank of China to confirm it had sent money from the Syndicate to Top of the Road's account, or for the Bank of the South to confirm it had received money in that account from the Syndicate. The question was how could she go about getting that information?

Johnny Yan came to mind. Ava had met him at York University, and they were part of a Chinese-Canadian cadre of friends who exchanged favours and helped each other advance in their careers. Johnny had a management position at the Toronto Commonwealth Bank, and had occasionally made bank-to-bank inquiries on her behalf. But those inquiries had required a plausible cover story, and in this case she didn't have one yet. There was, she knew, the option of approaching the banks directly to get confirmation. It wouldn't be easy, but it had the advantage of being quick since they would either co-operate or they wouldn't. But it would also require a story, she thought as she rose from the desk with her notebook.

She went to the mini-bar, took out a bottle of Chardonnay and a wine glass, and then walked out onto the balcony to sit and think. She was only a hundred yards or so from a major traffic artery, but all she could hear were the muted voices of people walking in the garden below. It was almost eight o'clock which meant the Bank of the South was probably closed, but given the time difference it was close to eleven a.m. in Beijing. What could she tell the Bank of China branch that would get her the information she wanted?

Ava mulled over several ideas and then decided she needed to know more. Her first call was to Chen.

"I got the banking information, so thank you for that," she said. "I also thought we should meet for breakfast at the Belvedere restaurant on the ground floor in the morning, to get organized. How's eight o'clock?"

"That's fine. Have you been able to do anything with what I sent you?"

"Not yet, but I'm thinking about it. I do have a question for you. Can you confirm when Christensen started becoming evasive? I know it was late July or early August, but I'd like to pin down as precisely as possible when his attitude seemed to change."

Chen hesitated. "It became really obvious in August, but I sensed something was going on earlier than that."

"So your best estimate is late July?"

"Yes."

"Then the way I see it, there are two possibilities," Ava said. "The Syndicate could have contacted Top of the Road while they were all in Cannes, and persuaded them to buy the rights on their behalf; or the Syndicate learned later that Top of the Road had acquired the rights and negotiated a deal after the fact. Given your interactions with Christensen it seems to me the latter is most likely, but what do you think?"

"I have been an agent for decades in a business where bullshit is a standard part of day-to-day dealings, and through trial and error I became proficient at detecting it. I also became a reasonably good judge of character," he said. "In Cannes, I thought Christensen was completely sincere. In fact, I would have never recommended going with Top of the Road if I hadn't been completely comfortable. So, unless he's the greatest con man I've ever met, I agree that your second scenario is the one that's most plausible."

"Which means Top of the Road was approached sometime in July?"

"That would be my guess, and if I had to narrow it down, I'd say later in July because before that I hadn't noticed any change in Christensen's attitude."

"That could be helpful, thanks," said Ava. "I may pursue this a bit more tonight. If anything happens, I'll let you know. Otherwise, I'll see you in the morning."

Making a logical assumption about when the money had been transferred was a start, but she still wasn't ready to approach the Bank of China. Instead she found the phone number for Dynamic Accounting in Hong Kong and called it. When a receptionist answered, Ava identified herself and asked to speak to Margaret Chew, the owner of Dynamic who had been Uncle's accountant for the last ten years of his life and who had on occasion done favours for him and Ava.

"Ava, it has been quite a while since I last heard from you. Is everything going well?" Margaret said when she came on the line.

"In general it is, but I could use some help with something."

"Why doesn't that surprise me?" Margaret said with a light laugh. "What is it this time?"

"Two things actually, but first let me give you some background…"

It took five minutes to explain the situation, and when Ava had finished, she asked, "So, what do you think?"

"I have no problem providing you with cover as Jennie Kwong and as a Dynamic employee, but Ava, I can't predict how the Chinese bank will respond to your inquiry, although your approach does make some kind of sense."

"I know it's a bit of a stretch, and if it doesn't work I'm going to have to repeat it in reverse with the bank in California."

"I'll make sure any calls from those banks are transferred directly to me, but other than that all I can do is wish you the best of luck."

"Thank you again, Margaret. I will repay you one of these days."

"There's no need, Ava. Every time you call, you brighten my day."

Margaret hadn't exactly been encouraging about her chances of getting what she wanted from the Bank of China, but Ava couldn't think of any other option. She did have a story to spin, and as she sipped her wine she began to embellish it to a point where she thought it was at least plausible. There was, though, only one way to find out if the bank would buy it.

Ava left the balcony and sat at the desk. She called Beijing, using the room phone so the L.A. area code could be seen at the other end. When a woman answered, Ava said she was phoning from Los Angeles and asked to be connected to the branch manager.

A minute later, she heard a tentative "*Wei*" in a man's voice.

"Is this the branch manager?" Ava asked.

"I'm the assistant manager. My boss hasn't arrived yet."

"I'm sure you can be just as helpful," she said. "My name is Jennie Kwong and I work for Dynamic Accounting in Hong Kong. One of our clients is considering making an investment in a Los Angeles–based company called Top of the Road Production and Distribution, and I've been sent here to examine its financial statements."

"By 'here,' you mean Los Angeles?" the man asked.

"Yes — I know it's a long way for me to come, but the client's potential investment is quite large."

"What does any of that have to do with our bank in Beijing?"

Here goes nothing, Ava thought. "The company records show that a substantial amount of money was sent in late July from an account at your branch to Top of the Road's account at the Bank of the South. Let me give you both account numbers," Ava said, and then read them out slowly and precisely.

"Okay, but I'm not sure why you're telling me this."

"I would appreciate it if you could confirm the sender's name and the amount of the transfer," Ava said. "The reason I'm making the request is that the transaction, both in terms of its size and the name attached to it from your end, is quite out of the ordinary when compared to Top of the Road's normal business. Our client is nervous about the prospect that money laundering could be involved."

"I assure you that our bank would never participate in that kind of activity," the man said sharply. "And I've accessed the account here that you mentioned, and I can guarantee that this client wouldn't undertake anything like that either."

"Of course not, and I wasn't suggesting otherwise, but you can't be too careful," she said. "Your client, though, did send a large amount of money to Top of the Road around the time I mentioned, did it not?"

"I'm not sure it is appropriate for me to acknowledge that."

Ava took his response to mean "yes," and felt a surge of adrenalin. But she hesitated before saying, "Why don't we try this — I'll tell you the name we have on the records here, and if it is the same as the one attached to the account, you can simply say 'yes,' and if it isn't you say 'no'? We're not asking you to give us information that's confidential. All we need is a few facts confirmed."

He didn't respond immediately, and Ava half expected him to hang up. Instead, to her surprise, he said, "What name do you have?"

"The China Movie Syndicate."

"Yes," he said.

She drew a deep breath, hoping that this small amount of co-operation would open the door for more. "And the money was wired in late July?"

"Yes."

She hesitated again, debating about whether to press her luck by guessing at the amount of money that had been sent. She would have only one chance, and if she was wrong it might raise suspicions at the Bank of China, and where could those suspicions lead? She didn't know, and that was sufficient for her to decide being cautious was best. Besides, the assistant manager had just as good as admitted that a large amount of money had been sent. That verified there was a financial connection between the Syndicate and Top of the Road, and the timeline fit perfectly with Chen's estimate.

Added together, it seemed to confirm her suspicions.

"I can't thank you enough for your help. My client will be pleased," she said. "But one last thing — I would appreciate it if you kept my inquiry strictly between us. I wouldn't want to offend Top of the Road by having them think that my client doubted their record-keeping."

"Our bank would have no reason to be in contact with Top of the Road."

"That is good to know, and thank you again," she said.

She ended the call and sat quietly at the desk, scarcely believing it had gone so well. Uncle used to tell her that things didn't always have to be hard, that sometimes luck took their side. This was one of those times, but even as she appreciated it, her mind was already starting to move on to the next obvious question — what the hell did knowing what had happened matter if she couldn't do something to reverse it?

26

CHEN WAS SITTING AT A TABLE ON THE BELVEDERE'S patio when Ava arrived for breakfast the next morning at eight. The sun was already high, but the table sat in shade of an umbrella. Ava had liked everything about the hotel's style so far, and the restaurant, with its white tile floor, glass-top tables, and wrought-iron chairs with white padding on the backs and seats, was no exception.

"How did you sleep?" Ava asked as she joined him.

"Soundly for about six hours, and then I kept waking and thinking about Christensen," he said. "How about you?"

"I slept really well. I wasn't in Thailand long enough to develop jet lag," she said.

"Do you want coffee?" he asked, pointing to a carafe on the table.

"I sure do," she said, reaching for it and pouring a cup. "Where's Silvana? I wouldn't have minded if she had joined us."

"She's still sleeping. Evidently she got less sleep at our apartment in Bangkok than I did in the cell."

"She was worried sick about you."

"I know. We've become very fond of each other."

"Speaking of which, I was talking to Fai last night and neither of us think that Silvana should be going to Hong Kong anytime soon."

"We've talked about that. We're going to stay in the U.S. until things are settled."

"That's wise," Ava said as a server arrived at the table with menus.

"I've eaten here before," said Chen, opening his when the server left. "The breakfast selection is very Californian."

Ava looked at her menu and smiled. There was no congee on offer, but she could have plant-based muesli, gluten-free muffins, homemade nut granola, various acai bowls, and a variety of fruit. "What are you going to order?" she asked Chen.

"The three-egg omelette with mushrooms and cheese."

"Do you think the server will think poorly of me if I have a couple of fried eggs on corned beef hash?"

"Probably, but I won't."

The server came back to the table as soon as she saw them close their menus. She replaced the carafe with a fresh one, and then they placed their orders.

"I had some good luck last night," Ava said when they were alone again.

Chen raised an eyebrow.

"I managed to confirm through the Bank of China that the Syndicate sent a wad of money to Top of the Road in late July," she continued. "I apologize for not calling you after I found out."

"That doesn't matter, I'm just glad you know," Chen said, his jaw clenched. "Now what do we do about it?"

"I've given that a lot of thought, and it seems to me the answer to that question depends on you and Lau Lau."

"You'll have to explain what you mean."

"How badly do you want the film to be seen?"

"As badly as I've ever wanted anything, and I'm sure Lau Lau shares that sentiment."

"And what about timing? Are you prepared to wait?"

"That depends on how long the wait would be."

"If we turn this into a legal battle then it would be months, maybe years."

"If we can prove that Top of the Road transferred or somehow gave control over distribution to the Syndicate, would it really take that long?"

"This isn't China, Chen. Getting justice here is a long, arduous, and expensive path. Besides, if we don't have a copy of the agreement between the Syndicate and Top of the Road, we have nothing to base a lawsuit on other than supposition."

"What if I could get one?"

"If the other side dug their heels in, it still wouldn't make things go any faster."

"I want the film to be seen this year," Chen blurted out.

"Why?"

"I'm speaking for Lau Lau now, as much as for myself. We spoke often after Cannes, and winning there sparked a dream for *Tiananmen* to be nominated for an Oscar. It would never be nominated for best foreign film because those nominees are submitted by selection committees in the countries they're from. In China, it is the Syndicate that decides who is nominated. So our only chance is for it to be nominated for best film, and not best *foreign* film."

"Has that happened before?"

"Foreign films have been nominated many times, but only one has ever won, and that was *Parasite* a few years ago."

"I loved that movie," Ava said. "But doesn't the fact *Tiananmen* was screened at Cannes qualify us?"

"No, and though I'm not sure of all of the rules surrounding the Oscars, I do know that a movie has to be shown commercially in the U.S. to qualify. And Ava, if we wait a year or longer to resolve the issues with Top of the Road, our film will be forgotten and we'll have no chance at all."

"A U.S. screening could be a challenge."

"Keep that in mind when we're talking to Christensen."

"Assuming he'll actually talk to us," she said. "Along those lines, I thought it might be smart if you called him before we go to their offices. If we show up unannounced, it only makes it easier for him to turn down a request for a meeting."

"Really?"

"He'll still be surprised to hear from you because I'm sure he was told that you were detained in Thailand, but if you're calm and pretend nothing has happened, he should find it hard to say no to you."

"Are you always this devious?"

"I prefer to think of it as being strategic, and not devious."

Chen nodded. "I'll call him as soon as we finish breakfast. Should I tell him that you'll be with me?"

"No, it might make him wonder why I'm tagging along, and we don't want to risk making him nervous or giving him an excuse not to meet with you," Ava said. "And by the way, I'll be going as Jennie Kwong. That's the name I used when I spoke to him about you. The real Ava needs to stay in the background."

"I understand," Chen said, and then he stared at Ava

across the table. "But I'm curious, if you don't think we have any legal leverage, what's left to use for pressure?"

"I didn't say we wouldn't take a legal stand; what I said was that it would be time-consuming with an unpredictable ending," she said. "But I wonder how he'll react if we tell him that we've confirmed he did a deal with the Syndicate to withhold the film from distribution. He'll deny it, of course, at which point we can say we have a source inside the Syndicate who has agreed to sell us a copy of the agreement, and that when we get it, we will make it both public and the basis for a lawsuit."

Chen shook his head. "That's one hell of an angle. Do you think it's enough to get him to bend?"

"I don't think he'll be afraid of a lawsuit, but he might not welcome that kind of publicity, and if we agree to buy back the rights for enough that he can pay back the Syndicate and still see some profit, he might see things our way."

The server arrived with their food, pausing their conversation. Ava looked at Chen and could see he was excited. He was a good man to work with, she thought — an experienced professional who she didn't expect to be intimidated or easily put off when he got in front of Christensen.

Ava forced herself to eat slowly, thinking over their strategy as she did. They had a solid jumping-off position, and from there it would depend on how Christensen reacted. Uncle had often told her that negotiations rarely proceeded in a straight line. It was important to be flexible and nimble, but without losing sight of the ultimate objective. She would let Chen start the process, but she imagined she would be the one finishing it.

When breakfast was over and the dishes cleared, she said

to Chen, "Are you going to call Christensen at the office or on his cell?"

"I'll try his cell first."

"Do you want me to leave, or are you comfortable with me listening to your conversation?"

Chen smiled tentatively. "Truthfully, I might feel a bit self-conscious with you here. Let me do this on my own."

"Sure," Ava said. "I'll wait in the lobby for you."

She found a corner sofa that had a view of the entrance to the Belvedere. There was a copy of the *Los Angeles Times* on a side table that she picked up and idly began to flick through. She was barely past the front page when she sensed a presence. She looked up, and to her surprise saw Chen standing there.

"You couldn't reach him?" she asked.

"The opposite, he picked up right away. He was hesitant when I told him that I had finally arrived in L.A. and would appreciate a few minutes of his time. I was totally non-threatening, and when I said 'please' a couple of times and generally grovelled, he told me he'd meet me at their offices at ten."

"Did he ask you why you were delayed?"

"He did, and I laughed and said I had a small issue with the Thai immigration department that needed to be resolved."

"Not only were you a good agent, you could have been an actor yourself," Ava said.

"Well, that's a lot of what an agent does," he said. "We spin, spin, spin, and spin, and try to avoid saying anything negative."

"That's not my style, but I think we're going to make a good team."

27

THEY LEFT THE HOTEL AT NINE FORTY-FIVE FOR THE
short walk to Top of the Road's offices. Ava kept glancing at
Chen, looking for any sign of nervousness. There was none,
and given what was at stake she found that encouraging.

The offices were on the eighth floor of a glass tower on
Santa Monica Boulevard. Ava and Chen entered a marble
lobby and walked towards a bank of four elevators. A list of
the building's tenants was on the wall separating the middle
elevators, and Ava saw that most of them seemed to be in
the entertainment business.

Top of the Road shared the floor with two other companies, and when Ava and Chen exited the elevator they
went left down a corridor to a set of double wooden doors
with the company's name stencilled in gold across them. The
doors were locked, and they had to buzz to request entry.
A woman's voice asked who they had come to see.

"My name is Chen Jie, and I have an appointment with
Mr. Christensen."

They heard a click, and Chen opened the door. They
entered a semicircular office that looked eerily similar to

Chen's in Beijing. The receptionist sat at a desk on the right that faced a sofa, two chairs, and a coffee table. The central space was unoccupied but was surrounded by offices, most of which had closed doors.

"Mr. Christensen will be with you in a moment," said the receptionist, who was wearing a T-shirt.

Chen and Ava sat on the sofa. He was wearing a suit and tie, and Ava had on black linen slacks and a button-down white Brooks Brothers shirt. She looked around, and the few people she could see were dressed similarly to the receptionist. "I feel overdressed," she said to Chen.

"Me too," he replied.

"Chen," a voice said.

Ava turned and saw a tall, barrel-chested man wearing a red polo shirt and jeans walking towards them. He had sandy hair that hung over his ears but was thinning on top. His close-cropped beard was slightly paler and accentuated his large jowls. She and Chen stood up to face him, and when they did he came to a stop.

"I was expecting you to be alone," Christensen said.

Ava could see her presence irritated him, and sensing he might use that as an excuse to cancel the meeting she said, "My name is Jennie Kwong and I spoke to you a few days ago about Chen, and I really want to apologize to you if I was rude or abrupt in any way. I was simply very worried about him."

Christensen ignored her as he spoke to Chen. "Could you tell me why you brought her with you? Does she have a position in your company?"

"She represents one of our major investors, and I would really like her to be able to participate in the meeting. Of course, if you have a serious objection . . ."

"No, I guess it will be all right," Christensen said with a flick of his right hand. "But I hope you aren't expecting a meeting in the usual sense. My schedule is tight, and given your short notice I've only been able to shoehorn you in for ten minutes."

"Then we should get started right away," said Chen.

Christensen led them to a corner office that was large enough to accommodate a large teak desk, several bookcases filled with binders, a credenza, and a conference table with eight chairs around it. A small, slim Asian woman who was sitting at the table stood when they entered.

"This is my assistant, Julie Park," Christensen said. "She'll be joining us."

Like everyone else Ava had seen, the woman was wearing jeans and a casual top.

"Take a seat, and tell me what I can do for you," said Christensen.

As they sat, Ava noticed that Park had a notebook open on the table. Christensen obviously wanted a record of what was said. *Why shouldn't we*, Ava thought, and she reached into her LV bag for her Moleskine.

Chen put his hands together and placed them on the table. "We are most interested in finding out what your plans are for our film. We seem to be on the verge of missing most of the festival season, so we're hoping at least for a fall release."

Christensen nodded, and then said, "Julie, why don't you explain what happened with the festivals."

"We had great difficulty getting positive responses," she said, speaking to him rather than Chen and Ava. "We're not sure why; it was all rather vague."

"Which festivals did you approach?" Chen asked.

"That is irrelevant," Christensen snapped. "The point is that we may have miscalculated the film's appeal, and frankly — if we had to do it over again — we probably wouldn't make the offer we did. The Palme d'Or doesn't appear to carry as much weight as people believe."

"All right, let's not discuss the festivals, but can you tell me when you intend to put it into general release?" Chen asked.

"We don't have a date," Christensen said without hesitation.

"How can that be? The major movie theatre chains plan runs months and months ahead. Are you telling me they won't give *Tiananmen* a slot?"

"No, we did approach them, but when we got some preliminary negative feedback we decided to back off and rethink our strategy. As I said, we may have miscalculated the film's appeal. Among other things, its length is an issue. The chains want to run a feature film at least twice and ideally three times an evening. *Tiananmen* would be tough to run even twice."

"What about the independent cinemas?" asked Chen.

"We aren't going to recoup our investment by going that route. We need the majors."

"You just told me that you think *Tiananmen* is a hard sell to them."

"Right now it is, but we're hopeful that they will be more receptive after New Year's," Christensen said, and then smiled at them. "I don't know how familiar you really are with this market, but when you get into the dog days of January, February, and March, there is always a dearth of product. *Tiananmen* could help fill a void."

"I know enough about the market to understand that those months are when studios release films that are duds and generally unwatchable," Chen said.

"That's not always the case."

"Assuming it isn't, are you then saying that you intend to release our film next January?" asked Chen.

"Not precisely. What I'm saying is that those dates are under active consideration."

Chen turned to Ava. "What do you think?"

"I think it's bullshit, and that it's time to discuss the China Movie Syndicate," she said.

Ava's attention was locked onto Christensen as she spoke, and when she saw his eyes flicker and his tongue ever so slightly lick his lower lip, she knew she had caught him off guard.

Christensen looked at her, and then at his watch. "I'm afraid your ten minutes is up. Julie will see you to the door."

"It would be rash of you not to hear us out, because if you don't, you will most certainly end up reading and hearing about what we have to say in the media," she said.

"I have no idea what you're talking about," he said.

"Yes, you do. Let's not play games."

"Julie —" he began.

Ava cut him off. "We know the China Movie Syndicate paid you to not release our film. We have confirmation from the Bank of China that the money was wired to you in late July. We also have a contact inside the Syndicate who is prepared to sell us a copy of your agreement with them. So, as I said, let's not play games."

"Why on earth would we pay ten million dollars for a film we didn't want to release?"

"Precisely — why would you? And the answer is that the Syndicate paid you far more than ten to bury it. Apart from being unethical, it also runs contrary to the contract you signed with Chen's company, which prohibits you from transferring or selling the rights in whole or part to anyone else."

Christensen shook his head as if he was frustrated by her lack of understanding. "Other than the opportunity to relay this ridiculous theory of yours — an opportunity that I've given you — what else can I possibly do for you?"

"We are prepared to buy back the distribution rights," she said.

"They aren't for sale," said Christensen.

Chen laughed. "That's ridiculous, you've just finished telling us what a bad investment you think the film is."

Christensen rose to his feet. "I am going to leave my office now. When I return I expect you to be gone. If you aren't, we'll be getting building security involved. Julie will see you out."

He left so quickly Ava didn't have a chance to respond. Instead, she glanced at an obviously uncomfortable Julie Park.

"We'll leave, so you don't have to bother with security," Ava said to her. "But tell your boss that this isn't the end of anything, it's only the beginning. We are going to come after him and this company. In fact, it might be a good idea if you started to look for another job, because Top of the Road may not be around when we're done."

28

AVA AND CHEN DIDN'T SPEAK UNTIL THEY HAD WALKED
out of the elevator into the lobby downstairs.

"He wasn't even interested in knowing what we were prepared to offer," Ava said. "What does that tell you about this
situation?"

"They've probably done a deal with the Syndicate that
includes more than our film," Chen said. "I'm sure the
Syndicate has done something like promise to green-light
distribution in China for any film that Top of the Road puts
forward."

"I was thinking the same," she said as they left the building. "And assuming that's true, it's going to take more than
money to get them to change their minds."

"So what can we do?"

"Do you know any top-notch entertainment lawyers in
L.A.?"

"No, but I know people who will."

"Then contact them and get us some names."

"We're going to sue?"

"We are going to explore our options, and a good lawyer

can help," Ava said. "Next, can you send me Harris Jones's contact information?"

Chen slowed his walk. "What do you think Harris can do?"

"I won't be sure until I speak to him."

"Okay, I'll send it to you as soon as we get back to the hotel."

"Lastly, we need to get a copy of whatever agreement the Syndicate and Top of the Road reached," she said. "And Chen, I can't emphasize how important I think that is. If we get it, and it describes what we think is going on, it gives us enormous leverage. Without it, it's our word against theirs, and our challenge is multiplied tenfold."

"I don't want to sound negative, but I've already told you how difficult that might be."

"I'm prepared to pay whatever it costs — and I don't care if I have to pay both a middleman and someone inside the Syndicate. Offer whatever you think will do the trick. We need a copy of that agreement."

"Ava…" he started to protest.

She stopped walking. "Chen, you *must* know someone who can get access to it — directly or indirectly. Take your time and think about who that might be, and if you're uncomfortable talking to them, put them in touch with me. I mean, there has to be a clerk or someone junior in the Syndicate's finance or legal department who needs money."

Chen hesitated, then said, "It was the staff at my agency who dealt with people at that level. I'll make some calls."

"Will they be discreet?"

"I have no reason to believe that my leaving the business meant a loss of the loyalty I spent years building."

"Chen, I apologize. I didn't mean to imply otherwise."

"Not a problem."

They continued their walk to the Peninsula in silence. Ava knew she was pushing Chen to do something he would rather not do, but a copy of the agreement would not only help them in a legal sense, it would also give them the moral high ground. But what if, she suddenly thought, there was no agreement? What if it had been a handshake deal? It wasn't logical, she told herself, but there was so much sensitivity in the Chinese government's hierarchy regarding the subject of the massacre in Tiananmen Square that maybe they had been prepared to waive normal processes.

"Ava, I've been thinking, what if there wasn't a written agreement?" Chen asked as the hotel came into view.

The fact his question mirrored her thoughts startled her, but she pushed her own negative views aside. "There has to be," she said.

"But if there isn't?"

"We'll still claim that one exists and keep going after them."

"Are you always this determined?"

"When I think I'm right, and in this case I'm certain that I am."

A moment later they reached the hotel and walked into the lobby. Just as they neared the elevators, Chen's phone started to ring. He glanced at the screen. "That's a Chinese number."

He answered, listened for a few seconds, then hit the speaker button and held the phone so both of them could hear.

"I understand that your trip to Los Angeles has turned out to be a waste of time and money," Mo said in his gravelly voice. "I'm not surprised to hear that, but I was surprised that you managed to get there. Let me be clear, getting out of Thailand was a reprieve and not a pardon. Sooner or later, Chen, you are going to pay for your sins. And we don't care where you are — California, Thailand, the North Pole — you will be found and you will be appropriately dealt with. Do you have anything you would like to say?"

Chen hesitated, and then said, "Yes. Fuck off."

Mo laughed. "Take care of yourself. I wouldn't want anything bad to happen until we have a chance to deal with you."

Chen hung up and looked at Ava. "Christensen must have called him."

"Undoubtedly he did, and probably to tell him not to worry — that he'd put us off."

Chen clenched his jaw. "You're right, there has to be a contract. I'm going to call everyone I know who might be able to help us get our hands on it," he said with more determination than he'd exhibited prior to Mo's call.

They got into an elevator, and as it started upwards another idea came to Ava. It was so obvious that she mentally chided herself for not having thought of it sooner, and she realized again that she had lost some of the sharpness that the debt collection business had honed. The elevator stopped at Chen's floor, and before he could exit she hit the button to keep the doors open.

"Do you remember the name of the law firm that Top of the Road used when they closed the deal with us?"

"Yes, it was Eli Brand Law."

"Do you think Top of the Road would use them to paper all of their deals?"

"Probably. In fact I'd be surprised if that weren't the case."

"I assume Eli Brand is a real person?"

"He most certainly is."

"And how many other people are involved in the firm?"

"It's his practice. He has no partners. There are some associates and staff, of course, but Eli calls one hundred percent of the shots."

"Is he here in L.A.?"

"Yes, and not far from the Top of the Road offices," Chen said. "Ava, what are you thinking?"

"We need to work both sides of the street. While you handle Beijing, I want to see if there's something that can be done here."

"You're going to try to get a copy of the contract from Brand?"

"Why not?" she said. "As I see it, there's nothing to lose in trying."

When Ava reached her suite she went directly to her laptop and entered the name *Eli Brand Law*. The firm appeared immediately. She went to its website. It was rather barebones, with a simple description of the firm's services and basic contact information. There were no pictures, no bios, and no mentions of partners or associates, which pleased Ava because it was always easier to negotiate when you were dealing with someone who made all the decisions for the other side.

She closed the website and accessed Eli Brand's Wikipedia page. It described Brand, a Yale law graduate, as one of the nation's leading lawyers in the entertainment field. He was fifty-four, but the photo of him from the waist up was of a younger man who was probably in his thirties. He had a full head of thick black hair combed back, a wide forehead, and a square jaw. He was wearing a white shirt that seemed to be at least a size too small for the chest, shoulders, and upper arms of someone who was into bodybuilding. Brand was staring stern-faced into the camera, and Ava couldn't help thinking that it was a weak attempt to be taken seriously.

There wasn't much information about his personal life, except for the fact he had been married and divorced twice and had no children. Ava was pleased to see the two divorces. They didn't come cheap in California.

She reached for her cell and then hesitated. Was there any risk in approaching him? Was it possible that Christensen had already told him about her and Chen's visit? While Chen was missing, could Christensen have mentioned to Brand that a woman named Jennie Kwong was trying to locate him? If so, she thought it was unlikely she'd get a meeting, although he might be shrewd enough to see her just to find out what she was up to. Why, for example, would she ask him for a copy of the agreement between the Syndicate and Top of the Road if she had access — as she had said to Christensen — to one in Beijing? She sighed, told herself she was overthinking things again, and dialled his office phone number.

"Brand law offices," a man answered.

"Good morning, I would like to speak to Mr. Brand, please."

"I'm afraid he's in a meeting right now. Can I take a message?"

"This is actually urgent. I live in Hong Kong and I'm here in L.A. on business, and I find myself in the immediate need of a lawyer. Are you in a position to make an appointment for me with Mr. Brand?"

"No, he does most of that himself."

"Then could you disturb him? Tell him I promise to be brief."

"I'll see if he will speak to you. Hang on," the man said.

If he wouldn't, Ava wondered, should she leave a message? She was debating the pros and cons when a deep voice said, "This is Brand. Are we acquainted?"

"No, Mr. Brand, we aren't, but a friend of a friend recommended you most highly to me. I'm here in L.A. trying to finalize a contract for a martial arts series, but some unexpected issues have arisen. I believe I'm in need of legal advice from someone familiar with how business is conducted here. Is it possible we could meet?"

"My calendar is full today, but I might be able to fit you in next week."

"The problem is I'm short on time. I have a meeting scheduled with the other parties to the contract this evening, and I have to leave for Hong Kong tomorrow," she said. "I thought things were cut and dried, but it appears I've been naive. Could you possibly find a way to squeeze me in, even for half an hour? I will gladly pay a premium on top of your normal rate."

Brand didn't reply immediately, but then said, "We bill at a thousand dollars an hour, or any part of an hour."

"Then I'll pay you two thousand for thirty minutes. I'll even bring it to you in cash if you wish."

"Cash won't be necessary," Brand said, and then went silent again.

"I know this is a terrible inconvenience, but I'm in a real bind," Ava said, afraid of losing him. "And I promise you that if you can help, this won't be a one-time thing. I'll make sure my company directs more business your way."

"Can you get here by noon? I have a lunch appointment that I can put off for half an hour."

"Yes, I most certainly can. I'm staying at the Peninsula on Wilshire, and I see your offices are on Santa Monica Boulevard, so not far away."

"Then I'll see you at noon," he said. "By the way, what's your name?"

"Jennie Kwong, and thank you so much for doing this."

"You're welcome, Jennie Kwong."

When the line went dead on his end, she put down her phone and resisted the urge to cheer. She was in the door, that was all, she thought, but now at least she had a shot at getting what she needed.

29

AVA SAT QUIETLY AS SHE THOUGHT ABOUT HOW TO
broach the subject of *Tiananmen* with Eli Brand. Then, deciding she could use more information, she called Chen's room.

"I have an appointment with Eli Brand at noon," she said
when he answered.

"Good grief, that was fast," Chen said. "And I've been
working too. Two people from my old firm are discreetly
trying to find out who at the Syndicate might be willing to
co-operate."

"Excellent, we're moving in the right direction," she said.
"But Brand is immediate and I'm sitting here thinking about
him. Can you help me?"

"How?"

"I'm wondering what kind of man he is. Have you actually
met him? What do you know about him?"

"I met him once in my former life, when an actor I was
representing was offered a role in a Hollywood film about
the samurai. The actor was Chinese, of course, but that didn't
matter to the producers. In their opinion, at the time, one
Asian was pretty much like any other. Things have changed

a bit since then, but not entirely," Chen said. "And when we were negotiating the *Tiananmen* agreement, I was involved with our lawyer in several conference calls, including one on Zoom, where Brand obviously participated."

"How did he strike you?"

"He reminded me of some actors I know. He came across as being very sure of himself, but underneath I detected a hint of insecurity."

"Was that self-confident attitude overbearing? Did you find it off-putting?"

"Not really, and he's too slick to be that overt. He didn't brag or drop names, for example, but rather subtly let us know he was connected."

"His Wikipedia photo is obviously that of Brand as a younger man. Am I wrong to think he's vain?"

"I never thought of him that way, and I never found him to be more concerned about his physical appearance than most of the people I dealt with in that business."

Which meant, Ava thought, that he was more concerned than ninety-nine point nine percent of the general population. "I noticed that he's been divorced twice, which means he might need to keep money coming in. When our side was negotiating the contract with him, did you ever think he was just dragging it out to maximize his billing hours?"

"It was a slog, but at the time I didn't find it especially unusual. Entertainment business contracts tend to be excessively detailed."

Ava felt slightly frustrated by some of Chen's answers, but she couldn't blame him for not knowing more. "Thanks for this. I'll let you know how it goes with him."

Given what she knew about Brand, she decided to look

her best for the meeting. The slacks and button-down shirt were replaced by a black pencil skirt and snug-fitting light blue silk blouse. She put on mascara, applied red lipstick, and dabbed Annick Goutal perfume on her wrists and behind her ears. Ava then pulled her hair back and fixed it with her lucky ivory chignon pin. At twenty to twelve, she slipped on a pair of black pumps and left the room.

When she stepped out of the hotel, she noticed the weather was warmer. Not wanting to arrive sweaty at Brand's office, she got into a taxi. The driver looked pained when she gave him an address that was so close. "Don't worry," she said. "I won't get out of your cab until almost twelve, so you can keep the meter running, and I do tip well."

The driver stopped the taxi about a hundred yards from the tower that housed Eli Brand Law. Ava sat and thought about what her approach should be until five to the hour, and then she gave the driver thirty dollars for what had been a twelve-dollar ride.

The building had twenty storeys, and Brand's offices were at the very top. When Ava exited the elevator she saw a sign that indicated the floor had two tenants, and Brand's offices were on the right behind a large oak door. She opened it and walked into a reception area that was designed to impress. It had hardwood floors, several large stuffed sofas, an enormous wooden coffee table that looked antique, and the walls were adorned with an array of oil paintings. A male receptionist wearing a suit and tie sat behind a wooden desk that also looked antique, and behind him on a credenza there was a marble sculpture of a nude female.

"My name is Jennie Kwong. I have an appointment to see Mr. Brand," she said to the man.

"Yes, he's expecting you. Let me show you to his office."

Ava followed him around a corner and down a corridor to a set of double doors. They passed several people as they went, all of them immaculately dressed. When they reached the doors, the receptionist knocked, waited a few seconds, then opened them and stood to one side. Ava walked into an office that was large and sumptuous. She guessed it was twenty metres between the doors and the desk behind which Brand sat. The floor in here was also hardwood, but partially covered by a sprawling Persian rug. Off to one side there was a conference table with twelve chairs around it. On the other side, three ice buckets sat on a table with the necks of beer, water, and soda bottles sticking out of them.

"Take a seat at the conference table. I'll be right with you," Brand said. "And grab some water or whatever you feel like from our selection."

Ava nodded, went to the ice buckets, and chose a bottle of sparkling water. When she sat at the conference table, she took out her notebook and pen, sipped at the water, and waited. Brand sat in a high-backed red leather chair that had a suit jacket draped over the back. He was wearing a white shirt and a paisley pink tie that Ava recognized as a Zegna because her father had one that was similar. Brand was reading and editing a document and seemed caught up in it, completely ignoring Ava. Finally, after at least five minutes, he put the document into a file folder, stood, and walked over to her. As in his photo, his shirt was tight across his chest, but the rest of his appearance surprised her. His face was taut around the eyes and jawline and suggested plastic surgery, and his hair was almost blacker than black and Ava assumed it was dyed. But it was his height that caught her most off guard. He couldn't be more than five foot four or five, she guessed, and his large chest and arms made him look oddly proportioned.

"I apologize for keeping you waiting," he said when he reached her, his hand outstretched. "I've been working on that contract most of the morning and wanted to finish it."

"I'm just pleased that you agreed to see me," she said, shaking his hand.

He sat in a chair two away from hers on the left, and then turned so he was facing her. She shifted her chair so she could do the same to him. "Truthfully, I didn't know martial arts series were still in vogue, but I guess they must be," he said. "So, what is this problem you need help with?"

Ava hesitated, and then decided there was no point in trying to ease her way into her reason for being there. "Mr. Brand, you have something I want, and I am prepared to pay you a great deal of money to get it."

His mouth fell open. "Huh?" he said loudly.

"And before you say anything, let me be clear that what I'm requesting isn't illegal, and in fact would be the morally right thing to do," she said. "It is also something that could be kept secret."

Brand shook his head. "I suspect I shouldn't listen to anything else you have to say, but your opening line is nothing if not intriguing. So, what in the hell are you talking about?"

"*Tiananmen*, the film *Tiananmen*."

"And that's supposed to mean something to me?"

"I'm told that you represented the company Top of the Road when they purchased the distribution rights to the film."

"Who told you that?"

"Chen Jie. He's the film's producer and an associate of mine."

"That's true, I did represent them, but what's the problem? It was a straightforward rights acquisition."

"There's no problem with that agreement per se, but Top of the Road subsequently cut an illegal secondary deal with the China Movie Syndicate that destroyed any plans they had to actually distribute the film," Ava said. "What we want to buy from you is a copy of that secondary deal."

"Who is claiming there's a secondary deal?" he asked. "And when you answer my question, don't throw the word 'illegal' around quite so casually."

"We've been told by contacts within the Syndicate."

"Have you seen any documentation to support that claim, or are you operating on hearsay?"

"Our contacts within the Syndicate are solid."

"Then why haven't you gotten a copy of the so-called agreement from them?"

This was a question Ava had expected, and she answered it carefully. "It would involve more than one person and would take more time. It would also be at least as expensive as paying you, without the security of dealing with someone one on one. Frankly, the fewer people who know about this, the better."

"And what are you going to do if I pick up the phone and call Larry Christensen to tell him what you're up to?"

"I think that would be counterproductive for you. We would go ahead and get a copy from the Syndicate, so you withholding it from us wouldn't benefit you in the least," she said. "We also met with Christensen this morning and told him we had a contact in the Syndicate who was going to sell us one. That provides you — I think — with the perfect cover.

He'll believe that's where we got it, and will have no way of knowing you're involved."

"Do you know how bizarre all of this is?"

"I don't think it's bizarre at all. It's a straightforward business proposal. You give us a copy of the agreement; we pay you lots of money, and your name is kept completely out of it."

Brand stared at her. She looked back at him with equal intensity.

"What the fuck," he said, finally averting his gaze.

"Aside from the money, I assure you it is the right thing to do. The Chinese government wants to destroy this film and everyone who is associated with it. You'll be standing up for freedom of expression, and what could be more American than that?"

"What if I believe that freedom of expression is overrated — especially in this country these days?"

"Then do it for the money," she said.

Brand's lips moved as if he were trying to smile, but the effect was lost. "I find this all very entertaining, but at the same time rather insulting since you seem to think I'd so easily breach lawyer-client privilege."

"I apologize if you're offended," she said, realizing he had stopped pretending he hadn't papered the deal. "I had a mentor who taught me that many acts could be forgiven if the end result was for the common good. I think this is one of those cases, and that lawyer-client privilege is trumped by the public's right to see a work of art that an autocratic regime wants to bury. If you help us — as I said earlier — you can tell yourself it was the right and moral thing to do. The fact we're willing to pay you for any inconvenience we've caused, you can regard any way you want."

"Are you a lawyer?"

"No."

"You should have been," he said, and then he stood and stretched. He was physically close enough that he would have towered over her if he'd been taller. Instead, he barely blocked her sightline. "Okay, let's say I am pre-pared to at least consider doing the right and moral thing. What amount do you have in mind to make up for the inconvenience?"

"A quarter of a million dollars."

"No, that won't do," he said quickly.

But Ava sensed that was a test of her limits rather than a rejection. "Okay, we'll go to half a million," she said. "And if you give me access to one of your computers, I can wire the money to any bank account you designate before I leave here."

"I need something to drink," Brand said abruptly, and walked to the table where the drinks were.

Ava watched him fuss with the cap of a diet cola and knew he was weighing his options. Her bet was that he was going to co-operate.

When he returned, he sat but stared past Ava. "Okay, I admit there is an agreement between my client and the Syndicate, but if I give you a copy for half a million dollars, what use would it be to you? I mean, from a legal viewpoint I don't think there's anything in there that you could use to your benefit. It's a tidy little contract which in my opinion doesn't violate the terms of the agreement Top of the Road reached with BB Productions."

"What we would do with it is our business."

"That's fair enough, but I wouldn't want you to come back to me claiming that you didn't get what you expected to get," he said. "And there's no way there will be a record of whatever we agree to."

"We'll take the chance on the contents, and we don't want a record either."

"And assuming I'm prepared to sell you a copy, what's to stop me from telling Larry? He and I are friends, and given that I think the deal is innocuous, he might find it amusing that you were willing to pay me for it. Hell, I might even give him a cut of the money."

"Mr. Brand, could you look at me, please," Ava said.

He turned his eyes to her.

"I know that last remark about Christensen was meant to be amusing, but if you ever did anything like that, the consequences could be severe. Chen has other partners who don't play by nice Western rules," she said.

There was a point in any complicated negotiation when it could go either way, and this was that point. She had laid out her case in a simple and logical manner, and she thought that Brand was warming to it. But although his comment about telling Christensen had been said flippantly, she sensed he was capable of doing it and this had triggered her reaction.

His response was simply to stare at her with a grim scowl that was meant to intimidate. Ava stared back. Then Brand reached for her left arm. She had totally not expected it and was too slow to prevent him from grabbing it.

"What do you think you're doing?" she asked.

"Little girl, I don't appreciate you coming to my office and threatening me with your supposed tough-guy Asian connections. This isn't a Tarantino movie," he said, squeezing harder.

"Please let go of my arm," she said as calmly as she could.

He smiled but didn't relax his grip.

This has to stop, Ava thought, and with her right hand she grabbed the elbow of the arm holding hers. Her fingers dug into its soft flesh until she found the nerve she was seeking. She pressed it with as much force as she could muster. Brand gasped, and then yelped. His hand dropped away and his arm hung limply by his side. Ava released her hold.

"I apologize if I hurt you, but I've had to learn how to deal with men who think their physical superiority gives them the right to bully weaker men and women. I may not look like someone who can take care of herself, but I assure you I have taken down men larger than you."

"Jesus Christ, that was unnecessary," he said, shaking his arm.

"Again, I apologize. Now, can we get back to the subject at hand?"

He lowered his head, and she saw the muscles in his shoulders tighten and wondered if that was a prelude to something more physical. She watched him carefully. Brand had gone from a man she was tolerating for the sake of getting a deal done, to someone she actively disliked.

"Are you completely serious about the half a million dollars?" he asked.

"I am."

"And you'll do it based on a verbal agreement?"

"I will, and I'll send you half a million dollars within the hour, and I won't leave your offices until the money is in the bank account of your choosing," she said. "I will also give my word that no one other than you and I will know any of the details of this transaction. All I want before I send the money is for you to give me a signed copy of the agreement and a few minutes to peruse it. You can stand over me and watch as I read. Regardless of its contents, I'll send you the money. The proof that the document exists is what matters most to me."

She saw his shoulders relax, and knew she had calmed him to some extent.

He pointed a finger at her. "Stay there," he said, in an attempt to assert some authority.

Ava watched him walk to his desk, shaking his arm as he went. He sat and began to work on his computer. In less than a minute a finger rose above the keyboard and then fell to strike a key. A printer on the credenza behind him hummed into life. Brand turned his back on her and he stood over the printer as it churned out paper. When it stopped, he gathered the printouts, scanned them, and then returned to the conference table.

"Here's the agreement," he said, placing it on the table in front of her.

She nodded, said, "Thanks," and went directly to the last page. She had hoped that Mo's signature would be on it, but it was Fong's. Still, he was Mo's deputy, and she knew from the encounter in Beijing that he was also head of the legal department. His signature was under the words *For the China Movie Syndicate* and had been witnessed by Ms. Hua. Larry Christensen had signed for Top of the Road, witnessed by someone named Dean Smith.

Ava turned to the first page of three and skimmed the contents. When she finished, she said, "Thank you again for this. Now, where shall I send your money?"

30

SHE WAITED UNTIL SHE REACHED THE STREET BEFORE she called Chen.

"There *is* a contract between the Syndicate and Top of the Road, and I have a copy of it. The BB bank account took another hit, but it was well worth it," she said when he answered.

"Where are you?"

"On my way back to the hotel, I should be there in about fifteen minutes. Where do you want to meet?"

"Why don't you come to my suite?"

"I'll see you soon."

She walked to the Peninsula, but didn't sweat as much as she had feared she would earlier. It was warm, but it wasn't Bangkok-warm, where a five-minute stroll left her underwear soaked and stuck to her skin. She rode the elevator to the third floor and made her way to Chen's suite. He was standing in the doorway waiting for her.

"Congratulations," he said. "I'll phone my people later and tell them they can back off."

Ava looked for Silvana when she entered the room, but there was no sign of her. "Is Silvana here?"

"She's shopping."

"That's probably for the best," said Ava.

"Do you want anything to drink?"

"No, let's get down to business. Here's the contract. I read it quickly. You read it and tell me what you think."

Chen took the document and walked to the sofa. Ava went into the bathroom to freshen up and to give him space. When she returned he was still sitting where she'd left him with the papers in his hand.

"Well?" she asked.

"Those fucking pricks," he said.

"Who are you referring to?"

"The Syndicate most of all, but Top of the Road run a close second," Chen said, waving the document. "This is intended to bury our film, make Top of the Road a lot of money, and do both things without breaching their contract with us."

"I understood that, but what I don't know is how Top of the Road can claim they're not breaching it."

"This is the key section," Chen said, and then read it aloud. "'Given the sensitivity and volatility of certain current political, social, and cultural issues in China, and the negative impact that the release of the film *Tiananmen* might have on them, Top of the Road Production and Distribution agrees to delay the release of said film until such time that the impact would be less harmful. In consideration of their thoughtfulness, and to compensate them for lost revenue in the interim, the China Movie Syndicate will pay Top of the Road twelve million U.S. dollars upon signing this agreement, and two million dollars for every three-month period from this date until the end of this calendar year. If conditions for release are still not considered appropriate by then, the Syndicate will pay Top of the Road a million dollars for every six months the film is withheld from release for a period of not more than five years.'"

"If my math is correct, then Top of the Road sold us out for a six-million-dollar profit this year, and potentially another ten million over five years."

"That's how I see it, and they can claim they haven't sold the rights or brought in a partner. All they're doing is delaying the release until those so-called conditions are more ideal."

"And we know they never will be," Ava said, and then drew a deep breath. "Chen, are you absolutely one hundred per cent sure that there is nothing in our agreement with Top of the Road that we can use to compel them to either distribute the film or sell the rights back to us?"

"God, Ava, how I wish there was, and I can't help blaming myself for the fact there isn't," he said, his voice full of emotion. "Their initial offer for the rights was less than ten million, but I used the fact they wanted total control to get them up to that number. I also never imagined we'd be in a situation where we'd want to buy the rights back, so I didn't think about putting a clause like that into the agreement. I mean, I thought I was dealing with serious, professional business people. How could I expect that anyone in their right mind would pay ten million dollars for the rights to our film and then not distribute it?"

"I'm not blaming you," Ava said, reaching out to touch Chen on the knee. "I'm just trying to find a way around this problem."

"While you were with Brand I did manage to find a law firm that comes highly recommended. I have an appointment at three," he said, checking his watch. "That's just over an hour from now. Do you want to join me?"

"No, if you don't mind I've had enough meetings for one day — and besides, you know your way around entertainment lawyers. You have our contract with Top of the Road and this one to show them. Maybe they'll find something in them that we can't," she said. "But you should stress two things. First, time is not our friend. You said you want the film to be shown this year. Let's stick to that as our objective. And second, if they can find a route to pursue that would make that possible, we don't care what it costs."

"I can hardly believe what this mess has cost us already."

"I agree it's unfortunate, but there are some things it's tough to put a price on, and this seems to be one of them. So, if you believe the lawyers can come up with a quick and sensible plan, don't hesitate to hire them."

The door to the suite opened and Silvana walked in. She was carrying bags from Louis Vuitton and Balenciaga.

"It looks as if the shopping was good," Ava said.

"I needed to do something normal. I've felt I've been living on another planet for the past week."

Ava stood. "Well, I'll leave you two alone. If you like, Chen can fill you in on what's been going on. But let's have dinner together. Silvana, why don't you find a restaurant you think we'll like? I trust your judgement."

"Sure, I'd be pleased to do that. Do you want to eat at any particular time?"

"Seven or later."

"I'll text you when I have something booked."

Ava smiled at Chen and pointed to the Top of the Road contract. "Could you make some extra copies before you leave? I may take a nap, so just slip mine under the door."

"*Momentai*," he said.

When Ava entered her room, she went directly to the mini-bar and took out a bottle of Chardonnay. She poured a glass, went to the desk, and opened her notebook. She recapped the events of the morning, wrote down addresses and phone numbers, and then made a heading that simply read *OPTIONS*. Chen's meeting with the lawyers could lead to one, but as badly as she wanted that to be the case, the earlier remark she'd made about the U.S. legal system being complicated, slow, and unpredictable was hard to refute. She hoped Chen would come back with an actionable plan, but it wasn't something she could expect. There had to be another way to pressure Top of the Road, she thought, then calculated the time difference between London and Los Angeles and decided to take a chance.

Harris Jones answered on the second ring. "Is this actually Ava Lee on the other end of this line?" he said.

"It is, and I apologize for such a late call."

"No need. I'm a night owl and it's just past ten o'clock here, so the night is young for me," he said. "But what's the time where you are? Are you still in Asia, or at home in Toronto?"

Ava had her cover story ready. "Neither, I'm in Los Angeles with Fai, and we've bumped into Chen. He's having a bit of a problem. Given how close we all are, I've agreed to help and thought that some advice from you could be useful."

"What kind of problem?"

"It might take a little while to explain."

"I have all the time you need."

"Okay, well, the bottom line is it seems the Chinese government has found a way to prevent Lau Lau's film from being shown," she said.

"What!"

"Let me explain from the beginning."

She didn't rush, and Jones listened quietly other than several grunts of exasperation. She wasn't sure how he would react, but smiled when the first words he spoke were "Those fucking dictatorial assholes."

"Except this time they aren't actually dictating, they're simply using their money to co-opt Top of the Road," she said.

"And how disappointing is it that Top of the Road would go along with it."

"They stand to make a lot of guaranteed money for doing nothing instead of taking a risk with the film," she said. "What we think is unethical and possibly illegal, they probably believe is simply good business."

"But taking a risk, trusting your judgement, is a key part of the distribution business."

"There could be more at play," Ava said. "I wouldn't be surprised if the Syndicate didn't also promise them preferential treatment when it comes to doing business in China."

"This is verging on becoming a trend," Jones said.

"What is?"

"The Chinese government trying to control how the world views them; they have total authority inside China, and now they're expanding their reach. My newspaper ran a story last week about how that government is buying up Chinese-language newspapers and media outlets all over the world so they can manage the content. And it's no secret that they've invested heavily in production companies in L.A., and again are trying to control content. This deal with Top of the Road could be their foothold in the distribution side of the business."

"Harris, as much as I agree with you about the dangers the Chinese government poses to the world's media, I'm only immediately concerned about the problems attached to Lau Lau's little film."

"What is it you want to happen?"

"All of us want the film to be seen in the U.S. Even more than Cannes, it could validate Lau Lau's talent and vision, and acknowledge the work that Fai and Silvana have done."

"Those are exactly the right reasons," Jones said emotionally. "Their work more than deserves to be seen."

"Except, if we can't find a legal route to make that happen, what are our choices?"

He hesitated, and then said, "We could embarrass Top of the Road. If I wrote an article explaining what they've done, it could force their hand."

"But what if they don't care about being embarrassed? What if they say that they're only delaying the release out of concern for human rights issues in China? If that was the case, how quickly would the issue disappear?"

"Truthfully, given news cycles these days, it might not take more than a day or two."

"And that won't help us with our problem."

"I'm sorry, but I don't have anything else to offer."

Some random thoughts came to Ava, and she quickly wrote them down in her notebook. "What if there was more than one article?"

"My story would get picked up by other media," Jones said, sounding slightly offended.

"No, what I mean is what if we co-ordinated it so the articles were all released at the same time?"

"That would have a greater impact."

Ava nodded, and the thoughts she'd had started to form into a plan. "I have another favour to ask you, although it isn't directly related — could you tell me about the Oscars? Chen and Lau Lau have been fantasizing about the film being nominated for one, but I have zero idea about how that could happen other than that Chen told me *Tiananmen* would have to be screened in the U.S."

"For the film or anyone connected to it to be eligible for a nomination, it would have to be shown to paying customers in an American commercial theatre for seven consecutive days with at least three showings a day, and one of those has to be in the evening. It would also have to be shown prior to December thirty-first. Typically, for late releases like that, the production companies choose an L.A. theatre."

"And how does the nomination system work?"

"You're really making me go into the weeds here," he said.

"Sorry, I've been thinking about what we could do for Chen and Lau Lau, but I'm working from a knowledge base that's sorely lacking."

"You have seen the Oscars?"

"More times than I can remember," she said.

"So you've heard of the Academy of Motion Picture Arts and Sciences?"

"Of course."

"Okay, the Academy has about nine thousand members who are divided into seventeen different branches, with each branch or guild representing a particular field — for example, directing or writing or acting. Early in the year, individual branch members submit a ranked list of five nominees for their particular area of expertise. Those lists are reviewed, and then the Academy sends a ballot to the members with the top five nominees on it. They're allowed to vote for only one. And that's how you get an Oscar winner."

"But what branch votes on best film?"

"That's an exception. Every member of the Academy can submit a ranked list of five to ten films. Points are assigned based on the number of mentions and the rankings, and the top five to ten films make the final list. This time, though, ballots are sent to all nine thousand members, and a week or so later, usually in mid-February, the nominated films and the other nominees are announced."

"It's simpler than I imagined," Ava said, making another entry in her notebook. "So we would need to find a commercial theatre, ideally in L.A., that would be prepared to work with us?"

"I beg your pardon?"

"Apologies, I'm thinking aloud," Ava said. "And finding a theatre would only be the first step. There are many more details that would have to be worked out."

"I'm guessing that isn't simply a stream of consciousness. Are you telling me that you're actually thinking about exhibiting the film yourselves? What about Top of the Road and the Syndicate? They'd have their lawyers all over you."

"That's one of the details I need to address."

"What are the others?"

"I have a short list I've just written down, but I'm sure more will come to me," she said. "But Harris, can our conversation be off the record for now?"

"I'm assuming you have a very good reason for that request."

"Yes, I've decided that I'm going to do everything I can to ensure that *Tiananmen* will be screened in L.A. I don't know how or when, but I'm determined that it is going to happen.

And when it does, I want the whole world to know about it," she said. "So I need time to get organized and co-ordinate those details I mentioned. I promise you that, as soon as I have a plan in place, you will be the first to know — after Chen and Fai and the others, of course."

"When I was in Taipei, Chen told me what you had done for Lau Lau and Pang Fai," Jones said. "To say he was impressed is an understatement. He doesn't quite think you walk on water, but it's close."

"He's a kind man."

"He is a cynic who you have somehow managed to convert into a believer," Jones laughed. "With that in mind, I will most certainly treat what you've told me as being off the record, in the expectation that you can pull this off and turn it into an even bigger story that you will give me first crack at."

"Thank you, and yes, you will have first crack."

"Then we have an understanding. And Ava, if there is anything I can do to help you with any of this, let me know."

"Actually, there is, but I didn't want to ask and I'm very pleased you offered," she said. "Would you mind acting as my sounding board?"

Jones hesitated, and then said, "How can I possibly say no?"

31

Los Angeles
November

IT HAD TAKEN MUCH LONGER THAN AVA HAD THOUGHT to formulate a plan that would result in *Tiananmen* being shown in a movie house in Los Angeles. Then, when she finally had one she thought had a chance of success, she had the challenge of finding the resources to implement it.

The first challenge was to find a theatre that would accommodate them. Harris Jones told her it was pointless approaching any of the chains and gave her a list of the best independent cinemas in the city. Luckily, there were quite a few, but when she contacted them she quickly ran up against a reluctance to commit to running one film for seven straight days — especially when Ava wouldn't disclose the title of the film. Keeping it secret was something that she couldn't see her way around until she met Noel Martineau.

Martineau was a transplanted Quebecer who had come to L.A. as an actor, had little success, and had decided to get out of the performing side of the business. He had taken a job managing the Westwood Revue Cinema, and when the owner died he was able to buy it from his estate. Over the next ten years, he'd put virtually every dollar of profit into upgrading it, and it was now often referred to as a "six-hundred-seat gem."

When Ava contacted Martineau, he was as reluctant as the other independent operators had been, but by mentioning that Harris Jones would vouch for her, using their connection as Canadians, and saying she was prepared to fly to L.A. from Toronto, Ava convinced him to meet her in person.

Martineau was a short, stout man with a beer belly and bright red cheeks. He grinned when he met her and shook her hand as if they were long-time friends.

"After we spoke, I called Harris Jones about you," he said. "He told me I should do whatever it was you wanted because I wouldn't regret it."

"That was very kind of Harris to say, and the last thing I would want to do is disappoint him."

"Then tell me what you have in mind for this mystery film of yours."

Ava looked at Martineau sitting across the table from her, and decided in that moment that this was someone she could trust. Uncle had believed in his instincts when it came to extending trust, and it was a trait Ava had adopted and rarely regretted.

"I'll tell you the name of the film, and then you let me explain to you the entirety of what's going on," she said. "My only request is that if you decide you don't want to participate, you'll keep everything to yourself."

"You have my word on that," he said.

Twenty minutes later Martineau held out his hand again.

"You have the full support of the Westwood Revue Cinema," he said.

With Martineau onside, Ava turned her attention to the two other key components of the plan. Working with and through Chen, she engaged a top-notch law firm, as well as a public relations/publicity company that Harris Jones had endorsed. Several weeks of meetings followed, which Chen and Ava always attended together, but it was made clear that she was there as a friend and not as a part of the film's team. By the beginning of November the team was ready to be brought together for a final review of the plan.

When they came together late in the afternoon, the group that Ava thought of as the war cabinet occupied the conference table in the main boardroom of the Hines and Ford law firm.

Pang Fai was there, having been in L.A. with Ava for a week, as had Chen and Silvana. Harris Jones had flown in from London the day before. The others around the table were local: Harold Hines, the senior partner in the Hines and Ford law firm, and two of his associates; Patricia Nolan, the CEO of the PR company Make Them Dream, and two of her senior people; and lastly, and very importantly, Noel Martineau, the owner of the Westwood Revue Cinema. The only person missing was Lau Lau. He was filming in Taiwan, but was on his way to L.A.

It was the first time they had been together as a group, and the only common thread was the film. Ava had hesitated when Chen asked her to chair the meeting, but she had finally agreed although it wasn't something she was accustomed to. She had been up late the night before trying to structure it, and had decided to start with Martineau.

"Thank you all for being here. This is going to be an important week, but it doesn't happen without the Westwood Cinema, so let me start by thanking Mr. Martineau for taking this on and by asking him if preparations are complete for tomorrow night and the rest of the week."

"We're ready as we'll ever be. We have hired and trained enough additional staff to handle three showings of *Tiananmen* a day for seven days," he said. "I'm rather excited about all of this. I can't remember the last time the Westwood was full to capacity, and if you're right then we're going to be."

"Do any of your staff know what our plans are?" Harold Hines asked.

"No, Ava was quite explicit about keeping things quiet. All I've told them is that the theatre has been rented to a corporation for a week of private viewings."

"Does anyone have any questions for Noel?" Ava asked.

Chen leaned forward. "No, but I have one for Harold. I have an idea what his answer will be, but I'd like everyone to hear it."

"Then go ahead," said Ava.

"How confident are you that Top of the Road won't be able to stop the screenings? I can't imagine them not trying to get an injunction as soon as the news about the film breaks," he asked.

Hines had been recommended by Chen, and Ava couldn't have been more pleased that he was handling this issue for them. He was in his fifties, tall and lean, with a thick mop of silver hair. Always dressed in a suit and tie, he had a sophisticated air that was reinforced by his calm, understated way of speaking.

"Our first hope, of course, is that they won't try. The news articles and advertisements that will appear tomorrow could prove embarrassing enough that Top of the Road won't want to make things worse by drawing more attention to the situation," he said.

"In addition, we're going to be emailing information about where and when to see the screenings — and what the Chinese Movie Syndicate and Top of the Road have contrived to do — to literally thousands of members of the Academy of Motion Picture Arts and Sciences," Patricia Nolan said. "If Top of the Road values whatever reputation they have left, they'll be issuing apologies rather than taking legal action."

"Where are the ads running?" Silvana asked.

"There will be full-page ads in every daily newspaper in southern California, in every trade publication, and in a select number of national publications," Nolan said. "We have also bought large blocks of time on the four local television stations that are part of national networks, and on the five most popular radio stations in the city. By the end of the day tomorrow, I don't think there will be many people in southern California who haven't heard about the attempt to prevent *Tiananmen* from being shown."

"I've seen the ads, and I think they are terrific," Chen said. "But we're not just dealing with Top of the Road. Knowing the Syndicate as well as I do, I don't think there's much that's capable of embarrassing them. And remember, the Syndicate is taking direction from the Central Chinese Government, which doesn't care what anyone thinks when it comes to the subject of the massacre. I expect there will be pushback of one kind or another."

"Given what's been going on in Hong Kong these days, I tend to agree with Chen that the Chinese government is not only impervious to criticism but has shown a tendency to overreact to it," Silvana said. "So what is our legal position if they force Top of the Road either unilaterally or in concert with the Syndicate to go to court to get an injunction?"

"We have a three-pronged strategy," Hines said. "Our first position is that Top of the Road has violated the terms of the distribution agreement they signed with BB Productions, and that all we've done is reclaim our rights. Technically that may not work, but there's no denying the spirit of the agreement has been broken. Depending on the judge we draw, that may be sufficient grounds.

"If there is resistance, then we're going to argue that the American principles of freedom of expression have been sandbagged by Top of the Road at the behest of a foreign government. In fact, one could make the case that the Syndicate is acting as a de facto censor, and in effect the Chinese government is trying to dictate what the American public can or can't see."

"I think that's a very accurate description, and a strong position for us to take," said Ava.

"Thank you, and we think so too, but if the judge decides to make a decision based strictly on the wording of the contractual agreement between BB and Top of the Road, then principles like freedom of expression won't matter, and that's why we're particularly pleased with our third position," Hines said.

"Which is a new director's cut," Ava said. "Over the last few months Lau Lau has revisited all the footage of the film. He was worried before Cannes that it might be too long so he took out more than twenty minutes. He has put that footage back, and for good measure he's also taken out a two-minute scene that he felt didn't work as well as he initially thought it did."

"We had to work like crazy to get the additional subtitles done, but they are now in place," said Chen.

"So, it's our position that this is a new film. Similar, of course, but with enough changes that we can make the case that — strictly interpreted — the contract with Top of the Road doesn't apply to it," said Hines.

"That is very clever, if a bit of a stretch," Silvana said. "Whose idea was that?"

"It came out of a discussion between Lau Lau and Harris. By the way, Lau Lau is arriving from Taiwan later today. He will most definitely be at the screening," Ava said, and then turned to Jones. "And Harris has been helpful to us in other areas. Would you mind taking a minute to explain what else you've been up to?"

"For the past few weeks I've been contacting critic colleagues and friends with influence in the business, telling them to be in L.A. tomorrow night at the Westwood for an event they won't forget. They all want to know, of course, what I'm referring to, and all I've been saying is that it's a fantastic film they need to see. Some of them saw *Tiananmen* in Cannes, but truthfully I think Lau Lau's new cut will be superior and I think they'll appreciate it all the more."

"So you've seen it?" Silvana asked.

"No, but he has described to me in detail what he's done."

"How many critics and people of influence do you think will be there?" Hines asked.

"I'll be disappointed if those that really matter don't show. I don't mean to sound egotistical, but over the years I've developed a reputation and a following, and if I say a film needs to be seen, I'm listened to. The fact that it is as yet unidentified has created additional buzz."

"We're grateful for everything Harris has done," said Ava. "We even offered to compensate him for his time and trouble, but he refused to take anything."

"This has been a labour of love," he said.

"When and how will the announcement about the screenings happen?" asked Silvana.

"Harris has written a story for the *Tribune* that will break at midnight, Pacific Time, tonight. His work is syndicated, so the reach will be much farther than the *Tribune*'s subscribers," Ava said, turning to Patricia Nolan. "Why don't you explain the rest of the program?"

"We've reserved space for the print ads, and we'll be sending the copy out after six this evening. The television and radio ads will start at six tomorrow morning and run all day. We'll be active on every social media platform and use them to provide links to Harris's story. The emails will be sent immediately after Harris's story breaks. All of the ads and the emails refer to the next seven days as the North American premiere week for *Tiananmen*, with the first screening being the actual premiere. We'll have a red carpet in front of the Westwood, and an area roped off for phototaking and interviews," she said, and then smiled. "We can't duplicate Cannes, but we'll provide a bit of pizzazz."

"Our hope is to catch Top of the Road by surprise, and hopefully delay any possibility of immediate legal action," Ava said.

"I have to say I'm surprised that you've been able to keep a lid on this," Silvana said. "With so many people involved, it's a minor miracle that word didn't leak out."

"I think that speaks to the quality and integrity of the people we're working with," said Ava.

"Well, when the lid comes off, I expect there will be a whirlwind of activity," said Martineau, and he turned to Patricia Nolan. "Am I wrong to suspect there will be tremendous interest from the media?"

"We certainly hope there is, and we are organized to handle it. I and my staff will be at the Peninsula hotel with Chen tomorrow, but simply to help co-ordinate. He's the lead spokesperson. I'm sure there will be some requests to speak to Fai, Silvana, and Lau Lau, but Chen will be deciding who speaks to whom. And, of course, he'll act as Lau Lau's translator if that need arises," she said. "Any legal questions will be directed to Harold."

"And I've left my day wide open so that I'm readily available if needed," Hines said.

"What time is the first screening?" Silvana asked.

"Seven o'clock tomorrow night, and then at eleven, three, and seven for the next seven days," Ava said, looking around the table. "Is there anything else anyone wants to add or ask?" When there was no reply, she said, "Then we'll see some of you in the morning and the rest of you at the Westwood tomorrow evening."

"Including spouses and partners, there will be ten of us at the cinema from our firm," Hines said. "I'm anxious to see the film that's causing the Chinese government so much aggravation. Not much seems to rattle them these days, and I'm pleased to be part of something that might."

"Well, I think that concludes things. My thanks to everyone, and here's wishing us the very best of luck for tomorrow and the next seven days," said Ava.

32

AN EVENING WHICH AVA HAD EXPECTED WOULD BE interminably slow while they waited for the Harris Jones's article to be published turned out to be anything but.

After leaving the Hines and Ford offices, Ava, Fai, Silvana, and Chen had several drinks at the Peninsula's bar. When Chen left to go to the airport to meet Lau Lau, Ava and the other women walked down Santa Monica Boulevard to Joss Cuisine, a Chinese restaurant they had discovered and now frequented. They had made a reservation for their first visit, but when the owner saw Pang Fai she almost swooned and told them that they needn't worry about making another; there was a table waiting for them anytime they chose to come.

Accompanied by two bottles of Chardonnay, they spent almost two hours enjoying Peking duck, Alaskan king crab in a clay pot, a crispy whole lychee autumn fish, and two Maine lobsters smothered in ginger and scallions and resting on a bed of homemade noodles. As they ate, they chatted about the week that lay ahead. They were uniformly nervous, if only because no one knew for certain how it would proceed. Ava's fervent hope was that the work done by Harris

Jones and Make Them Dream would cause Top of the Road sufficient embarrassment that they would do nothing to prevent the screenings. But if they did, she took some comfort in the fact they had capable lawyers and a sound strategy.

At one point, though, the conversation addressed the more long-term consequences in a way that made Ava slightly uncomfortable. It was initiated by Fai, who asked Silvana if she was worried about continuing in the long-running role she had in a Hong Kong–based soap opera.

"The show is on hiatus right now. We're scheduled to start shooting in a few months. I expect to be there on set," Silvana said without much enthusiasm, then looked around the table. "Mind you, after what happened to Chen in Bangkok…"

"They wouldn't dare try anything with you in Hong Kong. You're too big a star, and Hong Kong and its people still have rights," Fai said.

"Rights that seem to be diminishing by the day," Silvana said.

Ava touched her lightly on the back of the hand. "Tell me," she said softly. "Do you ever regret that you took on the role in *Tiananmen*?"

"When I was in Bangkok by myself, not knowing what had happened to Chen and hardly able to sleep, that's one of the things I thought about constantly. Part of me did regret the decision, but then I told myself that after more than twenty years of playing the same stereotypical roles, I had finally been given the chance to show I have more to give as an actor.

"You know, I loved every day on the set with Lau Lau and Fai. I've never been so happy or felt so much satisfaction practising my craft. And when I saw the finished product, I was so proud that I was able to contribute to it. No one can ever take that away from me," she said, her voice breaking ever so slightly. "And then, of course, I met Chen, a man I love wholeheartedly. He and I haven't talked about our future, but if we have one together, it isn't going to be in China, and unfortunately Hong Kong may be as inhospitable."

"I think…" Fai began, only to stop when Ava's phone rang.

"Yes," Ava answered.

"This is Chen. I'm in a taxi with Lau Lau and we're on our way to the Peninsula."

"Have you briefed him on everything that's planned?"

"I have, and he's pleased with our efforts."

"Let me have a word with him," said Ava.

"*Wei*," Lau Lau said seconds later.

"Welcome to L.A. We are anxious to see you."

"I feel the same way about you guys."

"Listen, we're in a Chinese restaurant close to the hotel. Would you like us to get you some takeout? And ask Chen the same question."

"He ate at the airport while he was waiting for me, and the crew on my EVA Air flight spoiled me with food. Flying first-class all the time will make me fat."

"I can't imagine you ever being fat."

"Fat-headed, maybe," Lau Lau said with a laugh.

"It's good to hear you so happy," Ava said.

"I appreciate everything you're trying to do with the film in L.A., and in a strange way I'm pleased that we ran into this problem," he said. "It gave me a chance to revisit and rethink what I'd shot. I honestly believe that what we're going to show in L.A. is a better film than the one we screened in Cannes."

"I can't pretend to understand your creative process, but I absolutely trust your judgement."

"Thanks, but I'm still a little worried about what Fai and Silvana might think about the changes I made."

"I'm sure they'll be okay with them."

"But I don't want them to see them for the first time tomorrow night," he said. "I brought the new version with me on a memory stick. I would like everyone to see it tonight."

"That's a great idea, we'll do that," said Ava.

Lau Lau paused for a moment, and then said, "Thank you."

"We're leaving here in a few minutes. I booked a suite for you at the hotel. Call me after you've settled in and we'll decide where to see the film."

"Talk to you then."

Ava put down her phone and saw Fai and Silvana looking intently at her.

"What's going on?" Fai asked.

"Lau Lau wants to show the recut film to us tonight. He seems nervous about how you and Silvana will react to it."

"He can't have changed it that much," Silvana said.

"I have no idea," Ava said. "But it will help get us to midnight."

"I'm anxious to see what he's done," said Fai. "He was always tinkering right up to the last minute with his early films, and to my mind they were all the better for it."

Fifteen minutes later, the group left Joss Cuisine and walked back to the hotel. When they got there, they went to their respective suites to wait for Chen and Lau Lau. Ava barely had time to go to the bathroom and change into jeans and a T-shirt before the room phone rang.

"Lau Lau is here in my suite. Come and join us," Chen said.

Ava took a bottle of Pinot Grigio from the mini-bar, and she and Fai made their way down the single flight of stairs.

When they reached Chen's floor, they saw him standing in the open doorway of the suite.

"Come on in," Chen said when they reached him. "Lau Lau is trying to connect his memory stick to the television."

Inside the suite, Lau Lau was in front of the television with a remote control. He looked up when they arrived. "This shouldn't take too long."

"I didn't know you were so technical," Fai said.

"I've been learning," he said without looking up.

The furniture in the suite had been rearranged so that two sofas and three chairs faced the television.

"I need to open this wine," Ava said.

Moments later they were all facing the television with glasses of wine in hand.

Lau Lau seemed to be struggling, and Ava began to doubt he was going to be able to transfer the movie to the television. Then he stood with his arms raised. "There, it's done," he said, and looked at his audience. "You know, I'm as nervous right now as I was in Cannes."

"You're among friends," Ava said.

"Yes, but friends whose judgement I trust, and who I know will be honest with me."

33

THE FILM NOW RAN FOR THREE HOURS AND TWENTY-
five minutes, and like the first time she saw it in Cannes,
time stood still for Ava. The others were equally caught in its
spell, and no one left their seats. The only movements were
when wine was poured, and during several scenes when tears
flowed and tissues were reached for.

Ava had no difficulty identifying the scenes Lau Lau had
inserted. Both were rather long, but she understood what he
was trying to do and thought his instincts were correct and
that he had definitely succeeded in strengthening the film.

The first scene was set in a large boardroom, where the
leaders of China's military and some senior politicians
discussed what to do about the ongoing — and seemingly
expanding — demonstrations being held in Tiananmen
Square. In the first cut that debate had been somewhat trun-
cated, and the decision to send in troops had been almost
perfunctory. Now Lau Lau had opened it up so that it was
more far-reaching in terms of the available options. As it
went it on, though, the positions of the people opposed to
dispatching troops — like the general played by Fai — were

rejected, and in fact they found themselves having to defend their patriotism. It was made obvious that the final decision was based on one thing — the need to maintain the government's power — and so the order was given to use military force to drive the protestors from the square, to arrest and jail the organizers, and to do whatever else was necessary to ensure that protests did not recur.

The scene closed with Fai's military superior speaking to her after the meeting. He told her that he was disappointed in her, and that unless she displayed a clear change in attitude her career was at risk. Fai responded by saying she just couldn't understand why unarmed students were seen as dangerous to the system.

He stared at her and then shook his head as if she had already said too much. "We can't allow dissent to damage or impede the progress this country has made," he said. "Even one dissenter is one dissenter too many. The direction we've been given is clear. They have to be permanently removed as a threat."

The second major addition was set in the square on the night of the massacre. The cameras tracked a young man and woman as they bravely tried to confront the first onslaught of tanks and troops. Realizing they were hopelessly outmatched and seeing the violence the troops were perpetrating on the demonstrators, the couple then fled to find safety. Except there was none; every street leading from the square was cordoned off, and as they ran from one to the next, their panic increased. Eventually they found themselves in a side street not much bigger than an alley, and thought momentarily that they might get away. That was when the rumble of a tank was heard. They turned and saw it rolling towards them. The young man stepped in front of his companion to face it. He held up his hand, asking it to stop. It did, briefly, before starting towards him again. The woman pressed her back against a wall, but he stayed rooted to a spot in the middle of the street, unflinching, his hand held up until the tank crushed him.

Lau Lau didn't show gore. The camera stayed on the man until it was obvious he was going to be killed, and then switched to the woman. She didn't scream or become frantic. She simply closed her eyes as her face collapsed, and slid limply to the ground. Then a shot rang out, and the white blouse she was wearing turned red.

Ava flinched and felt tears welling in her eyes. The deaths had been unpredictable and so cruel.

When the film ended, they sat in silence for at least a minute, everyone lost in their own thoughts, and then Silvana said, "That scene with the boy and girl was brilliant but I also found it shocking. Will you tell me why you added it?"

"It was shot early in production, and I found it almost melodramatic so I left it out. But as I kept thinking about the film, I began to believe that by focusing on the troop and tank movement on a larger scale, I had perhaps muted the human element. I'm sure all of you remember the photo of the young man standing alone in Tiananmen Square, in front of a tank?"

"Who can forget it?" Chen said.

"No one knows what happened to him, but I decided to recreate it on a smaller scale, and that was part of the initial impetus for that scene. The other was that I wanted to touch people more directly. A tank crashing into a crowd of people is horrendous, but it's hard to identify with. Seeing it go over one defenceless man you've watched running for his life and who is no danger to anyone personalizes it."

"But why shoot the girl?" Ava asked.

"She saw what happened, so how could they allow her to live? She'd tell someone what they did."

"I think you're right in terms of how they would react," Chen said. "But what was the impetus for the other scene, with Fai?"

"I felt that I might have been unfair in the first cut. From what I've read, there was considerable opposition in the party and the military to such an aggressive intervention, and evidently the debate went on for weeks. All I wanted to show was that there was a pro-reform faction within the party. It was, after all, the death of Hu Yaobang, the leader of that faction and a high-ranking official, that triggered the first demonstrations," Lau Lau said. "I may not be in agreement with the current regime, and I may accept that I have to live outside of China to be safe, but I can't believe that there aren't people inside the government — as there were then — opposed to what's going on."

There was silence again, and then Lau Lau asked, "Tell me what you honestly think. Have the changes diminished my film?"

"No, it is better," Fai said, reaching for his hand.

"I am more proud than ever to be associated with it," said Chen.

"I agree, but as I was watching it I became scared," said Silvana.

"Why, because of the China Movie Syndicate threat?" Fai asked.

"No — as I was watching, I couldn't stop thinking about

Hong Kong. According to the handover agreement with the British, the Chinese government has to leave policing to local authorities for another twenty-five years or so, but they still find a way to use the police, paid thugs, and the courts to shut down protests and arrest and jail the leaders of Hong Kong's democracy movements. One by one, they're eliminating our other liberties and slowly strangling the voices of anyone who doesn't toe the official government line. If it's that bad now, how much worse is it going to be when they have total unrestrained control? Are we going to have tanks running over unarmed civilians?"

"I share your fears about Hong Kong, but twenty-five years is a long time. Things can change, even in China," said Ava. "It starts with people being aware of what was and what is. Films like ours at least keep a part of history alive and meaningful."

"All of this talk . . ." Chen said, only to be interrupted by his phone ringing. He looked at the incoming number and picked it up. "Harris, how are you?"

Chen listened for a minute, and then said, "Everyone is here with me now. I'll pass the message along . . . and yes, of course I'll call you after we read it."

"What did Harris want?" Ava asked after he hung up.

"His story is dropping in ten minutes, which is earlier than he thought. He wanted to let us know we can see it online then. If none of you object, I'd like us to be together when we read it. It feels like something we should be sharing as a team," said Chen.

"I totally agree," said Ava, and held up an empty wine bottle. "But I wouldn't mind something to drink while we do it."

Minutes later, with bottles of Pinot Grigio and Cabernet Sauvignon opened, they sat facing Chen's laptop, which he had put on the coffee table.

"Did Harris discuss with you the thrust of his column?" Ava asked Chen as they waited.

"He's going to focus on the Chinese government's attempts to silence any creative expression they find objectionable, and the deplorable fact that an American company is prepared to take money to sacrifice a magnificent film, the principle of freedom of expression, and their own integrity in order to accommodate them," Chen said.

"Those are big-issue positions," said Ava.

"I can honestly say that's how Harris thinks. He isn't someone who nitpicks. He looks at the world in the broadest possible manner, and what is going on between Top of the Road and the Syndicate disgusts him."

"He's a tremendous ally," Fai said.

"But only because he believes in Lau Lau and the film. He wouldn't go to the extent he has if he didn't think the work deserved it," said Chen.

"Check the website again," Silvana said to Chen.

He did, and then said, "Wow."

Jones's story took up almost the entire front page of the *London Tribune*. The headline read: CHINA'S ATTEMPT TO KILL FILM MASTERPIECE DEMANDS RESISTANCE.

"Why don't you read it to us," Silvana said.

In English that sometimes faltered, but never badly, it took Chen five minutes to read Jones's praise for the film, a recap of its success in Cannes, and details of the distribution agreement BB had signed with Top of the Road. From that point on, it was a complete indictment of the China Movie

Syndicate's attitude towards the film, and Top of the Road's willingness to sabotage the very film they had agreed to distribute. Highlighted in darker lettering were key extracts from the contract that the Syndicate and Top of the Road had signed. Jones's article ended with him urging the entire film community to stand behind and support the screening of *Tiananmen* at the Westwood Revue Cinema in the coming week. Jones even included the contact information for the Westwood and the screening times.

"We couldn't have asked for more," Ava said.

"But is it enough to force the Syndicate to back down?" Silvana asked.

"I sure hope so," said Chen. "Now, I should call Harris and tell him how pleased we are with this."

"And I'll call Harold Hines and Patricia Nolan to let them know the action is about to start," said Ava.

34

AVA WOKE WITH A START WHEN HER PHONE RANG. SHE felt like she had only just fallen asleep, and a quick glance at the bedside clock, which read seven a.m., showed she had only slept for about five hours. She felt a touch of irritation, but then remembered where she was and why she was there. She picked up the phone.

"Yes," she said in a thick voice.

"I know it's early, and I'm sorry for waking you, but I've been up all night and I couldn't wait any longer to share things with you," Chen said.

"What's been going on?"

"Harris's article was picked up by just about every major media outlet in the world," he said excitedly. "I've been bombarded with requests for interviews and comments from me, Lau Lau, Fai, and Silvana. I talked to a few old friends before I realized I couldn't keep up."

"Have you contacted Patricia?" Ava asked, any feeling of tiredness now dissipated.

"I just finished talking to her and passed on the information. She'll respond to the requests on our behalf and start scheduling interviews," he said.

"As far as I know, Fai hasn't had any calls here, but she's using a Canadian number now."

"That's a good thing, because she would have been inundated as well."

"This is all so encouraging," Ava said. "I had a hunch we'd get support, but this is happening much more quickly than I imagined."

"On the negative side, I think we're going to need support from Harold Hines as well, and sooner rather than later," he said, his tone more restrained.

"Why do you say that?"

"Larry Christensen called me ten minutes ago. I wasn't going to answer, but I figured we were better off knowing what he had to say," said Chen. "In the back of my mind, I even nursed the idea that he might be embarrassed enough to be apologetic that we had been forced to go this route."

"I take it that he wasn't."

"Far from it. In between swearing at me, he told me that his legal team was preparing to prevent the film being shown, and when that was done, he would take great pleasure in ruining me personally."

"I imagine Mo is pushing him very hard," said Ava.

"I agree. Should I call Harold to let him know about Christensen?"

"There's nothing he can do at this time of day, especially when we don't know what the other side is planning legally. His office opens at eight, call him then."

"All right, but you may have to be the point person at times today, since I'm going to be tied up doing interviews."

"I would prefer to stay in the background, but if you need me, I'll be available."

"I do hope you aren't needed, and that Christensen was just venting for the sake of it."

"Well, if Harris's article has him venting, how is he going to react when he sees Patricia's email and the ads?" Ava said. "This could be a crazy day."

"I don't care what he has to say. After all these months of waiting for something to happen with the film, I'll take crazy all week long."

Ava laughed. "Me too. Stay in touch, and if anything important happens, call me right away. Fai and I will be here to help in any way we can."

"That sounded rather interesting," Fai said from the bed after Ava had hung up.

"Harris's article is getting a fabulous reaction. Chen already has more people trying to reach him than he can handle. I know you haven't told a lot of people about your new phone number, but I'm still surprised that you haven't had some calls."

"My phone is off, let me turn it on," Fai said, reaching for it. A moment later, she said, "Wow, nine calls and about twenty texts, but none of them are from China."

"That isn't surprising, I'm quite sure that they've blocked any access to Harris's article."

Fai scanned the texts. "Most are from friends working in other parts of Asia, and some of them are worried about how the Syndicate is going to respond. I should answer them."

"While you start doing that, I'm going to make coffee. Do you want one now?"

"Yes, and maybe we should order a pot from room service. It sounds like it could be the kind of morning for a lot of coffee."

Ava made two coffees, called room service to order a pot, and then sat at the desk and opened her laptop. She accessed the digital version of the *Tribune*, saw immediately that the top trending story was Harris's, and when she scanned down to the end of the story to the 'share this article' link, saw that six hundred and twelve subscribers already had. She closed the *Tribune* tab, went to her email, and had started to write to Jones when she saw she had just received an email from Patricia Nolan. It read: *Call me when you can.*

What had happened to trigger that request, Ava wondered? She dialled Nolan's cell.

"Ava, thank you for calling so quickly," Nolan answered. "Chen wanted you to know that the emails were sent last night to the Academy members."

"That's great, and Chen said he spoke to you about the response that Harris's article has elicited."

"The response from overseas is amazing, and we're already seeing the same here in the U.S. Every major newspaper on the east coast has already run with the story, and we're in touch with producers from the network morning shows."

"Now what we need is to get as many Academy members to the Westwood as possible."

"The nine thousand emails were nine thousand invitations. Our fingers are crossed that between them, the media attention, our ads, and the opportunity to do the right thing, we'll get a fair share of those living in southern California."

"Let's hope we do," said Ava. "When do you plan to be here?"

"My staff and I are following up with those who contacted Chen to arrange interviews with the various members of the film's team. We aim to be at the hotel by nine with the schedule. One of my people will sit in on every interview and tape it so we have a record."

"How long will all that take?"

"We'll try to finish the interviews by three, which should give everyone a chance to relax and grab an early bite to eat. The cinema is only a five-minute taxi ride from the hotel, so if we leave around six fifteen that should provide ample time for interviews there, and the photographers. What is Fai going to wear?"

"The same gorgeous cheongsam she wore at Cannes."

"I saw a picture of it. It's stunning, but it is slightly unusual for an actor to wear the same dress to two premieres," Nolan said.

"It brought her so much luck in Cannes that she chose to wear it again. She's very superstitious that way."

"I quite understand," said Nolan. "Now, I'll leave you to your morning. I still have a lot of calls I need to make."

"See you later," said Ava, and then glanced at Fai, who was still sending texts.

Fai looked up. "Everyone who knows Mo is telling me not to even think about going back to China."

"We knew that was the reality when the film was screened at Cannes. Nothing has changed."

"I know, they're just pointing out that continuing to poke the dragon the way we are is aggravating an already hostile relationship."

"Are they suggesting that we shouldn't be doing it?"

"No, in fact most of them compliment Chen, Lau Lau, and me for having the courage to take on the Syndicate. They're just telling me to be careful."

There was a knock at the suite's door. "That'll be our pot of coffee," Ava said.

A few minutes later they went to the balcony and sat with

freshly filled cups. Their relationship had reached the point that neither of them felt the need to talk just for the sake of it, so they sat quietly for fifteen minutes basking in the early morning sun and watching the garden below come to life.

"I'm nervous, but nervous in an excited way, not a fearful one," Fai said suddenly. "My only worry is that the American media won't respond as positively to our film as the Europeans did."

"Why wouldn't they? A great film is a great film."

"I know, but Lau Lau's others were only shown in arthouse cinemas here. They were never mainstream."

"I don't think a week's screening in the Westwood qualifies as mainstream."

"No, but with the ads and all the publicity we're generating, we're treating it as if it was."

"And why shouldn't we? We aren't going to attract the kind of crowd we want by being low-key."

Fai smiled. "One of the things I love about you is the way you go all out to support anything or anyone you believe in."

Ava leaned towards Fai and they kissed.

"What are you going to do today?" Fai asked. "Hanging around the suite listening to me answering the same questions over and over again won't be the least bit interesting."

Ava shook her head. "If Uncle was here, he would take me to the Santa Anita racetrack. If May was, she'd insist we go to Rodeo Drive to shop. On my own, I tend to do things that are more boring."

"Such as?"

"I think I'll go to the Getty."

"Who or what is that?"

"The who is J. Paul Getty, a deceased American billionaire

who lived in Italy and collected art and relics," Ava said. "The what is the Getty Museum, to which he left the things he'd collected. He also, I believe, contributed over a billion dollars towards its creation and maintenance."

"What kind of art?"

"Pre-nineteenth century, including painters like Van Gogh, Munch, and Cézanne, and then much further back than that."

"I know very little about art."

"I'm not pretending that I do. I simply enjoy looking at it," Ava said, and then glanced at her phone as it rang and saw Noel Martineau's name. "Good morning," she answered.

"And what a fine morning it is," he said.

"So you've heard about the reaction to Harris's story?"

"I've not only heard about it, I'm experiencing it," he said. "We've had so many online reservations that I was afraid our website was going to collapse. Tonight's premiere is completely sold out, as are most of the other evening screenings."

"That's fabulous."

"This town knows how to get behind a cause, and Harris and the work Patricia Nolan has done have quickly turned *Tiananmen* into that."

"I didn't expect this. I know we hoped for it, but this goes well beyond my expectations."

"Just goes to show that the good guys can sometimes win."

"Thank you for everything you've done to contribute," said Ava.

"I'm just pleased I had a chance to be part of the supporting cast," said Martineau. "I'm looking forward to seeing you and the film tonight."

"More good news?" Fai asked with a smile as Ava ended the call.

"Yes, but my natural inclination when things are going this well is to expect something nasty to happen," Ava said. "Uncle used to tell me he'd never met anyone who couldn't accept good things happening as much as me. I always thought it was just my survival instinct telling me not to take them for granted."

35

AVA'S INSTINCT TO NOT TAKE THINGS FOR GRANTED was justified at eleven, when Chen phoned her from the hotel.

She was in nearby Brentwood at the Getty Museum, looking in awe at Rodin's bust of John the Baptist, when the call came.

"Harold Hines just contacted me. Top of the Road has filed for an injunction to stop the film being shown. They are citing breach of contract, and somehow they managed to find a judge who is willing to rule on their filing today," he blurted out.

"Shit, but I guess we had to expect they'd try something, and I'm sure the Syndicate is behind it," Ava said.

"I was hoping that impact of Harris's article would embarrass Top of the Road enough that they would prefer to lie low. Taking us on like this makes them look even more despicable."

"They're being paid enough not to care about what anyone thinks. Besides, you know better than most that there's no way the Syndicate would let the film be shown without a fight. I'm sure they've been very direct in telling Christensen and his partners what they need to do."

"Still, I'm disappointed."

"So am I, but we've got to deal with it, and we have an excellent lawyer and a strong case so there's nothing to be gained by expecting a negative outcome."

"You're right. I need to start thinking more positively."

"Are you going to the hearing?"

"I'd rather not, which is another reason I'm calling you. It's scheduled for two-thirty. Harold would like one of us to go with him, and my afternoon is jam-packed. If it was simply interviews with me, I'd cancel them. But Lau Lau is in serious demand and he's very uncomfortable with a stranger interpreting for him."

Ava wasn't sure that was Chen's real reason for not going, but saw no need to argue with him. "I'll go. Where is the hearing being held?"

"In the Orange County Superior Court, and that's another issue, but I'll let Harold explain it to you. You should meet him at his office, and you need to get there quickly. You can go to the court together from there."

"Tell him I'm on my way," said Ava. "It'll take me about half an hour to get to his office."

"Thanks, Ava, and I'm about to call Harris and Patricia Nolan to give them a heads-up as well. It may not be too late to get some journalists to attend."

Her estimate of how long it would take to get to Hines's office hadn't factored in the heavy traffic her taxi encountered, and it was almost noon when she arrived. She was ushered into the boardroom, where Hines and two of his associates waited. Hines stood as soon as he saw her.

"Thank goodness you finally made it. I thought we were going to have to leave without you," he said.

"I thought the hearing was at two-thirty."

"It is, but the Superior Court in Orange County is about an hour-and-fifteen-minute drive from here," he said as he gathered papers from the table and then turned to a man who appeared to be in his twenties. "Jack, will you get the car now and bring it around to the building entrance? We'll meet you there."

As the man hurried off, Ava said to Hines, "Why Orange County, and why the Superior Court?"

"I know the term 'Superior Court' sounds grandiose, but it's actually the basic-level court in the state. As for Orange County, one of the principals of Top of the Road resides in the county, and that qualifies the court there to rule on the injunction request."

"On what grounds are they seeking the injunction?"

"I'm bringing copies of their submission with me. You can read it in the car," Hines said. "Now, we should get going."

"I'm quite ignorant about the American legal system, but I'm assuming this will be a hearing with a judge, and nothing more than that."

"That's correct. Although it will be held in a court, this isn't a trial, it's a hearing. Both sides will get a chance to present their position; I expect the judge will ask some questions, and then he has the right to make a ruling on the spot or to reserve his decision if he feels he needs more time to consider the facts."

Five minutes later, Ava found herself climbing into the back seat of a black Lincoln Navigator. Hines sat in the front with Jack, but as the car started to move he turned to face Ava and handed her a piece of paper. "As expected, they're claiming that BB Productions has breached its contract with Top of the Road."

Ava read the document quickly and saw that one of Christensen's partners, Justin Black, was applying on behalf of Top of the Road, and that he was using a lawyer named Robert Sanders. "I thought Eli Brand handled all of the legal matters for Top of the Road," she said.

"Sanders has his office in Santa Ana, which is where the Orange County courthouse is. He and whatever judge we draw will most likely know each other. I guess Top of the Road thought using local connections would help, especially when that county's court system has a reputation for being protective of county-based businesses," Hines said. "The fact they were able to get a judge to hear this so quickly is further proof of that."

"Is the system really that parochial?"

"That's an interesting choice of word, and in this case it's apt," Hines said. "Orange County has been hardcore Republican for more than half a century, and part of that mentality has been mistrust of anyone not from there. The fact that everyone associated with *Tiananmen* is Chinese, or at least of Chinese origin, won't work in our favour, but I'm hopeful that will be mitigated by Top of the Road's side deal with the China Movie Syndicate."

The car left the streets of Beverly Hills and headed onto Highway 105. Ava saw a sign indicating Santa Ana was forty-nine miles away. She read Sanders's submission again. It simply stated that Top of the Road had exclusive distribution rights to *Tiananmen*, and that those rights were in immediate danger of being violated. It went on to ask the court to issue a cease-and-desist order against BB Productions and the Westwood Revue Cinema to prevent them showing the film in whole or in part. A copy of the contract between BB and Top of the Road was noted as being attached, but there was obviously no mention of the Syndicate.

"Well, it is brief and to the point," Ava said, handing the paper back to Hines.

"I'm quite sure that Sanders will use more descriptive language when he presents his case," said Hines.

"I'm sure you'll be a match for him."

"I appreciate your confidence, but we shouldn't take anything for granted."

"You sound like me," Ava said, smiling. "So, tell me, what are our options if we lose?"

"We can appeal, but that does take time."

"And we don't have a lot of time," she said.

"No, we don't."

"But we'd still have the option of going ahead with the screenings, wouldn't we?" she asked. "Assuming of course we were prepared to pay whatever penalty the judge imposed for ignoring his order."

"Ignoring a judge's order is not something — as a lawyer in this state — I can recommend," Hines said. "The judge could impose a stiff fine or even threaten jail time, although I don't think the latter option would be on the table. And it isn't just BB who would be at risk. Considerable pressure could be brought upon Noel Martineau and the Westwood."

"We would make sure that Noel would be well looked after," Ava said. "But this is all hypothetical anyway, because I can't believe you're going to lose."

Hines shook his head in an amused way. "If I'm going to win then I need to take a bit more time to prepare my talking points. So excuse me while I work."

The rest of the drive was spent in silence, which suited Ava. Despite her words of confidence, she knew there was the possibility that the other side could win. She hadn't exaggerated when she'd told Hines that she had little experience with the American legal system. From what she did know, it struck her as being quite political and inconsistent. But what she had no way of knowing was whether that would work in their favour. If Sanders and the judge were friends, that could hurt them; but if Hines could exploit the angle of China trying to control what could be seen on a movie screen in America, that could benefit them. What she was certain of was that, with Hines, they were in capable hands; and regardless of how the judge ruled, she was determined that the screenings would go ahead.

Traffic flowed well, and they reached Santa Ana just before one-thirty. Jack parked near the three-storey, red-sandstone, red-tile-roofed courthouse that reminded Ava of Toronto's Old City Hall. As they walked towards it, she saw Harris Jones standing under one of three arches at the entrance. He was talking to a woman and a man, and Ava sensed they were colleagues. Off to one side, a TV truck was parked. "It looks like we have some media here," she said.

"That can't hurt us," Hines said.

"Hello everyone," Harris said as they approached. "The other side arrived fifteen minutes ago. I had spoken to Christensen on the phone but never met him in person. He wasn't particularly friendly when I introduced myself."

"Who else was with him?" Ava asked.

"It was four men, none of whom I know. One of them, interestingly, was Chinese."

"I'll try to talk to him," Ava said.

"Please, don't do anything brash," Hines said gently. "When we get inside, you'll see the lawyers will take seats at desks on either side of the court. The Top of the Road team may choose to sit with their lawyer. If they don't, they'll have seats on benches behind the railing that separates the court from spectators. I'm assuming you'll be on a bench."

"That's correct."

"Then let's go inside and get settled."

What Ava knew about U.S. courtrooms had been gleaned from various films and crime shows. The one in Santa Ana didn't disappoint in that it looked exactly like the ones she'd seen on TV. She figured the room would accommodate several hundred people, and to her surprise there was a scattering of maybe thirty already there.

She took a seat in the second row, as Hines and Jack walked to the desk on the left, unpacked their briefcases, organized their papers, and sat back to wait. The plaintiff's desk was as yet unoccupied, but a moment later a door behind and off to one side of the judge's bench opened, and from it emerged Larry Christensen, Eli Brand, two men who Ava assumed were the lawyer Sanders and Justin Black, and a forty-something Chinese man wearing a suit that looked expensive and custom-made. Ava saw Hines scowl, and watched him turn to Jack and mutter something.

The door on the other side of the judge's bench then opened, and a man and a woman in black robes came in and took up their positions on a dais. Ava guessed the judge's bench was a couple of feet above the courtroom, and the clerks' dais about six inches.

Ava watched as Christensen, Brand, and the two other Americans sat at the plaintiff's desk. The Chinese man sat on a bench two rows behind them, parallel to Ava. She eyed him. Upon closer inspection, the light grey suit looked like cashmere. He wore a white shirt, and a pink and blue tie that she thought was a Canali. He was cleanly shaven, his hair was neatly trimmed, and his overall appearance was immaculate.

She searched her memory, wondering if she had seen him at the China Movie Syndicate offices or at anytime with Mo, but couldn't place him. *What the hell*, Ava thought as she left her row to sit in his, no more than three feet away from him.

"Excuse me, but do I know you?" she asked. "You look very familiar."

The question seemed to startle him, then he frowned and shook his head.

"I'm sure I've seen you in Hong Kong," she said, taking Jennie Kwong's Dynamic Accounting business card from her bag and offering it to him. "My firm represents some of the wealthiest people there. We must have crossed paths."

He glanced at the card. "My home is on the mainland," he said.

"So you are just visiting Los Angeles?"

"No, and now I'd appreciate being left alone."

Ava considered why a sophisticated mainland Chinese, presumably living in Los Angeles with no connection to the Syndicate, was in the company of Christensen and the others and had such an obvious interest in the proceedings. One thing came to mind.

"Oh, now I know where I've seen you," she said. "It was few months ago here in L.A., at a Chinese cultural event. You're the Chinese Consul General — or at least a senior official at the consulate."

The eyes that darted in her direction said she had guessed right, but all he said was "I would appreciate it if you would return to your own seat."

Ava nodded, left his row, and went to the railing. "Harold, I want to speak to you," she whispered.

He stood and approached her, looking slightly annoyed.

"I apologize if I'm disturbing you," she said.

"It isn't you. I think that the Top of the Road team had a private session with the judge as we were arriving. I'm furious, and what's worse is I can't do or say anything about it, and I can't let it affect me," he said. "What is it you want to say?"

"See the Chinese guy sitting behind them?"

"Yes."

"I think he's connected to the Chinese government."

"What makes you believe that?"

"Obviously the Syndicate didn't have enough time to get someone here, so it makes sense that the Chinese government would send a local representative to observe and probably give direction. Someone from the L.A. Consulate General is the logical choice. When I told him I thought he was *the* Consul General, he became quite nervous."

"Do you have his name?"

"No."

"But you're sure he's with their government?"

"No, but what do we have to lose by trying to find out?"

Hines smiled and shook his head. "What was it you did before you got into business?"

"My partner and I chased down large-scale debts. It was a job that taught you to read people, and I think I'm right about that guy over there."

"Okay, but I need something — at least a name — to go on."

"I'll see what I can find. There should be something on the consulate's website," Ava said, opening her phone.

"If you get a name and it turns out to be wrong, we'll look stupid and our case will take a major hit," Hines said. "On the other hand, if you're right, they've handed us a gift."

36

THE JUDGE'S NAME WAS CHANDLER. HE WAS RUDDY-
faced, had grey hair thinly combed over, a belly that pushed
his robe to its extremities, and an arrogant manner that Ava
took an immediate dislike to. He looked down at Harold
Hines and said, "I don't always respond to requests for injunc-
tions as quickly as this, but the actions of your client haven't
left me much choice. I have to tell you I don't appreciate it."

"Well, sir, I have to say that I *do* appreciate *your* diligence.
The sooner this attempt at censoring a film that speaks to
the horrors of events that took place in Beijing's Tiananmen
Square in 1989 is set aside, the sooner the world will have
a better understanding of what happened and why the
Chinese government so ferociously tries to keep it a secret."

"Mr. Hines, I will not allow this hearing to be turned into
a series of political diatribes," Chandler said. "I have been
presented with a contract that your client signed, and that
your client now seems prepared to violate. Can we please
stick to the basic facts at hand?" he said, and then looked at
the Top of the Road desk. "Mr. Sanders, why don't you tell
us why you brought this petition."

The thickly set man sitting next to Eli Brand rose from his chair. "Your Honour, my clients signed a contract to acquire the exclusive individual distribution rights for the film *Tiananmen* this past June. They paid ten million dollars for those rights. Since then, they have run into a number of marketing and distribution issues that have delayed the film's release, but those in no way have affected their determination to make it available to the widest possible audience. In their view, it is a matter of finding the right time with the right marketing plan. The unilateral, premature, and illegal release of the film that has been trumpeted in various media deprives my clients of their rights and of any chance to recoup their investment. We therefore request of this court that the defendants be ordered to cease and desist in any public display of the film."

Chandler looked at Harold Hines. "Do you dispute that Top of the Road paid ten million dollars for exclusive distribution rights?"

"No, but we maintain they cut a separate, illegal, side deal with the Chinese Movie Syndicate that in effect transferred control to the Syndicate — something which was specifically prohibited in the agreement," Hines said. "The Syndicate paid Top of the Road twelve million to delay distribution until some unspecified conditions permitted. The longer the delay, the more Top of the Road will be paid. A copy of that side deal has been detailed by the media, but I have a copy of it here if you wish to see it. So, it is our contention that it was Top of the Road that violated the terms of the contract and not BB Productions."

"Mr. Hines, I am a stickler when it comes to the interpretation of contract wording," Chandler said. "On the one hand we have a clear-cut purchase of distribution rights, wouldn't you agree?"

"I told you I do."

"And on the other, a rather vague request for reasons that may be entirely valid for Top of the Road to simply delay releasing the film," said Chandler. "On the surface, I'm not sure that Top of the Road violated any of the terms and conditions of the original contract."

"Your Honour —"

"No, Mr. Hines," Chandler said forcibly. "I am prepared to make a ruling."

Hines hesitated, and then turned to look at Ava. She passed him a slip of paper, which he quickly read.

"Before you do," Hines said, the slip still in his hand. "I would like to address the issue of the Chinese government trying to exert control over what Americans can and can't watch . . ."

"Don't make me repeat myself," Chandler warned.

Hines turned away from the judge, looked at the Chinese man sitting behind the Top of the Road table, and said. "Mr. Wang Ping, will you please stand up."

Ava saw a panicked look cross the man's face as he stared at Hines, but he didn't budge.

"You sir," Hines said, pointing a finger at him. "Please stand and identify yourself."

"This is ridiculous," Sanders said loudly. "I don't know what kind of game Mr. Hines thinks he's playing. All I know is that it is completely inappropriate."

"Mr. Hines, explain yourself," said Chandler.

"Certainly, Your Honour. This man's name is Wang Ping, and he is the Consul General for China in Los Angeles.

Anyone who was in this courtroom earlier saw that, rather than being simply an interested party to this hearing, Mr. Wang is a member of the Top of the Road team that is trying to subvert this film," said Hines. "What is more troubling, and which must be noted, is that the team, including Mr. Wang, was seen leaving the judge's chambers before this hearing began. I have no idea what was discussed behind closed doors, and I have no way of knowing if Mr. Wang was introduced as Consul General, but there can be no doubt that his presence creates at least the perception that the Chinese government is so determined to prevent this film being shown that they are prepared to attempt to pervert our legal system in order to do so."

Ava heard a babble of voices behind her, turned, and saw that virtually everyone in the courtroom was talking to someone near them. She saw Harris Jones grin and give her a thumbs-up. She turned back and saw Chandler glaring at Hines.

"What are you implying, and be careful when you answer," said Chandler.

"I am implying nothing in reference to your actions, sir. What I *am* suggesting is the secret insidious involvement of a senior Chinese official in matters that should be of no concern to him or his country."

Chandler continued to glare, but Ava saw that Hines remained calm and in control. Finally, the judge shifted his attention to the other side.

"Is this man who Mr. Hines says he is?" he asked.

Ava held her breath, surprised at the question and suddenly fearful of any answer other than "yes." If he wasn't Wang, she knew they were doomed.

Sanders stood. "Your Honour, this gentleman has an indirect affiliation with Top of the Road, but is here only as an interested observer. He has not participated in any of our legal discussions."

"Which is exactly what you told me when you were in my chambers," Chandler said. "But you haven't answered my question. Is he the Chinese Consul General, Wang Ping?"

"Your Honour, his position has no bearing—"

"Enough," Chandler said. "Answer the question."

"He is, but—"

"There will be no buts," said Chandler. "And I am now assuming that the indirect affiliation you mentioned is the agreement an arm of the Chinese government reached with your client with regards to the film *Tiananmen*; and that Mr. Wang is in fact here officially representing the Chinese government's interest."

"We don't deny the Chinese government has an interest, but we believe it is legitimate and entirely justifiable," Sanders said.

"Then why wasn't I told that you were representing the Chinese government as well as your declared clients?"

"Because we're not. We have been engaged by Top of the Road and not the Chinese government."

"But who is pulling the strings?" Chandler asked, and then quickly continued. "Don't bother answering that, we'd only be splitting hairs."

The courtroom was really buzzing now, and Ava imagined the media would descend on both sides when the hearing ended.

"Your Honour, if I may," Hines said as he stood. "I think it is now crystal clear that the Chinese government has decision-making control over the distribution of *Tiananmen*, and this is in clear violation — in spirit and in fact — of the agreement my clients signed with Top of the Road. We believe that agreement should be abrogated…"

"That may be true, but that goes beyond the purview of this hearing," Chandler said. "We're here to deal with the request for a cease and desist order."

"You are correct, of course, so we'll save that fight for another day, and I assure you that day will be coming soon," Hines said. "But in the meantime, there is a screening of *Tiananmen* scheduled for seven o'clock this evening. Is it Your Honour's decision that it can go ahead?"

Chandler looked annoyed at the question, and for a second Ava wondered if he might still find a way to support Top of the Road. She watched as he looked down and shuffled the papers on his desk as if stalling for time. A moment passed before he raised his head and glared at both tables.

"This is a complicated matter," he said finally. "There are implications in terms of diplomacy and international relations that go beyond a business contract. Given the nature of those implications, I feel it is only appropriate for me to consult with others, including people in our government, who might have a stake in my decision. I have thereby decided to reserve my decision until I've finished those consultations."

Ava saw Jack turn to Hines with a smile on his face, but Hines didn't see it because he was getting to his feet.

"Your Honour, I am assuming that your decision to reserve means that the film can be seen this evening?"

"Of course. Without a cease-and-desist order there is nothing to prevent it."

"Thank you, Your Honour."

Then it was Sanders's turn to stand and speak. "We respect but are disappointed with Your Honour's decision," he said. "Is it possible, though, to provide us with some idea of when a final ruling may be made?"

"No," Chandler said, and then banged his gavel. "This court is dismissed."

(37)

AVA HUNG BACK AT THE FRINGES OF THE CROWD OUT-
side the courthouse while Hines gave an interview to a TV
crew and answered questions from other journalists. Nearby,
Larry Christensen was performing the same task on behalf
of Top of the Road with Eli Brand at his side. At one point
Brand glanced in Ava's direction. She shrugged as if to say,
"What else could you have expected?"

She had phoned Chen as soon as she'd left the courthouse
and asked him to pass the news along to Fai, Lau Lau, and
Patricia Nolan. He was understandably ecstatic. Her other
call had been to Noel Martineau, and he was just as pleased.

When Hines finally disentangled himself from the media,
he, Ava, and Jack made their way to the Lincoln. No one
spoke until they were inside the car, and then it was Jack who
said, "Mr. Hines, I thought things like what just went down
in the courtroom were only seen in the old *Perry Mason*
TV show."

"Me too, but there's a first time for everything. And that
isn't false modesty. I've never done anything like that before,"
he said, and then turned to Ava. "How were you sure who

he was? I know you said you were good at reading people, but that was more than that."

"The level of paranoia that exists at the most senior levels of the Chinese government about what happened in Tiananmen Square is something Westerners can't comprehend. People, even those in Hong Kong, who try to keep its memory alive or memorialize those who died are commonly arrested and jailed. Given that level of sensitivity, it made sense that they would have someone at a senior level at a hearing as important as this. I mean, they've already paid millions to buy off Top of the Road, and they went as far as to reach into Thailand and bribe local officials to kidnap Chen and ship him back to China. If they had been successful, we probably would never have seen him again."

"I didn't know that about Chen. Are you serious?" Hines asked.

"Absolutely. The only reason he's in L.A. is that we paid the Thais far more to get him released than the Chinese had offered."

"Good grief."

"Anyway, to return to your question, as soon as I saw Wang my first instinct was that he was a government representative. And as I said earlier, I thought if he was then he had to be local. But what made me think that he could be *the* Consul General was the way he looked," she said. "That suit he was wearing had to cost four or five thousand dollars, and the tie was a Canali. That isn't the way a run-of-the-mill Chinese bureaucrat dresses. He's probably the son of a wealthy senior party member."

"And you actually found his name on their website?"

"I did."

"Was there a photo with it?"

"No."

"So it was a shot in the dark, and one that couldn't have been more timely," Hines said. "I'm convinced Chandler was about to rule in favour of Top of the Road."

"I thought so too. I thought the fix was in, and I was actually surprised at the way he reacted learning about Wang Ping."

"I think saying the fix was in is a touch extreme," Hines said. "Chandler is even more conservative than the normal Orange County conservative judge, and given that this was a dispute between a domestic business and a foreign one, I'm certain his basic inclination was to side with the local guys. But the fact he's a conservative doesn't mean he doesn't have integrity. I don't know why Top of the Road met with him, but I'm sure nothing as tawdry as money changing hands took place. The mistake they made was to lie to him, or at least not tell him the truth about Wang Ping. The moment he realized what was going on, and that it was happening in front of the media, he knew his reputation was in danger. He may have done nothing wrong, but if he had ruled in favour of Top of the Road that would have been the assumption."

"But couldn't he have dismissed their request instead of reserving his decision?"

Hines smiled. "He went one better. By reserving, he eliminated any chance Top of the Road had to appeal his decision. There can't be grounds for an appeal if there's no decision to appeal. And I'd bet a lot of money that it will be more than a week before anyone hears from him."

"Will that be deliberate?"

"I think it will."

"That changes my opinion about him."

"Give it another week before changing it entirely," Hines said as the car started to slow.

"We're running into some heavy traffic," Jack said.

"We should be all right as long as we don't have to stop," Hines said.

Ava's phone rang and she saw Fai's name. "Hi babe, how did your day go?"

"Well enough, but evidently not as good as yours. Everyone is thrilled that we won."

"I'll tell you all about it when I see you, but for now I'd rather hear in detail about your interviews."

They talked for another fifteen minutes, but Ava began to lose her concentration as the car was now coming to a full stop regularly.

"Are we going to make it to the hotel before six?" she asked.

"We should be okay, but don't expect to get there much sooner than that," Hines said.

"Fai, we're in traffic. If I don't get to the hotel on time, you should leave for the Westwood without me and I'll meet you there. If things get really bad, I'll call," Ava said.

The stop-and-go traffic continued for another ten minutes, then suddenly, as if a dam had burst, they began travelling near the speed limit.

"This is our lucky day," Hines said.

Ava's phone rang again and she saw Noel Martineau's name on the screen. She was surprised to hear from him so soon, and it was with a touch of trepidation that she answered. "Hi Noel, is everything okay?"

"No, we have a bit of a problem here."

"And that problem is?"

"There are about sixty young Chinese people demonstrating in front of the cinema," he said. "Actually, 'demonstrating' is a gentle word for it. They are loud, aggressive, and being verbally abusive. Right now they're taking it out on my staff or anyone who looks like they want to enter the building. I've tried to speak to them, but they just shout me down."

"I assume they're demonstrating against the fact we're going to be screening *Tiananmen*?"

"That's the long and the short of it. They say the film insults China and propagates lies that the West is all too ready to accept."

"Of course, they haven't seen the film."

"Correct, but I don't think that's a fact that matters."

"Have you thought of calling the police?"

"Ava, some films I've shown have been demonstrated against in the past. The police response is always the same — people have a right to protest as long as they aren't violent," he said.

"If they aren't being violent then what is your concern?"

"They're still being aggressive and abusive enough that they could scare away quite a few of this evening's customers. And frankly, it also isn't a good look when it's Chinese protesting about us showing the film."

"Then how about hiring a security team?"

"I don't know any security companies, and even if I did, I can't imagine one would be available at such short notice."

"I guess you're right, but there has to be some kind of solution. Let me think about it. I'll get back to you."

She hung up, and saw Hines had turned to look at her.

"That didn't sound like it was good news," he said.

Ava shook her head and told him what was going on at the Westwood. When she'd finished, it was Jack, and not

Hines, who said: "They're probably students from UCLA. Every time the university has a guest speaker who has criticisms or doubts about what's going on in China, a gang of Chinese students shows up to shout them down. Everyone assumes their tuition and expenses are being paid by the Chinese government. I imagine when the government says do this or do that, they feel obligated."

"How do you know that?" Ava asked.

"I went to the USC Gould School of Law before my internship with Hines and Ford. We had a few Chinese students in our year, and they were always part of the group that went to protest."

"What should we do about them?"

"I don't know what you can do. They don't back down easily, and they'll probably be at the Westwood for every screening. You might just have to gut it out."

"It'll turn off a lot of people who would otherwise attend."

"I'm sure that's their intention," Jack said.

"And the day was going so well," Ava sighed, and then added: "There is one option I could explore, but it would have to be handled very delicately."

"Surely anything is worth a try," Hines said.

"You shouldn't say that so casually. If it's even possible, it could turn around and bite us in the rear," Ava said. "But what the hell, I'll call Shanghai and give it a go."

"Shanghai?"

"Yes, and I apologize in advance for the fact I'll be speaking Mandarin."

"No need for that."

Ava calculated the time difference between L.A. and Shanghai, and figured that Xu would probably be eating breakfast. In addition to being a Mountain Master, Xu was also chairman of the triad societies, and his influence went well beyond Shanghai. It was in that capacity he could influence the events in L.A.

The phone rang twice before Auntie Grace, Xu's former nanny and now housekeeper, answered with a brisk "*Wei.*"

"Auntie, this is Ava. Is Xu available to speak to me?"

"Good morning Ava, and for you he is always available. Just a minute, I'll take the phone out to the fish pond. He's having his first morning smoke."

Ava heard the front door of Xu's house open, and then a moment later he came on the line. "*Mei mei*, it's great to hear from you. Auntie Grace and I were talking about you last night. It's too long since we've seen you."

"*Ge ge,* this film of ours has made it impossible for Pang Fai to return to China anytime soon. I could come on my own, of course, but it would feel strange without her, and truthfully it could also be a risk for me. The Chinese government is doing everything they can to punish those who made it, and everything they can to stop it from being seen. That's why I'm calling."

"I know nothing about films, and aside from Fai, I know no one in that business, but tell me what you have in mind."

It took Ava about ten minutes to explain the situation with Chen, Top of the Road, the China Movie Syndicate, the court victory, and their hopes that the film would finally be screened in North America.

When she finished, Xu said, "*Mei mei*, I don't know how you get yourself into situations like this, but I will do what I can to help. You say the group that is protesting are Chinese students attending a local university?"

"Yes, but they're protesting at the bidding of the Chinese government."

"And you want them to leave?"

"Yes, but without causing an uproar."

"I'll make that request, in fact I'll stress it, but I can't promise that will be the outcome."

"Just making the effort will be much appreciated."

Ava heard a voice in the background and recognized it as belonging to Suen, Xu's Red Pole.

"Just a second," she heard Xu said, "I'm speaking with *xaio lao ban*."

She smiled — *xaio lao ban* meant "little boss."

"Okay, I'll make some phone calls," Xu said when he returned.

"There is urgency. The premiere is only about two hours from now."

"I'm on it."

"Thank you, and love you," she said.

"Love you too."

"Well?" Hines asked as she ended the call.

"My big brother is going to see what he can do," she said.

Twenty minutes later, her phone rang. She saw a number with the L.A. area code and answered it with a tentative "Yes?"

"Is this Ava?"

"It is."

"I'm Johnny Lam. You may not remember me, but I met you in Fanling at Uncle's funeral. I'm the Mountain Master in L.A."

"I don't remember very much from that day."

"I'm not surprised. You were distraught, which was

understandable. Uncle was a special man, and to none of us more than you," said Lam. "I'm calling you at Xu's request. He told me what's going on at that theatre and asked me to help."

"Can you?"

"My Red Pole, Chong, is assembling a crew as we speak. We'll have thirty to forty men at the theatre within an hour. Chong will nicely ask the students to leave. If they refuse, we'll remove them with the minimum of fuss. But truthfully, when they see our contingent I'd be surprised if they don't leave voluntarily."

"When Chong gets there, can you ask him to introduce himself to Noel Martineau, the theatre owner? He should be part of the process, so that the students know he has your support."

"*Momentai.*"

"Thanks, I'll give him a heads-up that your men will be there."

Ava hung up and then called Martineau. He answered immediately, his voice full of worry.

"Have you figured out what we can do?" he asked.

"In about an hour, a man named Chong will be arriving at the theatre with about forty other men. They will ask the students to leave, and if they refuse to go then Chong and his men will do what's necessary to get them to change their minds. When Chong gets there, he'll ask for you. I want you to be at his side when they confront the students. It's important they understand what kind of support you have — and you might emphasize that you have that support anytime you need it, so they shouldn't even consider coming back on another day."

"How did you convince a security company to act so quickly?"

"Chong is a triad, and so are the men who'll be with him. Their appearance alone will probably scare the students away."

"Are you serious?"

"Yes, and maybe one day I'll explain how it is I know them. For now we should be grateful they're prepared to help us. When the deed is done, you should make a point of thanking Chong, and you should go overboard with your thanks."

"If they get rid of those students I'll be effusive."

"Great, call me whenever it's over."

"Did I hear correctly? You're employing triad members to remove the students?" Hines asked.

"The triads are otherwise known as the Heaven and Earth Society, and not all its members are criminals."

"Are the men who are going to the theatre?"

"Probably — but to be clear, we aren't paying them. They have offered to help, and we can't afford to be overly fussy about who chooses to ally with us," Ava said.

38

THEY REACHED THE HOTEL AT QUARTER TO SIX, AND
Ava found Fai dressed, her makeup done, sipping a glass of
white wine on the balcony when she entered the suite.

"You look even more fabulous in the dress than you did at
Cannes," Ava said, bending over to kiss her lover.

"It fits better now. I think I've lost a kilo or two since then,"
Fai said. "Are you going to change?"

"No, there will be no red carpet for me tonight. I'm staying
strictly in the background," Ava said.

"After what you accomplished today you should be the
star of the night."

"That's sweet of you to say, but things aren't quite finished
yet. There are some students protesting against the film at
the theatre that we need to convince to leave. I'm waiting
rather anxiously to hear from Noel about how that's going.
The last thing we need is the students heckling or obstructing
people who want to attend."

"The problems never seem to end. What can Noel do to
get them to leave?"

"We're using some friends of Xu to do the persuading."

"Really, you're using triads?"

"Yes, I know it sounds a touch extreme, but asking them for help was a last resort. Luckily they said yes. Now all I can do is hope they don't go overboard. We don't need to make martyrs of the students."

Fai shook her head. "I've never been involved in anything that has had so many ups and downs. There are times I'm sorry I started it all by bringing you to meet Lau Lau."

"Don't be. Once the lights dim and the film starts, we can put all the crap we've had to deal with behind us," Ava said, and then leapt at her phone as it rang. "Noel, is that you?"

"They're gone," he shouted. "The students are gone."

"Thank goodness. Did it go smoothly?"

"There is nothing smooth about Chong or the men he brought with him. I've never seen a scarier-looking bunch. But he did get the students to leave without a fight breaking out," Noel said excitedly. "The students were cocky at first — definitely false bravado — but I think that was because they didn't comprehend who they were dealing with. Then Chong asked who was their spokesperson, pulled him to one side, and told him that they had to leave immediately. The guy started to argue until Chong discreetly stuck a knife against his ribs and told him that all of the men with him were armed, hated communists and communist sympathizers, and were itching for a fight, and so the students' two choices were to leave quietly or leave in pieces."

"And I'm sure he said that like he meant it."

"Yes, and when he did, his men moved in close to the students, as if they were preparing to attack. Truthfully, when I saw that my stomach did flip-flops," Noel said. "The spokesperson muttered something about how their right to freedom of expression was being abused. Chong stared at him, nose to nose actually, and started counting ten, nine, eight, etc. At five the guy turned to the people with him and said they had made their point and it was time to leave."

"A little face-saving — a time-honoured Chinese trait."

"I guess so, but before they left, Chong told them loudly that he was leaving men at the theatre. If they ever came back, he said, his men wouldn't waste their breath or time talking to them."

"Did he leave men?"

"There are five of them standing within a hundred yards of the theatre, and spread out so they won't look threatening to our customers."

"I'm going to owe someone a large favour for all of this."

"I'm still trying to believe it all really happened," said Noel. "I was so hyped when it was over that I rattled on and on when I was thanking Chong. He must have thought I was a fool."

"I'm quite sure he didn't, and the important thing is that we can have a conflict-free premiere," said Ava. "And on that note, I should let you get on with whatever you have to do. We'll see you around six-thirty."

"The red carpet is ready."

Ava put the phone down. "It's over. There should be no problems at the Westwood tonight, or for the rest of the week."

Fai smiled. "Now all I have to worry about is how the film will be received, and taking part in the Q&A session that will follow."

"When did you decide to do that?"

"Patricia says it is customary and builds goodwill. She

put together a schedule that she wants us to follow for every evening screening. Harris is the most natural choice to introduce the film, and he's agreed to do it. Chen, Silvana, Lau Lau, and I will join Patricia on the stage after the show. She'll ask a few easy questions, which she's already gone over with us, and then she'll moderate questions from the audience."

"I assume Chen will be translating?"

"Only for Lau Lau. Silvana's English is adequate, and I've decided it's time for me to take the plunge so I'll be trying to answer in English. All I've asked of Patricia is to speak slowly, and to repeat the questions that come from the audience."

"That's brave of you."

"Brave or foolish, I don't know. But since it's obvious that North America is going to be home for the foreseeable future, and I want to keep acting, I figured this is a chance to show members of the industry that I'm at least working on my language skills."

Fai's phone rang. "It's Patricia," she said to Ava. "Hi Patricia, Ava is back at the hotel, we'll be ready to leave on schedule." There was a pause, and then she continued. "Yes, I heard about the students at the Westwood, but they're no longer there. They left a little while ago and won't be coming back. If you want to know more, I suggest you call Noel... Okay, hold on, I'll pass the phone to her."

"Hi Patricia," Ava said.

"That was a wonderful job that Harold Hines did today in court. We've been getting terrific media coverage, and virtually all of it is sympathetic to our cause."

"You can tell Harold that tonight at the premiere."

"I intend to, and I also wanted you to know that Noel provided me with a list of the people who have made online reservations themselves or through their agents and PR people for tonight and the rest of the week. There are some heavy hitters among them from all branches of the Academy, as well as a who's who of film criticism."

"Which is what we prayed for, but now that we've got it, let's pray that the film doesn't disappoint."

39

TO CHARACTERIZE THEIR ARRIVAL AT THE WESTWOOD as stepping onto a red carpet was a bit of an exaggeration, Ava thought as she looked at the thirty feet or so of well-worn carpet leading to a large poster that contained the names of the film, the director, and the cast. The poster was roped off but there was no real security, and the ropes looked easy enough to climb over. But the people who had come to take pictures or simply to ogle were respecting what the ropes were intended to do, and Fai and the others took turns posing in front of the poster without any unpleasant incidents.

When they went inside, two other differences from Cannes were immediately noticeable. The theatre was a quarter of the size of the French one and so felt less intimidating and more intimate. And they were seated not in a row, but in chairs off to one side of the stage, where they could view the screen and part of the audience without being seen. Ava looked out at the sea of people and heard a steady buzz of voices. If she had strained her ears, she might have been able to pick out some of the things being said, but instead she held on to Lau Lau's hand and whispered encouragement.

He wasn't as nervous as he had been in Cannes, but his palm was still slightly sweaty and every now and then his hand trembled.

Harris Jones walked past them to the stage in front of the screen promptly at seven, to a smattering of applause. Using a microphone, he said, "Let me tell you a little bit about the career of the director Lau Lau..."

The "little bit" was a full ten minutes, but Harris was a talented speaker and the story he told of Lau Lau's creative emergence, of the handful of years of brilliant films, of the beginning of the deterioration that had ended with him penniless and unemployable, and finally of his resurrection, was done so skilfully that Ava heard sobs and gasps.

"Did you know he was going to do this?" she whispered to Lau Lau.

"He went over it with me. I agreed to it all. It's my life, why should I lie about it?"

When Jones finished speaking about Lau Lau the man, he turned to the film *Tiananmen*. He recounted seeing the rough cut in Taipei and how impressed he had been with it, and then spoke about the success in Cannes that had triggered the campaign by the Chinese government to prevent the film from ever being seen again.

"Fortunately, a number of us came together and decided to wage our own campaign to liberate it. Thanks to the American legal system and this country's dedication to free speech, that campaign culminates tonight with you here in this movie house. So, ladies and gentlemen, it is my honour, it is my privilege, to present... *Tiananmen*."

Despite the film's length, Ava didn't detect any restlessness in the audience at the Westwood, and in her mind the hours seemed to fly by. When it ended, there was the same thoughtful silence that there had been at Cannes, and then the same eruption of clapping and shouting. Lau Lau gripped her hand so tightly that it hurt.

Patricia Nolan approached them. "Huge congratulations, but I expected nothing less than this kind of success," she said. "Now it's time for the stars to emerge. We're going to put four stools on the stage in a minute, and after that's done I'll go on. I'll introduce myself, and then introduce each of you one by one. In order it will be Chen, Silvana, Fai, and Lau Lau. When we're settled I'll ask you the questions we went over earlier, and then we'll take questions from the audience. I will repeat those questions and direct them to who should be answering. In Lau Lau's case, Chen will be interpreting. Is that all clear?"

They nodded. Ava noticed Silvana and Fai looked composed while the men seemed nervous.

The Q&A session went on for nearly an hour. Many of the questions were accompanied by compliments, and if those were anything to go by, the film was being rapturously received. As it proceeded, Lau Lau became increasingly relaxed, and at one point went on for several minutes when asked about the challenges of shooting the film surreptitiously in Beijing and on location in Taipei. Ava became nervous herself every time Fai was asked a question, but to her delight she managed to answer almost entirely in English, only turning to Chen a few times to ask him to translate a word for her.

The session ended on a dourer note than Ava would have liked when a Chinese man rose to ask in English if Lau Lau, Chen, and Pang Fai were concerned that they might be considered traitors by the Chinese government. The three chatted briefly among themselves in Mandarin, and then Chen spoke for all of them when he said, "We are Chinese born, citizens of no other country but China, and we consider ourselves to be patriots. But that shouldn't mean that one must stay quiet about our country's history, and that one should accept that everything that goes on there is beyond constructive criticism."

The man raised his hand again. "You must know that there is no way any of you can return to China without facing the severest of punishments."

"None of us have any immediate plans to return, but who knows what the future holds."

The man started to speak once more, but Patricia Nolan cut him off. "I believe we have used all of our allotted time for questions and answers. On behalf of the *Tiananmen* team I would like to thank you all for coming, and remind you that the film will be shown here three times a day for the next week." Then she smiled. "Please be sure to tell family and friends about it, and feel free to return to see it a second or third time."

Ava met the group as they left the stage. She threw her arms around Fai's neck and hugged her. "You were wonderful. You spoke English so well."

She hadn't seen Harold Hines in the theatre, and now she saw him coming up the few steps that led to the stage.

"We lawyers don't get to work that often on things of which we can be so proud," he said when he reached them. "The film is fantastic. My wife and daughter were both in tears, and I felt like crying more than once myself."

"Thanks Harold, that's very kind of you. We're getting

together for a small party at the hotel. Can you join us?" Chen asked.

"It's almost past my bedtime, but I daren't say no or my wife and daughter might kill me."

Harris Jones then joined them, a huge grin splitting his face. "You're going to get some terrific reviews tomorrow, and I just told Patricia that she'd better start organizing your Oscar campaign."

"Harris, we can't thank you enough for everything you've done for us," said Chen. "I wish there was something we could do for you."

"Well, actually," Jones said, looking uncharacteristically sheepish, "I have written a script that I would appreciate you reading. If you like it, it's yours to produce."

Chen smiled, looked at Ava, and said in Mandarin, "This is the film business. If friends don't scratch each other's backs, nothing much gets done."

"Then read it. We owe Harris that much," she said, "And, if you like it... well, maybe we can find a way to help."

40

THE WEEK WENT AS WELL AS THEY COULD HAVE HOPED.
There were no protests; an almost full attendance for every
screening; and good reviews kept coming in. At the end of
the week it was with a satisfied feeling that Ava and Chen met
Noel Martineau for breakfast at an IHOP not far from the
theatre. Martineau wanted to extend the run indefinitely —
and had another proposal to present, which was why he had
suggested the meeting.

"After eating breakfast at the Peninsula every morning,
I thought this would be a nice change of pace for you," he said
as they settled into their seats. "I normally have the breakfast
sampler — two eggs, bacon, sausage, ham, and hash browns
with pancakes on the side — but it isn't for everyone."

When the server came to table, Ava ordered cranberry
vanilla pancakes, and Chen an egg white and mushroom
omelette. "I've put on three kilos since I've been here, and
I was overweight to begin with," said Chen.

They ate before getting down to business. When they did,
it was with a spirit of co-operation.

"Have you been contacted by any of the large or regional

movie chains looking to book the film?" Martineau began.

"No," said Chen.

"I'm not surprised. *Tiananmen*'s length would be an issue for them, but the real reason is that they probably don't want to offend any of the major studios, production companies, or distributors, who in turn don't want to do anything that might anger the Chinese. That market is just too big for them to risk gambling it away by hooking up with you."

"Both points that Larry Christensen made," Ava said.

"He may have been an asshole, but he wasn't entirely wrong," said Martineau.

"Where is this leading?" Chen asked.

"To an alternate plan," Martineau said. "There are hundreds of independent movie theatres across the country. I only know relatively few of the owners personally, but we're all loosely associated, and I think through networking I could get in touch with most of them...I would like to do that and offer them the chance to screen *Tiananmen*."

"So in essence you want to take over distribution?"

"Only in the U.S., and only to the independents."

"Truthfully, Noel, I haven't given much thought to where we'd go or what we'd do after our adventure with you. I've just been focused on getting through the week," Chen said, and then looked at Ava. "Do you think this is something we could consider?"

"I'm going to leave that decision up to you," she said. "I trust your judgement in these matters, but I do have to say that I think Noel has earned our gratitude."

Chen nodded, and smiled at Martineau. "Then let's you and I put our heads together and see what we can come up with."

"Thank you, I think . . ." Martineau said before being interrupted by Ava's phone ringing.

"It's Harold Hines," she said, picking it up. "Good morning Harold, I'm having a late breakfast with Chen and Noel."

"I'm glad you're all together. That should make this easier," he said.

"Make what easier?" she asked, immediately sensing trouble.

"Judge Chandler has ruled on the request for an injunction against BB Productions. He did it in writing, which I found slightly cowardly, and emailed a copy to my office — the original document will follow," Hines said. "He found in favour of Top of the Road."

"What!"

"I believe it's what he wanted to do last week until we ambushed him with Wang and created that media frenzy. He waited until things calmed down and then reverted to the norm. For him it's win/win. No one can accuse him of stifling free speech or being prejudicial, since his actions allowed the film to be seen all week, and now this will restore his pro-business reputation in Orange County."

"What justification did he give?"

"He wrote that while it could be argued that Top of the Road had violated the spirit of the agreement, that was a subjective position open to multiple interpretations. On the other hand, there was zero doubt about the exactness and meaning of the wording in the contract that assigned exclusive distribution rights to Top of the Road. In terms of contract law, you can say he was exercising tunnel vision, but you can't actually accuse him of being wrong or, as I said, prejudicial."

"What about all the consulting he was going to do in the diplomatic arena?"

"I'm sure he didn't make one phone call. He simply sat and waited until the seven days were up."

"Do we have any options? Can we appeal?"

"Of course we can, but it could take months — actually, many months — before an appeal is heard."

"You sound as if you don't think it's worth making the effort," she said.

"Ava, I'm just not sure how much you would gain by it," Hines said. "You wanted the film seen by people in the industry for seven days at the Westwood, and you accomplished that. In a way, being forced out of circulation again might add to its mystique. And if your objective of getting Oscar nominations for Lau Lau and the others comes to fruition, I almost guarantee that the pressure on Top of the Road to release the film might be too much for them to bear."

"That might be the case, but I still want us to appeal. I want us to be on the record that we won't accept a decision that is so unjust."

"Then we'll prepare an appeal, and we'll get something to Patricia to release to the media that reiterates our position."

"Thank you, and I hope you don't think I'm simply being pig-headed."

"Not in the least. I admire your determination to stick to your convictions."

Ava saw Chen and Noel were staring at her, both of them looking downcast. "I'm sure Chen and Noel have heard enough of our conversation to figure out what has happened. But is there anything else I should be telling them?"

"Yes, Chandler assigned a penalty to any breach of

his judgement," said Hines. "Any theatre which shows *Tiananmen* is subject to a ten-thousand-dollar fine per individual screening, and the same fine would apply to BB Productions."

Ava sighed. "We were just speaking about Noel's wish to expand distribution to other independents. The ruling obviously crushes any chance of that happening."

"It would be rash and probably financially ruinous not to obey it," said Hines. "If the Chinese government is as determined to stop the film being seen as it seems, you have to believe they will be monitoring it."

"I think you're right. They won't stop until it's completely dead and buried," Ava said. "So we'll appeal, and if we have to, we'll appeal again."

"Then I should leave you to Chen and Noel and get started on that process," said Hines. "Please tell both of them that I'm sorry things turned out this way."

Ava put down the phone. "I know you've probably figured out that Judge Chandler ruled in favour of Top of the Road."

"That son of a bitch," Martineau said.

"His ruling also includes a financial penalty clause that makes it impossible for the film to be shown by someone who has common sense and even the tiniest regard for money," she said. "I'm sorry, Noel, I think that puts an end to your plans."

"Just like that," he said, snapping his fingers.

"That's how it happens sometimes. You can't plan for everything, and you just have to learn to adapt to whatever is tossed at you."

"I'm not complaining. I'm just a little disappointed," he said. "Oh well, it was a hell of a ride while it lasted."

"Indeed it was, and you heard me tell Harold to launch an appeal. Who knows, maybe we'll win."

Chen shook his head. "Now what do we do?"

"We file the appeal and then wait. Harold said it could take months to get a hearing, so there's no need for us to be here. Fai and I will head to Toronto. What about you and Silvana?"

"She has work in Hong Kong that she wants to return to. I'm really nervous about her going back, but it's a career she's spent many years building," Chen said. "I'm going to go to Taipei. I'm going to sell off everything I have elsewhere and make that my headquarters. It may be the last place in Asia that the Chinese can't infiltrate."

41

Toronto
February

IT WAS LATE WINTER IN TORONTO AND THE CITY WAS
recovering from a recent snowfall. Ava and Fai sat in the
condo kitchen looking down on streets lined with grey slush
and dotted with puddles that pedestrians were mainly able
to avoid, although that wasn't so true of the sheets of dirty
water that passing cars sent flying onto the sidewalks. It
had been Fai's first Canadian winter, and Ava thought she
had handled it well. Mind you, she had been busy, spending
most weekdays at the nearby English language school and a
number of long weekends in the Bahamas. In fact, they had
just returned from the Bahamas when the snow came. Ava
would have gladly spent another week or even two at the
resort near Nassau, but Fai had an exam to write.

They sat at the kitchen table, Ava's laptop open in front of
them and mugs of coffee in their hands, as they waited for
the announcement of the Oscar nominations.

"I didn't think I'd be this nervous," Fai said.

"Why wouldn't you be? Can you imagine what Lau Lau is going through right now?"

"He must be bouncing off the walls."

"I'm glad Chen is with him."

"And wouldn't he be? They live two blocks apart in Taipei."

"I know, but I'm sure some people prefer to hear this kind of news on their own so they can cheer or mourn as they see fit, without worrying about what anyone else thinks."

"Not me," Fai said, pulling her chair closer to Ava's and resting her head on her shoulder.

Ava kissed her on the forehead. "I actually don't care if we get nominations or not. I'm just happy we're in the discussion."

"I'm greedier than that," said Fai. "I want it all."

Ava looked at the time. "Ten minutes to go," she said, and then her phone rang. She saw the number and answered immediately. "Chen, where are you?"

"I'm with Lau Lau and Silvana. She flew in from Hong Kong for a few days. Can I put you on speaker?"

"Of course, and I'll do the same on this end."

"Hi guys," Fai said.

"Hey," they chorused.

"Ava, I wanted us to Skype with you, but Chen is so old-fashioned," Silvana said.

"It has nothing to do with that," he said. "I'm afraid I'll get too emotional if we're looking at each other, and the last thing I want is for you girls to see me cry."

"I understand how you feel," Ava said. "I'm never more self-conscious than when I'm on Skype or something like it. My mother is the opposite, and she's constantly pushing me to sign up for this and that."

"What's your gut feeling telling you about our chances?" Silvana asked.

"I don't have a clue, I'm just hoping for the best," Fai said.

"I'm the same, but I was talking to Harold Hines earlier today and he said he's convinced we'll get some nominations," said Ava. "By the way, Harold called me to say that a date has been set for our appeal on that Top of the Road decision. It will be heard in the California Court of Appeal on July seventeenth."

"That's good news," Chen said.

"Lau Lau, you haven't said much. Are things going all right for you?"

"Just fine. I'm clean and sober, I've met a man I like, and I'm directing a TV series about a religious cult that is a bit weird, but well written and the cast is terrific."

"And Chen, how is Harris Jones's script coming along?"

"It's almost ready to be sent to you. A couple more tweaks should do it."

"They're showing the podium where the nominations are going to be announced," Silvana broke in. "It looks like they're ready to start."

"Here we go. Good luck everyone," Ava said.

A moment later, the host and hostess took their positions, welcomed everyone to the event, and began to announce the first category. As they spoke, the entire thing suddenly became surreal to Ava. Watching Oscar nominations was something she had started doing with her mother when she was in her teens. That this year she knew people who might be nominated, and that she had something to do with it, was almost fantastical. Even more so was the memory of how it had started. What had she actually seen in the wreck of a human being sitting half-naked on a bed in Beijing? She hadn't seen the man in front of her; instead it had been images from the brilliant films he'd made, and she had somehow transposed those into an image of what Lau Lau had been and perhaps could become once again.

"What are you thinking? You look like you're somewhere else," Fai whispered.

"I was thinking about meeting Lau Lau for the first time, and about the journey we've been on. It's something so improbable that it could never be made believable in a film."

"I lay in bed thinking about the same thing last night. But it was one step at a time, wasn't it. Just the way you like to do things. Get Lau Lau into rehab, convince him to write a script, get Chen onside, and then somehow find the money to secretly finance it all..."

"And the nominees for best supporting actress are..." the hostess said, bringing Fai's recollection to a stop.

"I can't listen to this. I'm going to put my fingers in my ears," Silvana said.

"There's no need for that anymore," Chen shouted seconds later. "You're nominated."

"*Aieee*," cried Silvana.

A few minutes later, *Tiananmen* captured a second nomination when Lau Lau made the list for best original screenplay.

With the best actress category next in line, Ava glanced at Fai. She was staring at the computer screen, and the only emotion Ava could detect was determination. *St. Jude, please let her get a nomination*, Ava prayed silently.

When her prayer was answered, she threw her arms around Fai's neck and they hugged so ferociously that

Ava's arms began to hurt. "I'm so pleased. I'm so proud," Ava said.

"Me too, but I want that best film nomination," Fai said, almost out of breath.

Soon after, Lau Lau was nominated for best director.

Ava and Fai smiled when they heard the commotion that generated in Taipei. It wasn't surprising to hear Chen and Silvana celebrating, but Lau Lau seemed to be yelling louder than either of them.

"I never imagined I'd hear him so happy," Fai said.

The last category was best film, and they all became eerily quiet as the names were read out. When *Tiananmen* wasn't among the first four named, Ava's stomach began to knot. How could Lau Lau be nominated for best director and the film not get a nod?

"The last nominee for picture of the year is . . ." the host said, then smiled and paused before saying the one word they wanted to hear. "*Tiananmen.*"

Pandemonium broke out in two households thousands of miles apart. As Ava and Fai jumped up and down in their kitchen, they were matched shout for shout by Chen, Lau Lau, and Silvana. Ava carried on until she felt her throat start to burn.

"This is so crazy," she said.

"We did it. We did it," Chen yelled.

"And now, onto Los Angeles. You're going to meet us there for the awards ceremony?" Silvana asked.

"There is nothing that could stop us from going," Ava said.

"Do you have any plans to celebrate today?" Chen asked.

"It's just past nine o'clock in the morning here, and that's a bit early for celebrating. Maybe we'll take a long, slow walk and think of a place — somewhere special — that we can go tonight. How about you?"

"I reserved a table in a private room at Le Palais — the restaurant I took you to when we were shooting in Taipei. Lau Lau didn't join us, but it was the first time the rest of us ate together as a team."

"That's the three-Michelin-star restaurant in the Palais de Chine?" Ava asked.

"It is."

"That was a fabulous meal."

"I'm sure it will be fabulous again tonight. I made the reservation more than a month ago, in the hope we'd have something to celebrate, but I was determined to go even if we didn't. Now the food is going to taste that much better and champagne will flow," Chen said. "I wish you guys could be here with us. Lau Lau's boyfriend is coming, and some of the cast from the TV series he's making, so we'll be a healthy crew, but it's just not the same without you."

"We wish we could be there as well. Think of us when you're eating the roast duck, and toast us at least once."

"That's a promise."

"Go and enjoy. We'll be in touch soon," said Ava.

When the call ended, Ava collapsed onto a chair. "That was so exciting, but now I feel drained."

"I guess this is what you call anticlimactic," said Fai. "Maybe we *should* go for a long walk."

"Let's, and do you know where I'd like to go?"

"I have no idea."

"The Broken Bicycle monument."

"What's that?"

"You'll see."

They left the condo fifteen minutes later, made their way west to Avenue Road, and then Ava turned south. They passed Bloor Street, where Avenue Road turned into University Avenue, and walked down the west side past the Royal Ontario Museum, the Planetarium, and onto the grounds of the University of Toronto.

Ava had found the monument by accident, just before she committed to finance *Tiananmen*, and had been awed by it but hadn't visited it since. She and Fai held hands as they weaved their way through the maze of buildings. The campus was busy, and they passed a large number of Chinese students. Several recognized Fai, but were content to shout her name and wave at her.

They reached Hart House Circle, which was home to a number of buildings. Ava led Fai directly to the one that contained the student union. "There," Ava said, pointing.

"There what?" Fai asked.

"We need to move closer."

They stopped just short of a wall that had a large plaque-like memorial affixed to it. "Oh my god," Fai said. "Now I see."

The memorial was a crushed, upside-down bicycle, but it wasn't until you were almost on top of it that you could see there were tank treads embedded in the bronze.

"This was a gift from the Toronto Association for Democracy in China to U of T's student union, in memory of the student uprising in Tiananmen Square," Ava said. "It was given in 1992, only three years after the massacre, but people were already kind of nervous about discussing it. The university's administration distanced itself from the project and wouldn't allow it to be displayed on any of its buildings.

But the student union building is not technically part of the university, so that's why it's here."

"It's so simple, but so moving," Fai said.

"When I saw it, I realized that the movie needed to be made, and I made my commitment," said Ava, and then glanced at her ringing phone. "Silvana, we didn't expect to hear from you so soon," she said when she answered it.

On the other end of the line were the sounds of car horns, a siren, raised voices, and screams.

"Silvana!" Ava said. "Are you there?"

"My name is John Tam. I'm in the TV series that Lau Lau is directing. I was going to dinner with him and the others," a man said in trembling voice. "Silvana called your number but she's not in any condition to talk."

"What happened?" Ava asked, feeling her legs start to buckle and reaching out to grab Fai's arm for support.

"When we arrived at the hotel, two men came out of lobby. They said they wanted to congratulate everyone on their Oscar nominations, and then they took out guns and started to shoot."

"Oh no," Ava gasped.

"The men targeted Lau Lau and Chen. Silvana wasn't hurt, but she's in a terrible state of shock."

"And Chen and Lau Lau?"

"They're dead."

"What makes you so sure?" she asked in disbelief.

"The gunmen put at least six bullets into each of them. When the police arrived, they took one look and covered the bodies."

Ava felt tears coursing down her cheeks. "I know that Silvana may not be able to speak to me, but put the phone to her ear," she sobbed.

"It's done," he said.

"Silvana, I promise you that whoever did this will pay for it," Ava said, and then waited for a few seconds. "Did you hear me? They will pay for it."

ACKNOWLEDGEMENTS

THIS IS THE FIFTEENTH BOOK IN THE AVA LEE SERIES, and that's a number I find astounding. But I guess if you write almost every day — as I do — the pages accumulate, and one book rolls into the next. I have been fortunate in that I've always had a story arc propelling me forward, and in this case the arc for *The General of Tiananmen Square* began in the eleventh book, *The Goddess of Yantai*. And it is an arc that will continue into the sixteenth book — tentatively titled *The Fury of Beijing* and already written. The first fourteen books were edited by either Janie Yoon or Doug Richmond, but because of Doug's absence from House of Anansi on parental leave, this book fell into other hands — all of whom were very capable. So my thanks to Gemma Wain, Jenny McWha, and Michelle MacAleese.

IAN HAMILTON is the acclaimed author of fifteen books in the Ava Lee series, four in the Lost Decades of Uncle Chow Tung series, and the standalone novel *Bonnie Jack*. National bestsellers, his books have been shortlisted for the Crime Writers of Canada Award (formerly the Arthur Ellis Award), the Barry Award, and the Lambda Literary Prize. BBC Culture named him one of the ten mystery/crime writers who should be on your bookshelf. The Ava Lee series is being adapted for television.

NOW AVAILABLE
from House of Anansi Press

The Ava Lee series

Prequel and Book 1

Book 2

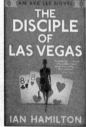

Book 3

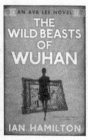

Book 4

Book 5

Book 6

Book 7

Book 8

Book 9

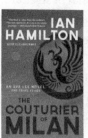

Book 10

Book 11

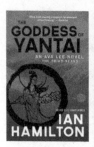

Book 12

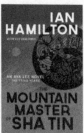

Book 13

Book 14

www.houseofanansi.com • www.facebook.com/avaleenovels
www.ianhamiltonbooks.com • www.twitter.com/avaleebooks

ALSO AVAILABLE
from House of Anansi Press

The Lost Decades of Uncle Chow Tung

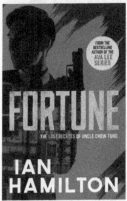

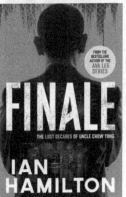

www.houseofanansi.com
www.ianhamiltonbooks.com

ALSO AVAILABLE
from House of Anansi Press

"Hamilton, author of the Ava Lee mystery series, turns in a stellar performance in this stand-alone...Hamilton pulls us into the story with carefully crafted characters, and keeps us involved by increasing the complexity of the tale: introducing a mystery here, uncorking a shocking revelation there. The book is a departure from the author's more traditional mystery fiction, but his fans will find much here that is familiar: realistic dialogue, characters they can care about, and a gripping story."—*Booklist*

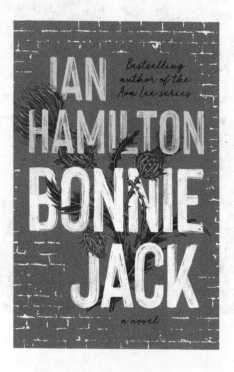

www.houseofanansi.com
www.ianhamiltonbooks.com